GAMES OF CHANCE

"As you wish. All-Fours is the game then, and we shall play to eleven points?" Belle began to deal the cards, giving six to each of them. "What do you suggest as a wager? I have little with me that you might want. In fact, all I really have that you might want are my riding boots, and I do not think that you would fit in them."

"I believe that I saw some ink and parchment downstairs," Stephen said. "I could fetch it up for our use."

"You would accept a promissory note from me?" she asked, both flattered and charmed. She had never had a debt of honor and found that she rather liked the idea.

"I should do so, of course," he assured her. "But that was not what I was intending."

"What, then, shall we stake?" Belle asked, intrigued.

"I propose that we handle our wager thusly. The paper will be quartered and we shall each take two pieces. On one, we shall write down what we would like to have from the other person—this may be anything which is not injurious or illegal. On the other, we shall write down what we would give in wager—for instance, a bauble, a song . . . " Stephan looked at Belle's lips and added: "A kiss."

Belle

Melanie Jackson

LEISURE BOOKS NEW YORK CITY

To Chris, the resurrection man

A LEISURE BOOK®

March 2002

Published by

Dorchester Publishing Co., Inc.
276 Fifth Avenue
New York, NY 10001

ISBN 0-8439-4975-9

The name "Leisure Books" and the stylized "L" with design are trademarks of Dorchester Publishing Co., Inc.

Printed in the United States of America.

Visit us on the web at www.dorchesterpub.com.

Belle

Prologue

A portion of a burned letter found in the grate of a guest bedroom at Ormstead Park.

. . . I would rather embrace the Popish church than face the anguish of a union with a man so wholly unfit for the contemplative life I intend to pursue.

Sir, your heartlessly expressed—and ill formed—opinions of the brilliant minds that founded the Society for the Propagation of the Gospel and Christian Knowledge (and I do not even mention your vulgar connection to the East India Trading Company and The Society for the Encouragement of Art, Manufacture and Commerce—though this intercourse with the lower classes is something for which you should reproach yourself daily!) has led to my belief that we shall never suit each other. Your character has obviously been degraded by your time spent abroad among the heathens of foreign lands and must render you unacceptable to any woman of breeding, even had the circumstances of your birth not been so regrettable. It is true that your scarred face proclaims your scarred morals.

I have no ambition to become wife to such a godless and forsaken man! Therefore I must insist that you speak to my father immediately about withdrawing your acceptance of his proposal for our marriage. Indeed, I should prefer a lingering death to a place in your household. . . .

Chapter One

Two hours before, while standing in front of the looking glass with his clefted chin craned toward the ceiling as he tied his cravat, Stephan Kirton had felt like the unluckiest bastard alive. In fact, he had briefly wondered if he shouldn't have been tying a noose rather than a neck cloth. Now, though, all the melancholia of the day had dropped away. His bleak mood had departed when he'd sat down to dine at Lord Duncan's lavish table. There was a *lady* present.

Actually, she was not such a lady. There were no genuine ladies at Ormstead Park.

He grinned suddenly, studying his prize through the eye slits of his mask. There were ladies at the table, of course, and gentlewomen of other degrees,

3

but they were not *ladies*; they were well-born strumpets.

Oh, this girl played the part of an innocent debutante well enough now that they were assembled in the dining room and there were witnesses to her actions, but he had caught her first bold stare when he entered the parlor where they'd gathered before dinner. It was the look of a woman who either knew a man very well, or was making an appraisal of one that she would *like to know*. He was fairly certain that they had never met.

She was pretending to be cold now, but Stephan had hopes that in private she would prove as honest about her attractions as she was beautiful. It would be all the better for him if she were not bent on playing out that tiresome role of a woman of virtue who needed to be seduced into doing what she, too, desired. Such false delicacy could be amusing but, tonight, with wax dripping down upon him from the chandelier and ruining both his soup and second-best coat, he wished for a more straightforward transaction.

His campaign to attract the girl's wandering attention had begun with the meal's first course. So far, she had largely ignored him in favor of listening to some unabating discourse about ill-bred horses from the old man to her right. She would not be an easy victory as long as they remained in a large group, for she would make no overt signs when there were gossips about. That was not how the game was played.

But he didn't mind a few hours' wait. The anticipation of seduction was half the fun. Or so he dimly recalled from the days when he'd had time for such pleasant pursuits.

Of course, he *would* have her before the night was through. He would not be thwarted. Normally, he was not much into the petticoat line—he didn't feel the need to make conquests of supposedly virtuous women, and he had no interest in whores, whatever their pedigree—but this girl was different. He *wanted* her, *needed* her, in a way that was in no part connected to reason.

What a pity she was not well-born! She would make the perfect life companion. Of course, if she were truly a lady, she would have nothing to do with him.

Stephan leaned back in his chair and sipped at his wine while he pondered. He was used to dealing with jointured widows who preferred their freedom to a second marriage with a man whose fortunes might fluctuate with the weather or season, and it seemed to him that the case must be somewhat similar for a girl like this. No thoughts of marriage would ever enter her mind. And if that were so, then it only remained to negotiate her price: a bauble, some trinket, perhaps a new gown. He was a little hazy about what he should offer her for a few days of her company. Sadly, he was not prepared to take her on as a mistress when this pleasure party was through, and she was certainly not some dockside whore to be had for a few hours and even fewer coins.

This in-between status made things difficult. Women who were able to simulate the manners of those of gentle birth were bound to be expensive, and were used to offers of extended protection. She might even be insulted by the proffer of such a short liaison as a weekend. Perhaps, though he disliked the idea, he should speak to Lord Duncan and learn her particulars.

"What shall it be, m'dear?" he asked quietly. "I have little experience with this bewildering state. It is for you to name the price I am to pay."

Her shoulder twitched as though feeling the weight of his gaze across the table, but she did not answer.

He knew that he had made his prey aware of him but, so far, the girl was proof against his generous attentions, remaining as cold and aloof behind her tiny mask as an angry moon goddess to the petitions of presumptuous mortals. From a true lady, this behavior would have been daunting. But Stephan felt certain that with time, this earthbound deity would consider his appeal in a more favorable light. The slight blush, which mantled her cheeks below the strip of black velvet that masked her eyes, coupled with the odd sidelong looks she occasionally bestowed, told him that she was not unaware of him, for all that she pretended indifference.

She looked the daintiest piece, residing over her place at the table in a velvet gown whose white hue rivaled the snowdrops of earliest spring. The costume was cut low on her bosom and the pointed sleeves showed off her narrow wrists and delicate hands to great advantage. Tiny fingers peeped past her half-gloves, (which were cleverly knitted out of golden threads). The wrap of delicate zephyrine that had been her veil was now loosely draped about her shoulders. However, she was careless about its mooring and allowed it to drop from time to time so that the cream of her fair skin was exposed to dazzling candlelight.

It was an alluring show. Yet somehow, despite these calculated tricks, she still managed to look pure and innocent. It was puzzling how she managed the illusion. It had to be an advanced form of female alchemy that he had never seen.

Stephan knew that he was inebriated—was in fact, to use the vulgar parlance, drunk as a wheelbarrow. He didn't drink often and had completely misjudged what those extra glasses of Lord Duncan's special brandy would do to his senses. But some dimly recalled female lore, relayed to him in his youth, proclaimed that no woman would dress up like a virgin sacrifice if she were truly intent on rebuffing all suitors.

His eyes moved upward, continuing his appraisal. She had not bound up her luxuriant hair. Her head was, in fact, completely naked now, except for a spray of orange blossoms: an oddly virginal choice of blooms for a woman of experience to wear. In all other respects, she was dressed as any other lady at a costume ball might be, but her long, unveiled tresses were a badge of availability that no real woman of virtue would ever wear in company—even to a private masked ball. It was a propitious sign for his campaign that she had chosen to appear with her coiffeur *en deshabille*. It had to be a message.

"Mais ravissante!" he said in a nearly inaudible whisper, giving her bare shoulder a toast, as she stubbornly toyed with a fugitive grape. The fruit evaded her careless fork and threatened to escape her dish altogether.

She would leave the table soon. It was not the sort of party where formalities were seriously observed, but before the dancing and flirtation and other less innocent sports, there would have to be brandy and cigars for the gentlemen as they passed the chamber pot.

And there would be brandy and cigars for the rich, base-born like himself. It was a ritual, and for a gentleman—*and those aspiring to be gentlemen*—rituals were everything. That was one of the first lessons he had learned about polite society.

Ah! She departed, sedately following their hostess, Lady Duncan, with only a slight backward glance for those at the table. Without her, the board was empty. What charms could candlelight hold when there was only the cold sterling and crystal to be graced by its fiery light? What use was more brandy when the lady—and a deal of preprandial wine—had flooded his spirits with more emotion than they could readily hold? He needed nothing else upon his lips but her soft, white skin.

Still, he did not follow his heart's desire. *Bastard Kirton will be on his best behavior tonight,* he thought, running a finger over the narrow scar that marred his left cheek. *Or at least his most polite behavior.* Tedium would have to be courteously endured for another hour or two.

And there would be tedious moments. The evening's dancing would begin with Bach. All Lady Duncan's dances began with Johann Bach's music because she was prodigiously—and tiresomely—fond of him. But more lively tunes would follow and, after a fast turn about the floor, it was pleasant to take a stroll through gardens—always well-lighted by their thoughtful host, who enjoyed spending a fair amount of his own time in the various summer houses and gazebos placed on his well-manicured acres. For a long moment, Stephan lost himself in pleasant reverie as he imagined lying with the girl in white in one of those frivolous structures.

He blinked blearily as those around him started to rise. At last, it was time to leave behind the smoke and idle masculine chatter. If he needed to fill his ears with chit-chat then let it be from softer voices than these! His host's conversation was stupefying and coarse. It put him off of the idea of trying to negotiate for the girl's favors with Lord Duncan. Mentioning her to anyone else no longer seemed agreeable. He did not want to share so much as her name with another man.

But where was she now? He pulled off his mask in irritation and tucked it away. It was so difficult to see with the halls so dimly lit and those infernal curtains swaying about until it seemed the very floor pitched beneath his feet. What meant his host in having so many rooms open for his guests to get lost in—and all of them cluttered with ugly, sharp-edged furniture? It could take him half the night to find—*ah, there she was!* Seated in a parlor at a little writing desk, shoulders again turned against the room, almost as though she were planning to compose a secret letter and was seeking privacy as she gathered her thoughts.

Stephan smiled triumphantly and stepped into the room. The desk was a pretty one, with fine brass marquetry inlays, which were picked out clearly by the low fire's flame, but of course, it did not do her justice. Nothing could. No setting was lovely enough for this living jewel. Sapphires could not rival her eyes, nor pearls her skin, nor rubies her lips. Mere brass inlay was . . . was . . . he couldn't think of a metaphor. Just trying to think made his head ache.

"Good evening, Miss Winston," he said softly, hoping he had her name right. He closed the study door. Behind it, the orchestra struck up the predicted Bach cantata. It was not played with much precision because Lady Duncan kindly supplied her musicians with wine, and they were not so puritanical or devoted to their craft as to abstain from the offer.

"Mister Kirton." The girl did not feign surprise at his arrival. It was difficult to tell behind the narrow mask that turned his way, but it seemed as though her delicate brows—surely they were delicate on one so fair—drew together. "So, you do remember me after all?"

"Belle Winston. Of course I remember. I would not forget your name," he said gallantly, though he wondered if the lady might actually be vexed at the idea that he did not recall meeting her earlier in the day. Or was she simply pretending to be?

Stephan frowned slightly. *Had* he met her earlier in the day? He truly could not recall. Or, was she vexed for some other reason, wishing him away because some other man had beaten him to the gate and she was no longer looking for a patron?

But that couldn't be it; she was quite alone here in this room, and a new lover would never let it be so.

Reassured of his welcome, Stephan advanced.

"I see that you have sought out some privacy," he said, walking over to a rosewood sofa table where someone had laid out a selection of games, including backgammon, chess and cribbage. Feeling a bit awkward beneath her continuing gaze, and uncertain where to begin negotiations for sexual favors with a moon goddess, he added: "I vow that the noise in the dining room was enough to give anyone an aching head. Conversation was very difficult."

The lady's brow seemed to relax, and her lovely lips twisted slightly.

"It was a trifle boisterous at times," she allowed, her voice as soft and appealing as he had hoped. He could not abide shrill women. "But I thought that you enjoyed many such weekends here at Ormstead Park."

He shrugged.

"I have been here a time or two. It is one of the few places where I am made to feel completely welcome." Stephan was pleased that he did not sound bitter. Lately he had felt most sour about the subject of his birth and the social constraints it put upon him.

"I see." The lovely eyes dropped.

"Not all of society is anxious to welcome a bastard into their home," he was appalled to hear himself say. Clearly either the brandy or her beauty had loosened his tongue.

The eyes fluttered up again, plainly startled.

"I have not seen any doors closed against you," she said gently.

"Ah, but have you been welcomed into every home that you might judge this?"

"No, I have not," she admitted. Her head cocked, not flinching at his rude observation.

Aware that he was close to blundering into the land of insults, Stephan made an effort to turn the subject and recover a lighter tone.

"Missing out on those invitations is not so terrible, is it?" he asked, taking a seat in the delicate chair at the table where he pretended to study the chess-board. "What would one do in the sacristy of some great lady's home? Nothing amusing, I'm sure."

"I had not previously found the exclusion inconvenient, since I had no desire to visit those hallowed portals," the girl admitted. There was a strange undercurrent to her words, but Stephan could not grasp what it might be. Truly, the brandy had fuddled his wits.

"But now it is inconvenient?" he asked idly. Then, seeing an opening, he suggested hopefully: "Perhaps because you are looking for someone particular to suit your needs and feel that your selection has been limited by such closed doors?"

"That is exactly so." She sighed. "But do not let us speak of that. You still try to play chess?"

"When I must," he answered, frowning as the marble figures seemed to wander about the checkered board on their own. He made a promise to himself never again to mix wine and brandy in a single afternoon. "Tonight I am rather preoccupied by something more serious. A terrible blight has been cast over my happiness, and I seek succor."

"And what is it that occupies your unhappily blighted thoughts?" she asked politely. Standing suddenly, she brought her chair to the table.

Stephan looked up, unable to understand why the girl looked and sounded amused when he told her that his life had been utterly destroyed. Probably she did not believe him.

13

"You know, it's deuced hard talking to that mask. I can't see your eyebrows," he complained, surprising his companion into a small laugh. "Do act like a sensible woman and take it off. It doesn't go with the sacrificial virgin fashion anyway."

"Voila!" she said, pulling the black velvet strip away and shaking out her golden hair. "Behold, a sensible woman! I don't know why Lady Duncan insisted we wear these at dinner. They give one a headache, and it is not as though there is any mystery about who we all are."

"Stupid idea. Lady Duncan likes masked balls, though. Still, it's a damned shame to hide a face like yours away from the world," he proposed, staring hard at the object of his compliment. The visage was certainly worth some study in its own right, but suddenly the face seemed vaguely familiar. Perhaps he *had* met her earlier in the day. He hoped that, if they had exchanged words, he had not been rude. His mood after receiving his fiancée's letter had been dangerous.

"Thank you, but at the moment I would as soon keep it hidden from the other guests." She paused and then began to smile. "Mister Kirton, you are staring rather hard. Have I a smudge upon my nose? Or perhaps your memory is returning?"

Stephan finally recalled himself and looked away from her face. Absently, he took hold of one of the milling chess pieces from the table and studied it. A pawn. He thought he recalled how those pieces moved and carefully relocated it to an appropriate spot on the board.

"Mister Kirton?" the girl asked again, her voice and expression now openly laughing. "Forgive my impertinence, but are you very intoxicated?"

"I am pretty high up in the world," he confessed. Then alarmed: "Does it show?"

"Your cravat is not mussed," she said soothingly. He'd reached for the neck cloth at his throat, worrying for a moment that he had in fact tied a hangman's knot while dressing. "Your locks are perhaps a shade disarranged, but you needn't be upset. The effect is most dramatic and fashionable, and I do not in the least mind such a small degree of untidiness."

Stephan blinked at the praise, uncertain of what to say.

Undeterred by the silence, the girl took a seat at the chess table and studied the black pieces before her.

"Your own hair is very demure," he complimented at last, recalling that females liked praise about their appearance, yet feeling that comparing her to jewels might be excessive. He did not want her to think him irrational, though why her opinion mattered so much, he could not say. "I remarked it immediately."

"I know. I chose this style deliberately—for all the good it has done me," she said, moving her own piece forward. "It was intended as a reproachful reminder, but it rather missed the mark as Quincy has departed."

Quincy? Stephan frowned, trying to call to mind anyone by that name. The only person he could remember seeing was Andrew Marvelle's youngest rakehell. The thought of this girl having anything to do with that Quincy made his gut clench in protest.

"Have you seen the gardens yet?" he asked abruptly, hoping that they might avoid both the game of chess and the discussion of a potential rival he had inadvertently inaugurated. When she didn't answer immediately he added: "The many hedges strike the eye pleasingly, and it is planted with many rows of flowering trees. Withall, it is kept in excellent order. In fact, it is quite easy to stroll there at night, for among the trees are placed a number of globe lamps and torches."

"Indeed." The reply was polite and perhaps a bit amused, but not enthusiastic.

"Any number of people shall be strolling about already," he suggested again, aware that he sounded stiff and formal, but for some reason was quite unable to relax. "And the music is much more enjoyable when heard from a distance through fresh air."

The young woman chuckled, showing her pearl-like teeth. Stephan stared, entranced.

"Exercise is better for the digestion than chess?" she asked innocently.

"Just so."

"And it might even clear your head."

"One never knows," he agreed, but without much eagerness. He did not particularly want his head

16

cleared. In the back of his mind, he feared that any return to sobriety would spoil the divine madness that had seized him.

His companion stood. "Very well then. Let us take a turn through the garden. The night is already a complete disaster, and my plans are all awry. What matters one more error? I do believe that my reputation is quite ruined anyway." The last was said quietly and with a touch of anger.

"You are only recently ruined?" he asked with interest, struggling to his feet. "I thought you might be. The ravages of a life of disrepute do not yet show."

"Yes, I am quite recently—*and quite utterly*—ruined, I should think. Ladies don't come here to Lord Duncan's weekend house parties, or so I have been lately told."

"That is true," he agreed, swaying slightly as he offered his arm. "I can never recall having seen one here before."

"It would have been convenient to know this two days ago." The beauty in white stared at him for a moment, making Stephan wonder if he had said something wrong.

"You aren't going to fall down, are you?" she asked at last, as she laid her fingertips upon his sleeve. "I do think that I would be unable to catch you if you fell. At least, I might catch you, but you would surely be pulled from my grasp as you weigh a great deal more than I am used to carrying."

"I shan't fall," he promised.

"Why ever did you drink so much tonight?" she asked curiously as they walked slowly toward the double doors, which opened onto a terrace and then the garden. "Surely such inebriation makes dining difficult and in no way lessens the pain of whatever you are suffering."

"I was rather the worse for brandy before I knew that you were here," he excused himself. "And I have never found drink to impair my use of cutlery."

"Yet why were you drinking so deeply?" she pursued, pausing as he fumbled with the door latch. "Because of the great blight on your life?"

"Why drink?" he asked. "Because I was supposed to get married. This week," he added morosely. "And I was endeavoring to forget that for a while."

Her huge blue eyes turned his way. "You were getting married this week?"

"Aye, so I was told. But now I have met you and seen what loveliness exists. It makes my fate more difficult to swallow. Assuming that my bride is still among the living and has changed her mind about wedding me."

"What!" the girl exclaimed, horrified, all mirth fleeing her face. "Your affianced is ill? Mister Kirton, I am so very sorry."

"Constance is not ill—except in her temperament. If she is dead, it is from spleen." Stephan added feelingly: "She is not at all like you. Respectable females never are."

The young woman blinked and then ducked her head.

"Why, thank you! That is quite a compliment, I believe." She sounded like she might be laughing again, but Stephan wasn't certain.

"You are welcome," he said mournfully, feeling the earlier oppression covering his spirits.

"This is a most strange coincidence because, as it happens, I was also to marry a most ill-tempered—*what are you doing?*" she asked as he turned away.

"Let us bring some wine with us. I am suddenly able to recall my affianced's face, and I like it not. In fact, any thought of my intended and of the financial nature of my impending union makes my liver bilious. Look! In my upset I even burned my sleeve."

"Burned your sleeve?"

"I was trying to get rid of her letter in the grate and ruined my lace instead," he explained. "How convenient if one could get rid of any thought of Constance the same way. I'd as soon marry a feral cat as she."

"I see." The young woman examined his scorched cuff when he thrust it at her. "How . . . how truthful of you to say so. It is most refreshing to hear such honesty. I am still rather puzzled though."

"Truthful? If you enjoy such honesty then I will tell you that *truthfully*, there is nothing more corrosive to a good mood than thinking of being purchased for Constance Wrawby. She doesn't like me, you know. Said she'd rather take the orders than marry me—and she isn't even Catholic. She also said that she would be a spiritual slave in my household." He added fairly: "Don't blame her really for disliking me. I wasn't very understanding about her religious mania. And I wouldn't want to marry a bastard myself. Particularly one who never liked me above half. But she had no reason to get so insulting about my politics when she is the one who is completely mad about joining strange societies and organizations!"

His companion eyed the nearly full decanter in his fist but, apparently understanding his dejection, did not raise an objection to bringing it.

"It is strange that you should have to marry someone you dislike this week for I, too, had planned such a wedding," she repeated, reaching again for his arm. "Or, at least, one was planned for me. I actually had no hand in the decision and was presented with it a *fait accompli*."

"Truly? What an odd coincidence," he marveled with genuine astonishment. "And was your fiancé very plain and cold and religious?"

"No, he was very faithless and had a weak chin. I came with him here this weekend because he insisted. And then I discovered him *cavorting* with another woman in the shrubbery. We quarreled," she said simply. "I hit him in the eye and now he has left in a huff, and I am abandoned in this den of iniquity with nothing to do but wait for the *ravages of disrepute* to mar my name."

"Ah, then it *was* Marvelle's cub you spoke of earlier. Quincy always has been a loose fish. That is quite hard luck for you not discovering his true nature before being abandoned here." Stephan was much struck by this tale of woe, and he offered the girl the decanter with a consoling air. He said in commiseration: "Here, have some brandy. It is something of an anodyne. And at least my chin is not weak. Did you really hit Quincy in the eye?"

"Yes, though not nearly hard enough. It didn't even blacken. I should have used a deal more force if I had known he was going to abandon me." She stared at the etched crystal for a moment and then shrugged her delicate shoulders. Taking the decanter, she sipped directly from the rim. The first swallow made her exhale violently.

"You probably have not been taught the proper science of fisticuffs," Stephan consoled, patting the girl on the shoulder. Her skin was deliciously soft.

"Very true. Somehow that was neglected. I must admit that I was not truly looking forward to this match, but my stepfather was quite insistent." She gasped again as she took another swallow, and fought a cough as the fiery spirits raced for her stomach. "He wants me married to someone connected to the peerage, if not a peer himself. Andrew Marvelle was the only one he still had business ties with who might be interested in acquiring a daughter from the shops."

She handed back the decanter. Stephan reluctantly abandoned her shoulder and offered his arm a third time. They turned out toward the night.

"And who is your stepfather?" Stephan asked, happy to discuss something other than his own affairs.

"Hippolyte Lydgate."

Stephan started.

"Your stepfather is *Nabob Lydgate*, the East Indies plantation owner and shipping magnate?" He whistled and handed her the decanter again. This time the girl took it with less reluctance and managed to drink without shuddering. "If you must be from the shops, that is certainly the most magnificent of them to spring from."

"Yes, that's my latest stepfather." Her tone was sepulchral. "He said not to come home until I was married, but now I think that I shall have to go home regardless. And things are bound to be very unpleasant for a while if he discovers that I am returning without a husband. However, I hope that they will not be so unpleasant as remaining *here* where people are quite rude and horrid. It isn't as though I was actually born in a shop, you know. My real father and first stepfather were quite respectable. It was a pity they had to die so young."

Stephan ignored the last part of her speech.

"I am somewhat acquainted with your stepfather and agree with your summation of his mood. Personally, I might stay and brave the storm here in England for a while."

The girl thought for a moment.

"Perhaps there is some other way. I could tell him

that I wed Quincy and then was widowed in an epidemic or some such thing. Has there been any cholera about recently?"

"Not very recently," Stephan answered, as they carefully negotiated the stairs down into the garden. "I can't think of any real plagues this year. In any event, I doubt that tale would work. Marvelle would probably think it strange when he received a letter of condolence on the loss of his son. He'd be bound to write back eventually and correct the misapprehension."

"Probably. The whole family seems most disobliging and would do it out of sheer meanness." She took another drink of brandy.

"Perhaps you might go to France? Or Holland? There are any number of disenfranchised French nobles looking for heiresses. Some of the new nobility are not of the best blood, of course, but they do have titles if that is all your stepfather wants."

The girl shook her head.

"No, it won't do. I had already thought of this. It is a good notion, but my stepfather abhors foreigners. He says that he wants a man of sense—that means someone English, or at least American—who would be able to take over some of his burdens. He plans to enlarge his fleet so that he might do more overseas trade."

"Truly?" Stephan was impressed. "It is a strange coincidence, for that was my thought as well. This is a good time to expand one's business. I have one ship already and she is doing well in her ventures. But it will take time to gain enough profits to buy another. Unless my uncle is willing to back me."

"And your uncle isn't willing?" the girl asked, though it was easy enough to guess the answer.

"Not unless I marry his daughter, Constance Wrawby. And since it is time I marry, and no other respectable woman will have me . . ." He shrugged.

"I recall Constance," the girl said, drinking again from the decanter. "She always was very . . . studious."

"Aye, that she is. And vocally moral, too. That is quite bad enough from a distance. But twice a year I must go and see my uncle and look at her face across the coffee cups for a fortnight, and it is unmitigated agony. Until now we have managed to tolerate each other. But now my uncle is insisting upon marriage, and she has started treating me as a leper. She said that men like me were the cause of female self-defenestration."

"*Defenestration?*"

"I believe it means to throw someone out of a window."

"Ah . . . and Constance now wants to join a nunnery?"

"So she says. That, or she wishes to kill herself by jumping out of a window or becoming infected with consumption." Stephan turned and said earnestly: "I tell you, arranged marriage is an Evangelical blight cast over the relations between women and men.

24

What is the matter with these old codgers that they must try and force everyone into deadlock with the wrong sort of people? Why should we not marry where our heart takes us?"

"Wedlock," his companion corrected, then added warmly: "And I haven't any notion. It seems quite cork-brained to me, for it is bound to end in misery. I do not see that my marrying some lord who despises my stepfather's family for its humble origin can lead to anything except disaster. Yet my stepfather insists."

"Better to be of humble origins and wealthy, than a well-born but sometimes impecunious bastard."

The girl in white nodded. "I have never been reduced to hard straits, but suspect that I should not enjoy poverty in the least."

They stepped onto a graveled walk and began listing in a less than straight line toward the nearest lighted structure. The mood was harmonious.

"Sorry, didn't mean to be so tedious about my troubles. Anyway, I am not really poor anymore. It is just that large ships are very expensive, and I have two homes to keep up as well." Stephan shook his head. "Did you say that you actually knew Constance?"

"Yes, my mother and father were neighbors of your uncle's for a time when I was young. My name was Wrexhall, then. I recall seeing you upon occasion as well."

"*Annabelle Wrexhall! I know that name!*" Stephan

was bowled over. "I thought you looked a little familiar . . . after you took the mask off," he added. "Yet I only dimly recall meeting you as a child. You used to visit the stables?"

"Yes, and you were usually galloping by on that great chestnut brute you liked to ride and had no time to stop and talk to lowly, unmounted females. We did play chess once, though, on a day when it was raining and my stepfather went to call upon your uncle."

"Hm." Stephan almost blushed. "How foolish and impolite of me not to remember."

"Not at all. What would there have been for you to say to the nursery set? In any event, you were paying a great deal more attention to the game than to me. Too, it was not so long after your mother died," she said with easy forgiveness. Her words were slurring slightly and she was obviously finding it expedient to cling more tightly to Stephan's arm as they negotiated the shadowy walk.

Stephan did not want to think about his mother.

"Be a little careful of the brandy," Stephan belatedly warned her. "It is some strange concoction infused with sherry, and it rather creeps up on one."

"I feel quite well."

"It seems grand now, but trust me, it could make things a bit embarrassing later if you start casting up your accounts, or got lost in this mausoleum on your way back to your room."

"Later?" she asked absently, as they circled the gazebo, looking for an entrance. "Why would I get lost later or have anything to do with accounts?"

"You might actually get lost at any time. Happened to me earlier, and I've been here many a time. The thing is . . ." Stephan cleared his throat. "Well, you wouldn't know this since you've never visited before, but the Duncans do not segregate their guests by sex. Both wings are mixed. It would not do to have you wandering into the wrong apartment this evening. Not all the men here are gentlemen."

"You are right," she admitted, stopping at the steps, which led up into the fantastic gazebo. "In fact, I don't think any of them are. Though I am quite ruined already, so I don't suppose that it would truly matter if I wandered into the wrong room."

"It *would* matter."

Stephan looked up at the small white pavilion. The golden light showing through the draperies was soft and lovely, much more modest and welcoming than the original structure in Brighton it had been patterned after. He wondered fleetingly if it had been in just such a place that his own mother was seduced.

"Truly, it could matter," Stephan assured the girl again, frowning slightly as he ushered her into Lord Duncan's nearest love nest. "There is ruined in *name* and ruined *in fact*. Not the same thing at all."

The ceiling above them was a dome of gilded scallop-shaped shells nestled in a sea of exquisite blue and held in place by marble palm trees where clever globe lamps were hung like miniature coconuts. All about them, light shed from the amber globes. Scattered around the floor were a number of low settees, strewn with matching cushions, and there were a bounty of thick rugs piled upon the floor. It was quite idyllically romantic and rather recalled him to his earlier intention of seducing this beauty. Only now, it didn't seem quite so wonderful an idea.

"Belle?" he asked, forgetting all formality as his embryonic attraction was rekindled. An idea began to form in his befuddled brain. "Are you quite certain that you are ruined? Socially, I mean."

"Oh yes, quite." She sank onto a settee and lounged back, as boneless as the draperies that shielded them from the night outside. Her eyes closed. "Do you know, I believe I might be intoxicated."

Stephan sat beside her and possessed himself of her hand. It was so much smaller and softer than his own that he had to marvel at the difference.

"Well, I know for a fact that I am—drunk, I mean. Though, I suppose I am ruined, too, more or less. Have been since birth," he said frankly. "But I do believe that I have come up with a capital notion anyway."

"Yes?" Her eyelids half-opened.

"What if we were to marry each other instead of someone else?"

"What?"

28

Seeing her surprise, Stephan tried to sort out his periods and form a coherent argument.

"I had thought that we should perhaps just be lovers, but I can see that you are in the suds here, and I feel I ought to make a push to set things right since we were practically children together. There are other men here who might say that they would help you, but they can't be trusted for they would never marry you. They would only give you a diamond trinket or perhaps some rubies. And they would expect—"

Belle blinked at him, and Stephan managed to stop his tongue before she accused him of raving.

"But what of Constance Wrawby? And your uncle? And your new ship?"

"Well, if you're an heiress I don't need my uncle. In fact, I don't need him anyway. I shall manage some other way. And Constance won't mind a blink. In fact she'd be bloody grateful. And as for your problem, I can certainly run your stepfather's company, for I am already in shipping and not going to sneer about doing work. Nor would I sneer about your family. Many would say that your birth is better than mine. Wrexhall is a respected name."

"So you say now, but that is just brandy." Belle was staring at him as though he had grown horns. "Later you would resent everyone saying that you had to marry money."

Stephan waved her words away.

"Nonsense. Also, though I am not a peer, I *am* the

son of a duke. A bastard son, of course." Stephan frowned and put the decanter on the floor, scooting it a safe distance away with his boot. "And when Uncle Wrawby dies I shall be landed with a second estate. He can't prevent the estate coming to me even if he does disinherit me now. My father's attorneys set up the entail with my uncle at a time when he was in financial trouble and made it all legal and binding. It was good of him, as my mother was by then long dead."

"Well, it seems a very tidy notion, Stephan," she said kindly. "There is just one problem."

"What is that?" he asked, staring first into her sea-deep eyes and then down at her milky white bosom.

"Quincy's behavior has quite put me off the notion of matrimony, and I have decided that I don't want to get married now. Especially not just because I am ruined," she told him in a rush. "Truly, I am not anything like Constance, but I do understand about feeling shackled to some man. My stepfather does not seem to realize that slavery was abolished last year. It is illegal everywhere, you know, I think even in the East Indies. I don't see that I should have to do this just because he—or society—says so."

"You don't want to get married just because you are ruined," Stephan repeated, eyes snapping to her face. "But why ever not? It is a time-honored tradition. In any event, I should think you would like being married to me a deal more than being ruined all alone. Believe me, being alone and ruined is most

uncomfortable. Particularly for females. If you don't know this, it is only because you are too innocent. Or intoxicated."

"I'm not so certain of that," she answered. "Anyhow, I am only ruined *here*. There are many places where I might go and still be quite respectable. You said yourself that I might go to Holland or France."

Stephan shook his head, frowning at what he was sure was some sort of insult to him.

"It doesn't work that way, Belle. Gossip travels. Especially when you are a Lydgate, which someone is bound to discover. You will be quite ruined everywhere by the end of summer unless some gentleman offers you the protection of his name."

"Do you truly think so?" She sighed. "But what is there in marriage to tempt me, beyond saving my face? You certainly don't seem thrilled at the prospect. Yes, my stepfather will get a business manager, but I do not see that this is any great advent for me. And all the *gentlemen* I meet are drunken wasters—I do beg your pardon, Stephan, but it is the truth. Having no occupation, they simply spend their days drinking and gaming. Why should I want to saddle myself with that sort of companion?"

"Well, I am not habitually drunk," he complained, growing more offended and somewhat defensive. "And I am not a waster. Not at all. Why, I don't even care for gambling above half. I only take wagers when I have no other choice. And you misunderstood. I shouldn't mind getting married—only not to Constance."

"That is comforting knowledge," she answered wryly. "But I still do not see what would tempt me to marriage with you. Or anyone. There is nothing in it for women after the wooing . . . and most men have no notion of how to go about that part either. You are all quite monstrously selfish."

Stephan leaned forward, his eyes narrowing. "That sounds like a wager. Are you saying that I could not win you to me if I put my mind to it? Do you truly think I am incapable of wooing you in a romantic style?" They were so close that their noses nearly touched. "Or do you really believe that because a woman is innocent that she is shielded and cannot be taught to desire?"

" 'Tis not a wager. Don't be foolish." The girl struggled up onto one elbow and tried to pull her ruffled skirts back into place about her ankles. Her skirts did not move far, for Stephan was sitting on them. Her unbound hair had also become ensnared with the pillow fringe.

Stephan saw how her pulse increased when he said *desire.* Watching the blood pounding in her throat, he smiled knowingly. "I tell you that there is one thing that would tempt you into marriage, Belle, and that would be a place in my bed. You just don't know it yet," he claimed. "After all, that is what you were made for. It is your purpose. Destiny brought us together. If you were not so innocent, you would already feel the attraction here between us."

"Well, it seems I may have a place in your bed anyway," she replied crossly. "You all but said that you were planning on seducing me."

"That was before," he rebutted immediately, caging her with his arms. "Stop thrashing about."

"Well, I do not plan on being seduced into either your bed or into marriage—at least not tonight," she informed him, though her voice was not as certain as it might have been. Her heart began a noticeable pounding that made the lace at her bosom shiver.

Stephan's eyes swept over her, and he smiled at the creeping blush that heated her chest and cheeks.

"Then I suggest that you begin making plans," he said. Leaning over her until their bodies actually met, he watched her lovely eyes go wide. Then he announced: "For I have decided to have you to wife before any of these other bounders has a go at you. I can't believe that idiot Quincy let you go. His family is quite done-up, you know."

"No, I didn't know, but I thought it might be the case. It is the only explanation that makes sense." Belle tried to scoot away, but Stephan halted her efforts by laying some of his weight upon her. Her heart's pulse fluttered visibly in her throat as she grew breathless and quite pink lying there beneath him. Her restless shiftings teased him to a distracted state that made him ache, but he forced himself to ignore his body's demands.

"I assure you that they are. That cad will be back

as soon as his father hears what happened. Wouldn't you truly prefer to have me in your bed than a man who loves only your uncle's purse?" He lowered his head until his lips hovered over hers, their breath mingling. Her eyes were very large and a little anxious, but she did not look away. "For I do want you quite for yourself, Belle. I did from the moment I saw you."

"Um . . . yes, I did gather that much. And I am not completely unattracted to you, Stephan. Obviously not, since I came out here with you. But to *marry* where there is not love, or even acquaintance . . . that is surely nothing but mad—"

"Arranged marriages happen all the time. Is it not better that we arrange one for ourselves? Our marriage of convenience could be so much more than merely expedient." He watched her beautiful lips, hoping to see them form into agreement.

"But . . ."

"Kiss me, Belle. That will begin to acquaint us." Unable to completely resist, Stephan touched a finger to her mouth.

"Stephan, please." She tried pushing him away with a trembling hand, but he did not budge. After a moment the touch at his chest became a tentative caress. She whispered breathlessly: "It is not that I am uncurious about this . . . this side of life, especially now that I am ruined. But I think it best I begin making some arrangements for my departure. I need to leave at once, particularly if you think that Quincy will return straight away. I am quite determined not to see him again."

"You *shall not* see him again," Stephan promised.

"Then you must let me go now, for kissing me will not help matters if I am to leave. And you will certainly regret this moment of idiocy in the morning."

"I shall regret the brandy certainly, for I shall probably have a devil of a head. But not the rest of this. Do kiss me, Belle. Put your arms about me. I believe that it will make everything seem much clearer for you."

"I am not so sure of this reasoning," she answered. Yet her hands lifted and slipped around his ribs and over his back, where they sought purchase in his coat. Her eyes were very wide as she studied him.

"I am very sure. One kiss, Belle,"he coaxed. "And then I'll let you go—if you still wish it. On my word of honor."

Chapter Two

Belle watched as the handsome, if slightly marred, face draw nearer. Stephan's broad shoulders blotted out the lamps above them, and she could feel his greater weight bearing her back against the cushions. The heat of his body tingled against her skin. Doubtless the brandy had been a mistake, for she could not seem to summon the words of rejection she should be uttering. Ladies of virtue simply did not cooperate in their own ruin when a well-made man asked them to.

Of course, if she were truly a woman of virtue, she would not be battling this desire. She should be defending herself from the bliss promised in Stephan's passion-darkened eyes. It spoke volumes to her diminished state that she was having to fight against herself not to capitulate immediately.

Belle closed her eyes as Stephan's head bent slowly toward her. She sensed that he hesitated, studying her, but then when she felt that she could stand the scrutiny and anticipation no longer, there came the soft and unexpectedly sweet caress of his lips upon her shoulder.

Won over, Belle sighed and relaxed.

He kissed her gently on her collarbone and then moved unhurriedly to the hollow where the pulse in her throat still danced erratically. His face dipped lower, and his cheek and then lips brushed over the top of her breasts, which were doing their best to escape the neckline of her dress.

She swallowed convulsively, as her heart seemed intent on trying to break out of her throat. Her actions failed; the fluttering organ seemed to break free, tearing itself loose from her will as Stephan slipped a hand beneath her skirts and curled warm fingers around her calf.

"Will you not smile for me, Belle?" he asked as he playfully tickled the back of her knee.

She gasped softly and surged up against him in an involuntary contraction of her stomach muscles.

"Stephan!" she cried. She was nearly certain that she felt him smile at her response to this invasion of her skirts, but Belle did not open her eyes to search for the proof of this teasing. The moment was too wonderful to spoil with such an unnerving sight.

"Ah, Belle," he murmured, stroking her gently, drifting ever higher up her leg. "My sweet, I knew you would see reason. Is this not what you have been waiting for all this time? I know that it is what I want."

Reason? She was not feeling at all reasonable. As for what she had been waiting for—could he have known all along about her secret passion of so many years before? Surely not! He had to be speaking solely about physical passions.

Yet this grown Stephan seemed able to see into her mind and know her secret wants . . . and he was much more alluring than the boy she had been half in love with all those years ago. Doubtless he had shattered many silly female hearts since those long-ago days. He was certainly causing carnage in her own breast. She was nearly certain that she should not confess that he was right about what she desired, and yet . . .

Belle sighed. She could not speak of this rising wantonness that filled her, but there were other ways to tell Stephan what she was feeling. Against her better judgment, she laid a hand upon his scarred cheek and guided his lips to her own.

The kiss surprised her. It was not at all like the hasty and sometimes clumsy busses snatched by other would-be suitors who worked for her stepfather. Stephan's lips were soft and nearly leisurely. The brandy he and she had consumed tasted different—kinder and sweeter—when diluted by their kiss. Surprised, she let him nibble her mouth and then, when he asked to be let inside, she began to kiss him back in that teasing manner that touched tongue to tongue.

Modesty was forgotten. Desire seemed to pour from his mouth to hers, sneaking deep down inside her with every inhalation. She finally opened her heavy lids and looked into his face. He had beautiful eyes, the color of fine sherry. She recalled her mother saying that they were a gift from a noble French grandmother who would not acknowledge her son's merrybegot, even if he was the Duke's only male child.

Stephan's gaze burned down at her as he waited. Belle's will, not firm to begin with, softened further.

She allowed her hands to explore his face and then bury themselves in the silk of his black hair. She did not protest his hand's invasion as it traveled up her calves and over the edge of her stocking. He was gentle, even adoring as he traced up her hips and the curve of her buttocks. When he moved to the inside of her thighs she did not protest, but instead allowed him closer to the heart of this strange new fire by bending one knee and curling against him. Her shoe, falling silently onto the rug, went all but unnoticed.

"Close your eyes again, love," he whispered. "This is just a dream. Never fear it. Nothing bad shall happen here."

Coaxed by his voice, she allowed her eyes to drift shut once more, the glow from the lanterns above her being replaced by the fire burning within. It was a heady mixture, Stephan and the brandy and this new desire.

He touched her again and then again, whispering softly of her beauty and charm. All at once, something blazed bright, a splash of liquid fire that consumed her thoughts and convulsed her body.

Belle's hands tightened in Stephan's hair and she heard her voice breathing out a prolonged *ooohhhh*. She was catapulted into some other place of blazing fires.

"Belle," she heard Stephan whisper.

The explosion skyward finally ended, but rather than plummeting back to earth as a fiery Phoenix would when its glory burned out, she found that she was floating down as softly as snow to settle again in Stephan's arms.

"So very beautiful," he whispered. "There is nothing more beautiful in this world than watching a woman's surrender."

Somehow, she thought that she should say something, but the other words that she might have used to describe the sensations that had raced through her—*explosions and temblors and meteor showers*—somehow failed to express the emotion that went with the moment. It was both terrifying and wonderful. She was at a loss for what to say and so contented herself with sighing his name.

Stephan laughed softly, triumphantly.

The sound, though joyous, disturbed Belle's languid peace and firmly recalled her to reality.

Surrender, he had said. Belle forced her reluctant eyes back open and found Stephan's gaze still blazing above her. His face was flushed and taut, and he looked more than a little wild with his hair loose and disarranged and his cravat untied.

She had not seen naked desire before, but recognized it anyway when it looked at her out of Stephan's eyes. It was not a tame or gentle beast that wanted her, whatever the soft voice had whispered.

"Ah, my beautiful, Belle," he said tenderly, his teeth gleaming as he smiled. "How I wish you were to be my lover instead of my wife."

"Why?" she asked, after she had swallowed once and gained control of her voice.

"Because I might have you now. Still, I do not regret this. The gods have thrown you into my lap and I mean to take up their most generous offer."

"Have me?" she repeated, feeling at once stupid and a bit dizzy, and wondering what there was to regret—*or not regret*—in what had just happened.

Shaken, and striving to repossess some measure of sanity, she turned her eyes away from his forceful gaze and focused on the small scar on his left cheek. She touched it lightly with fingers that were still uncoordinated and asked: "How did this happen? You did not have it when you were a boy."

Stephan froze, his expression hardening. He turned his head to the side and kissed her palm before pulling her hand away.

"It was a duel," he said, sighing regretfully, closing

41

his eyes and finally sitting up. He twisted half away from her and took a deep breath as he pushed the hungry beast away.

"An affair of honor?" she queried, shivering as the evening chill crept over her. Once freed of Stephan's embrace, she was uncertain that it was what she truly wanted. "You fought for a lady?"

"It was an affair of idiocy conducted by a callow youth. There was nothing honorable or gallant about it, or the woman whose name I defended." Stephan's voice was not cold, but it had turned practical and no longer caressed her. Somehow, he had snuffed out the desire that a moment before had seemed to blaze between them. "Come along, Belle. We'd best be getting back to the house."

"Why?" she asked, accepting his offered hand as her knees were unaccountably shaky, and she needed the comfort. She was suddenly feeling as naked in his presence as she did when entering her bath. Perhaps even more naked than she did then, which was odd because she was still fully clothed.

She also did not want to begin thinking about this other woman in Stephan's past life.

"Because too many people are wandering by this place. They've had the tact not to come in, but I think we'd best away before someone less sober discovers us." He sounded as brisk as a man of business laying out his report for his employer on quarter day. The abrupt change of mood left her shaken and questioning the sincerity of his expressed desire for her.

"Oh." Belle tugged her décolletage back into place and started for the door. Suddenly, she badly needed the privacy afforded by the garden's comparative darkness.

"Wait, let me go first," Stephan called, adjusting his own clothing and then stepping around her.

Disappointed that he did not kiss her on the way past, Belle hung back from him as he peered into the garden, checking to see if it was safe for them to depart. Her feeling of embryonic affection for her childhood love was fading quickly, and more appalling emotions were beginning to creep into her thoughts to chastise her.

"I'll never touch that brandy again," she vowed, even as she regretted her returning sobriety.

"That is probably a sound notion," Stephan said, but reminded of the decanter, he turned back to the pavilion to retrieve it. "This is vile stuff."

Belle finally noticed that she was missing a slipper and had a quick hunt about for it. She found the absent footwear beneath the settee, lying on the opulent rug in clear reproach of her wanton behavior.

It took her a moment to tie the laces with her shaking fingers, but at last she was ready to depart. Since neither he nor she recalled which door they had exited from the house, they headed for the first open set of doors that were lighted but quiet.

They found themselves standing in the armory—a room Lord Duncan rather fancied as his own *curia regis*. He had made a fine display for his antique collection of mainly French and Spanish armor, which did not actually belong to his ancestors but had been purchased when the romantic revival had brought such trophies of war into fashion. He would have preferred to have had all English armor, but the style had become so popular that native metalwork was not to be had except at prohibitive prices. Fortunately, his chair of state was an actual family heirloom and carved with a coat of arms, however spurious.

Belle thought that the anthemion that ringed the room with its elegant and feminine honeysuckle-and-vine motif, and the knotted axminster carpets on the floor did not truly compliment the objects of war. But they were doubtlessly more comfortable for the family when they used the room in the winter, and would serve the chamber's architecture once this craze for armor had passed and regular furniture was returned to the room.

The prosaic household thought demolished her few lingering romantic feelings.

Belle was lost at first, but Stephan seemed to know where they were going inside the rabbit warren of connecting rooms. Under his guidance, they soon found an empty back stair and once on the second-floor landing, Belle was finally able to orient herself and lead the way to her assigned bedchamber.

She was surprised, but not entirely displeased, when Stephan followed her into the room and eased the door shut behind them.

There was a small fire burning in the grate, an unnecessary luxury for April, but welcome to Belle who was feeling rather cold and cheerless.

Stephan set the brandy decanter on her dressing table and thoughtfully lit the candles in the triolet, being careful that they were adjusted so they did not set the nearby drapes ablaze.

"It is probably a mistake," he said, smiling warmly at her reflection in the glass. "But shall we have a last drink to toast our betrothal?"

"Stephan," Belle began, feeling horribly confused and increasingly dizzy, "we are not actually betrothed. At least, we are not betrothed to each other."

Stephan's reflection frowned at her, a line appearing between his dark brows.

"I had forgotten about that. But it doesn't matter. It is just a pesky detail that I shall deal with tomorrow," he assured her, lifting the nearly empty decanter and tilting it up so that he might drink the last swallow. He turned around. "To our marriage, Belle. It shall be a grand one, my sweet."

"Stephan," she tried again, but her voice was weak. She was truly feeling poisoned and very unsteady in her legs and head.

"Aye?" With a less-than-stable hand Stephan returned the crystal decanter to the triolet. He took a step toward her. "Will you kiss me good night, Belle? Doubtless it is the act of a masochist, but I should very much like one last kiss to take to bed with me."

"I am not certain that this a sound notion, Stephan.

I am feeling all at sixes and sevens, and your kisses only confuse me."

"So, too, am I all on end," he answered, slipping a hand about her waist and leaning over her. Somehow his body felt right pressed up against hers. Again, she found herself wanting to give herself to this man instead of defending her honor.

Truly, she was ill and hallucinating!

"You've invaded my brain, my sweet Belle, and taken away all reason. But is this madness not enjoyable?" he murmured, lips brushing enticingly against her ear as he smoothed her hair away then sighed deeply.

"Very, but . . ." Belle had the sensation of falling and then realized that it was not just the brandy running about her head that caused the feeling; Stephan had actually collapsed upon her, and they were in reality tumbling down upon the bed.

"Stephan," she gasped as they landed, struggling to free herself from his alarmingly limp body. Breathing was difficult with his full weight pressing down upon her. "Wake up, Stephan. You cannot be that intoxicated. You must get up at once and go to your own room. I shall smother, else."

His only answer was a soft snore and to finally roll onto his side when she pushed hard against him.

Belle had to fight to free her skirts and escape to the other side of her bed, which now seemed very narrow and unsafe.

"Stephan, can you hear me? Awake!" she commanded, shaking his shoulder, but he only grumbled unintelligibly into her pillow.

"This is too impossibly horrible. It cannot be happening." She wondered briefly about emptying a vase of cold water onto her almost-lover, or maybe rolling Stephan into one of the Persian rugs that graced her floor, then dragging his body to another chamber— any chamber! But her own head was reeling so sickeningly that her very room seemed to be spinning about her.

Momentarily defeated by the brandy, she closed her eyes and laid her head upon the bolster.

"I shall rest for just a moment," she said to the fire crackling in the grate. "Then I'll pour some water onto Stephan and force him awake."

The fire didn't answer, but Belle wasn't awake long enough to know it.

Chapter Three

Belle found herself awake for dawn's arrival but was quite unable to appreciate the glory of sunrise in the country. The gory color of dawnlight flooding her eastern window underscored the unfamiliar pain in her head and pressed mercilessly against her inflamed eyelids. To add audible insult to the morning's ocular assault, a dozen cockerels began to crow in disharmony right outside her casement. The blessed oblivion of sleep was ended.

Belle opened her eyes and noted unhappily that the mattress beneath her was listing toward the right, suggesting that some weight greater than her own was laid upon it.

With a growing pall of resignation, Belle turned her head to see if she truly had a companion in her bed. At the sight of Stephan Kirton's pale face on the pillow beside her, Belle's stomach rolled over and announced that it, too, was dissatisfied with the early hour and her precarious circumstances.

Though Belle would have preferred to do any retching in private, she thought it wise to immediately seek the nearest repository for her over-indulgence in case she was bested before her will could assert mastery over her stomach.

Fortunately, though standing upright made her head pound, it did seem to settle her stomach, and she did not disgrace herself by cascading onto the floor. By walking slowly, she was able to reach the triolet and the basin resting upon it.

Mistaken as to her intent, her stomach tried to avail itself of the perceived invitation to rid itself of the remainder of the previous night's excesses. The battle for control was short but pitched, and in the end she won by dint of staring fiercely out at the day and breathing deeply of the clean air.

Putting the unused basin aside and avoiding the unforgiving image in the glass, she made an effort to smooth her badly crushed costume, then checked once again to be certain that Stephan's presence in her bed was not simply a brandy-induced hallucination.

It was not. Her careless foray into the garden of desire had netted her a snake that was curled up in her bed. And this time her would-be husband's eyes were slitted open. His expression was as filled with suffering and rue as she imagined her own to be.

Given his complexion, she thought it merciful that he did not seem inclined to the rigors of remorseful conversation, for his grim expression said plainly that it could only be an unpleasant exchange. Belle decided that whatever witch's brew they had been drinking the night before would have been more properly served in a skull than a goblet.

She would have been content to simply stand in silence and stare at Stephan for a while, for even pale and worse for drink he was still quite the handsomest man she had ever seen, but when he groaned and rolled onto his side, she pointed at the basin and lifted a brow.

"I am never ill," he declared and waved her away with a weak hand. He followed with a few deep breaths and a study of the rug upon the floor near the bed.

A clock chimed six times below stairs. Reluctant to break the hush, Belle nevertheless felt obliged to remind him that there was a morning of vigorous exercise in the offing for them, and that servants would be around shortly to help them prepare for the activities.

"Do you recall this morning's planned events?" she asked in a rusty voice.

Stephan groaned again. Belle sympathized at the atonal sentiment. That day's entertainment was to include a ride to the local cavern where there was an underground pool, and an archery tournament for the ladies. Personally, Belle could not see the charm

of going to stare at a dank, dark hole filled with ex-
cruciatingly cold water, but she would have happily
fallen in with the scheme had this been a normal pleasure party where transportation by carriage was offered to the ladies.

But that was not the case. This was not a normal
sort of gathering, but one composed of sport-mad
gentlemen. Everyone going to the cavern was expected to choose a mount from Lord Duncan's stable
and ride briskly over rough country to reach the cav-
erns.

Belle liked the English countryside as much as the
next woman, but that morning, not even the verdant
grass and promise of multitudinous wildflowers
could tempt her into riding with boisterous crowds
that would be making up the gathering. She had also
been warned that in order to discourage the ladies
from destroying the gentlemen's fun, grooms had
standing orders to give them nothing but sluggish
mounts.

"Are you promised to the party?" Stephan asked,
propping himself up on an elbow. His cravat had
gone missing in the night, and his shirt gaped open
to reveal a few tufts of crisp black hair.

Belle shook her head once and then stopped, regretting the action immediately.

"Saddle boils," she said darkly. "I was warned
about the mounts given to the ladies."

"Aye." Stephan sighed, beginning to hunt through
the covers for his missing cravat. "Lord Duncan's

horses are all the worst hacks. They should have been taken out and turned into burned offerings years ago."

"But they weren't, and instead I am to shoot arrows at targets and doubtlessly listen to the women titter about Quincy," she said a trifle pettishly, feeling suddenly put-upon and more than a little embarrassed at having Stephan in her bedchamber. She looked out at the too-bright sky, which was already showing black on the horizon and added morbidly: "In the rain, too, if those clouds are an indication."

Belle began hunting about for a robe. Her nightrail was lying unused on the floor, but of her dressing gown there was no sign. Finally, she contented herself with pulling on her rumpled wrap and folding her arms around her waist. She tried not to look at the snarled hair that intruded on her face in a reproachful veil.

"They shan't titter for long," Stephan consoled her.

Belle rolled her eyes, but he did not see her.

"I don't mean to be rude, Stephan, especially when you feel ill, but you simply must leave now. The servants will be up with hot water and chocolate soon, and you must not be discovered here."

"I suppose not," he agreed, swinging his legs onto the floor. He was also missing his shoes, but Belle was relieved to see that everything else was in place.

Stephan cleared his throat.

"I know that this is not the best moment to bring this up, but I am of the same mind as I was last night.

More so even, for I have truly compromised you now. You must do me the honor of becoming my wife."

Belle closed her eyes against the unromantic words and said earnestly: "Indeed, this is not the time for such a discussion. And I shan't be any more compromised than I was yesterday if you just leave now."

"You know that is not true, Belle. Not after what we did last night. I shall set about acquiring a special license on Monday. One must get it from the Archbishop of Canterbury, so I shall have to leave first thing in the morning." Stephan draped his rediscovered cravat around his neck.

Belle wanted to protest his assumption that they would marry because of what had passed between them last night, and even more so at the speed at which her circumstances were deteriorating. But she could hear the stealthy footsteps of departing lovers in the hall outside her door and felt completely unequal to the task of railing at either Fate or Stephan with danger and discovery so close at hand.

"We'll discuss it later," she promised in a whisper, as someone staggered against her door and gave a pained grunt. Then, unable to help herself, she asked: "You know the Archbishop of Canterbury?"

"Aye, and he is perennially short of funds—fortunately for us, as he will likely be happy to sell us a license." Stephan looked away from the door and began pulling on his shoes. His dark locks were no longer neatly confined at his nape but were quite as mussed as her own.

Belle blushed when she remembered how they had gotten that way.

"Couldn't we just have a regular courtship and then publish the banns later if we still feel it is a good idea?" she asked reasonably, if with some duplicity. "You said that you could woo me in proper style. Why all this unseemly haste? It shall only lead to wild speculation, perhaps even scandal. Especially since you are already betrothed to Constance Wrawby."

"Unfortunately, we cannot wait. I'm sorry, Belle, but I shall have to woo you after we are wed. Did I mention last night that Lord Duncan saw us in the gazebo?"

Belle's heart stuttered as the implication of his words sank into her brain.

"In any event," he went on, completely unaware of how he had stopped her heart with the infelicitous news. "It isn't likely that Constance will sue me for breach of promise since our engagement is not widely known and she is the one who wrote to break it off."

"But—"

"And Quincy would not dare bring suit after abandoning you here. In fact, I should probably call him out for being such a bounder. Only that, too, would cause a huge scandal. I'll have to consider what to do about this."

Belle stared, sorting through the appalling list of observations Stephan had just casually reeled off and then finally said: "Lord Duncan saw us last night? No, I do not believe that you mentioned that."

There was only one moment when Lord Duncan might have looked into the gazebo and Belle not notice him. The thought would normally have made her go pale, but her hangover had left her feverish and flushed. All the news did was increase the pain in her head.

"Are you quite certain that he actually saw—*oh, do hurry!* This is no time for vanity," she snapped, as Stephan made his way over to her glass and began to attempt to retie his rumpled cravat.

Even in her misery, she felt guilty when she noticed that the candle sockets on the triolet were nearly empty because she had allowed the candles to burn down. They were fortunate that no window had been left ajar. A stray breeze might well have blown the drapes into the fire and set the entire house aflame.

"Don't look so appalled. Lord Duncan won't say anything when I tell him that we are to be married," Stephan explained as he looked up at the ceiling and began forming a knot.

This time Belle did moan. Her mind could all too easily conjure the image of what such a pronouncement would bring. Lord Duncan might not say anything while they were in residence, but his wife would spread the tale the moment they were gone from the house.

"You cannot tell him this. I forbid it."

"And we shall suit well enough," Stephan went on, ignoring both her protest and her demand. "Last night proved that much, I trust."

"I feel ill," Belle announced.

"Belle." Stephan shot her a stern look with his bloodshot eyes. "I am doing you the courtesy of assuming that you have a sense of honor."

She blinked and then looked quickly away. She was quite unprepared to recall her actions on the evening before. She completely disowned that dissolute, immoral creature who had invaded her body and made her behave like a common wanton, and she had no intention of honoring any of her implied promises.

And that thought made her heart twist a peculiar and painful way that was wholly new to her.

"Stephan, perhaps this sort of conversation is *de riguer* in these circumstances," she said desperately. "But I have not previously had experience with this precise situation, and I am quite unable to appreciate your—"

"I am trusting in your principles, Belle," he interrupted, turning from the glass. He did not level a finger at her, but he might as well have, so severe was his tone. "You are not to try and run away, or invent tales to tell the others. They will not believe you. And if you do, there'll be nothing for it but for me to disavow any stories and then chase you down. That would mean making a run to Scotland and an anvil wedding. And if you think that things are difficult now—"

"Things are appalling now. That is why we must allow ourselves a period for quiet reflection. I know that you have always craved respectability. We—"

"Well, the servants will only gossip more if you run away, and that will surely get word to the *ton* and subsequently to your stepfather . . ." Stephan stopped, his brow furrowing. "I wonder if it might not simplify things though."

"Running away to Scotland?" She stared, aghast.

"No, letting the servants catch us together. There wouldn't be any need for explanations then, and public outcry would ensure that Constance wouldn't have me, no matter what her father said."

"Are you still drunk? Don't say that," Belle pleaded, sinking down upon the bed and putting her hands up over her face. Even in her agitation she noticed how Stephan's warmth clung to the linens. Aware that desperate measures were now called for, she said: "I assure you that I have no plans to *run* anywhere this morning. I couldn't manage even a brisk walk. I feel too wretched. Do you think that the servants might have a methradate to cure my head? Surely, given the constant drunken revels here, they must have a supply of headache powders on hand." Belle peeked out through her fingers to see how this speech was being received and watched Stephan's face soften.

"Poor Belle! Never mind the devilish details. I am deuced sorry about giving you that brandy. Next time we'll have champagne and celebrate properly. Shall I see you at breakfast?"

Belle shuddered. "No."

"You might try some coffee and toasted bread a

little later," he said kindly, either immune to her glare or mistaking it for a wince of pain.

"I think I shall try lying down in the armoire," she muttered. "It is nice and dark and quiet in there."

"I wish that I could join you," he said ruefully. "However, I had not your foresight to refuse the entertainment and am promised to Lord Duncan this morning for his pleasure expedition. Besides it will allay any gossip."

Stephan walked over to her, and pulling her hands from her face, bowed quickly over them, breathing a warm kiss into her upturned palms. Her heart twisted again to have him so near, and she marveled that he could seem so unaffected.

"I am so grateful that my ride at least shall be smooth. My head would burst, else."

"Did you bring your own mount?" Belle asked, shaken by the tingling in her hands and both relieved and saddened when finally Stephan dropped his grip and went to the door to lay his ear against the panel.

"Aye, Roi is with me." Carefully, he opened the door a scant inch and put an eye to the crack. Seeing the hall was empty, he pulled the panel open and stepped out into the corridor. "Good-bye for now, Belle. I'll see you at tea. Take a walk if you can. The fresh air will make you feel more the thing."

He turned, smiled once, and then was gone.

"Don't wager any money on that," Belle muttered unhappily, standing up immediately and going to the armoire. Tempting though the dark, peaceful interior was, she began hunting for her riding habit. "I shall have to do more than walk. I am going to have to run far, far away so that you will forget this madness."

She wondered if any place would be far enough away to forget Stephan.

Belle's mood turned unusually morbid. It disturbed her tremendously that she had lied to Stephan, especially after he said that he trusted her sense of honor, but she simply could not agree to marry him by the end of the week. And probably not ever. He was betrothed to another woman—however reluctantly—and she was probably completely ruined as far as polite society was concerned. If he married her, Stephan would likely never be welcomed into polite society again.

She could simply refuse him, she supposed; in this day and age no woman could be married against her will. But the peculiar twist of the heart that happened when he'd touched her intimated that her will could not be trusted to hold out in his presence. She had to leave. At once.

"Damnation."

Though her heart wished her to believe otherwise, Belle knew that Stephan was wrong about their marriage putting an end to the gossip. And to marry her immediately after this weekend would cause a dreadful scandal. Certainly it would bring about an irreparable breach with Stephan's uncle, whatever Constance Wrawby's feeling about a union might be. It was also probable that such an impulsive act would enrage her stepfather. He would doubtlessly be disappointed that his scheme for her to marry Quincy had fallen through, and she would need time to convince him that Quincy was not the proper person to be running his empire.

Belle took a last regretful look at her bed with the twin indentations that marred the pillows and then began to struggle out of her velvet gown, careless of any damage she inflicted on the detested garment, which made a mockery of her bridal plans.

She hoped that Lord Duncan would not mind her borrowing one of his horses and then leaving it in town, but she had to ride into the village and discover how to get a seat on the north-bound stage. She had already decided that she could not journey south toward London, as that was likely the first place Stephan would look for her. And though there was a part of her that might wish him to catch up with her, she knew that she had to remain resolved upon a sensible course of action.

She had no notion of what a seat on the stage might cost, but fortunately she had a generous fund with her and could draw upon more once she was able to contact her stepfather's people.

Belle made another sigh as she resumed her cold morning ablutions. It would be polite of her to leave a note so that her host and hostess did not wonder at her sudden disappearance. It would also be most convenient to have them send her limited luggage after her, as she could not possibly take it all along when she left.

However, she had no definite notion of where she was going and absolutely no conception of how to go about composing such a difficult epistle. None of her governesses or friends had ever mentioned writing a letter under circumstances such as these. The whole situation was enough to make her feel ill.

Of course, without other instructions, her bags would likely be sent back to her former fiancé's aunt, since that was where she had previously taken shelter. That was not at all convenient, as her sojourn under that lady's roof was quite certainly at an end. She would simply have to overcome her squeamishness, make a sound plan, and somehow find the right way to word her request to Lady Duncan.

Belle was stymied about where to take refuge until she looked out the window and spied a clump of white marguerites swaying in the morning breeze. The common flowers recalled to mind her old friend, Becky Claremont, who resided in York at a small estate called Ashlars. Becky was widowed and lived much retired from society, preferring to spend her days reading and tending to her flower gardens. Her home, though reputed to be very odd, would be the perfect sanctuary. Belle was certain that Becky would welcome her, even without warning of her arrival, as she had written not a fortnight ago asking Belle to come for a visit when she had time.

And her friend, who had not enjoyed a particularly

happy marriage, would likely aid her by refusing to receive Stephan Kirton—or, heaven forefend, Quincy Marvelle—until Belle was a little clearer in her thoughts about what she wished to do about her present predicament.

All that was needed was that she reach Ashlars ahead of Stephan. It would be difficult if Lady Duncan betrayed her destination to her other guest, which she might very well do if Stephan demanded to know her whereabouts, but possibly she could still manage the trick with an entire day's head-start.

There wasn't any time for dithering.

Belle took a seat at her dressing table and opened the drawer where she had seen paper, ink, and pen stored. She did not waste time on artistry, but simply requested that Quincy's aunt send her bags on to Madame Becky Claremont at Ashlars, near York. She put Lady Morton's name and direction on the outside of the note, regretting that she did not have a wax jack so that might seal the missive tight against servants' prying eyes.

Belle shrugged, deciding that privacy didn't matter. By now, every servant at Ormstead Park probably knew about her quarrel with Quincy and wouldn't wonder at her seeking asylum somewhere else.

There was, of course, the little matter of her night with Stephan, but if Lord Duncan kept his mouth shut, Stephan's role in her flight would never become known to the rest of the household.

"Stephan." Belle sighed. She looked at the remaining paper and thought what she might say to him. Her mixed-up emotions were all too horribly complicated to be put into writing, and there was also the danger that any missive could be intercepted by servants. If that happened, Stephan could end up with his name firmly coupled to hers, which was something she wished to avoid. She simply couldn't risk it—even if she had the time and imagination to compose such a letter of parting. Instead, she wrote a second note to Lady Duncan.

It took her but a moment to pack a small bandbox with essentials and open the stubborn window near the triolet. She peered at the ground, which was damp with dew and infested with wandering chickens, and frowned. She did not fancy tossing her belongings out into the wet, but she could not very well walk downstairs carrying luggage, so she flung her box and heavy cloak into the nearest stand of shrubbery beneath her window to be retrieved later.

The chickens were not happy with her bombardment and fled squawking, but Belle felt they deserved the scare since they had been so unkind as to wake her that morning.

The dining room was nicely deserted, except for the chafing dishes, but Bell's stomach said that breakfast was still something to be avoided, so she bypassed the breakfast parlor and went directly to the stables to request a speedy mount.

Though she had prepared a lie for anyone who

might ask her plans, the lads were completely incurious about her devices, only telling her that she must ride sharpish to the west if she was to catch up with the rest of the pleasure party.

For once, Belle was glad that she was staying at the Duncans'. At any other house, a groom would have felt compelled to ride behind her until she was safely with the rest of the expedition, which would have been most inconvenient as she was headed in the exactly opposite direction.

Of course, the downside to staying at Ormstead Park, she realized the moment she mounted and headed for her abused luggage, was that gossip was for once accurate and she had, in spite of her request, been given a horrid horse. In fact, so poor was his gait that she leaned down to check that he was actually an equine of some sort.

Belle fetched up beneath her window and slid off the animal's back and onto the damp ground. She looked about as she hurriedly attached her bandbox to the cinch and then struggled back into the saddle without a mounting block.

Though urged to speed, the horse shambled away from the house at only a plodding gait.

Belle groaned at every aching jolt, feeling sorry for herself. Her mount would probably have been shot for vermin by the members of the Jockey Club. It was not just that the beast was an ill-favored color—a most unattractive mix of liver and soot—but it also had an evil gleam in its red eyes and bony withers, which it endeavored to poke into her with every swaying step. The monster managed to accomplish the feat because her light saddle had not been properly secured, and with the added weight of her bandbox, it was slipping more askew with every step.

The beast also had the temperament and pacing of a slug flung out on rocky ground on a cold winter day. She did not blame him for disliking the chill. She was none too pleased to see the lowering sky and to feel the pinch of a rising wet wind, but she did resent his ambling pace, which he would not increase beyond a bone-jarring trot. It made her head throb.

And then, when she finally lost patience and railed at him, threatening to beat him as he deserved, he just rolled an ugly eye and sighed as though the perfectly flat road they were traveling was, in fact, the most difficult steeplechase ever devised by cruel humankind. He simply would not hurry.

"I am lost," Belle moaned, slumping in the saddle. Her horse turned his head and snorted in agreement.

As though to underline her unpleasant predicament, a few scattered raindrops began to fall.

"Come on, you slug!" she urged as the droplets hit her face. "We shall be found drowned in a ditch if we do not make haste, and that will spoil everything as well as being unpleasant."

When her mount yet again refused to gallop, Belle began to worry that in spite of her head-start, Stephan would catch her before she reached town and could procure a seat on a stage going north. It would almost certainly happen if it began to rain in earnest and the pleasure party turned back for home.

The rain might also delay the stage somewhere along the road before town.

"Bloody hell. Now I know why they did not give me a crop."

She had to move quickly. She could save time by setting off across the heath, cutting short the greater distance that traveling by road would require.

This was not something that she would normally do in an unknown place, and as an admonition to caution and the necessity of speed, more gray drops began hurling themselves out of the sky, which was suddenly torn by a bolt of lightning.

"Oh no! You can't. Have you no heart?" she moaned at the sky as it upended a heavenly bathtub upon her.

The weather was merciless but she kept on riding. She could not risk a doubling back to the road now as the pleasure party would surely be returning on it.

The way grew increasingly rough. Coarse shrubbery clutched at her skirts and the occasional thickets she and her horse pressed through seemed all to be inhabited with hostile, thorny greenery, which scratched and pricked at her legs even through the thickness of her riding habit.

Worse still, she was no longer certain that she was headed toward the village. With the sun gone, and no familiar landmarks to guide her, Belle was fearful that she might have gone astray.

"And you would let me," she accused her horse bitterly, glaring at her mount's twitching ears. In answer, he turned his head and snapped at her foot.

"You'll eat this boot, if you try that again," she warned angrily.

She and her mount glared at each other in damp unhappiness.

Her precipitous flight, she was finally willing to admit an hour later, had been a bit of ill-conceived folly. She should have waited for the morrow and left Ormstead Park—in a carriage, with all her luggage—after Stephan went off to see the Archbishop of Canterbury. Or she should have commandeered one of the grooms as a guide to the village and the gossip be hanged. But it was as she had complained to Stephan that morning: she had no previous experience with this sort of situation. Being ruined and hungover simply destroyed rational thought.

In any event, it was too late for regrets now. There was nothing for it but to press on toward where she believed the village to be, and pray it didn't begin to snow or hail, or some other freakish weather event, before she got to shelter.

Belle sneezed violently, causing her mount to start and shy as though confronted with a wolf or dragon.

"Stupid sluggard," she muttered. "This is your fault, too. If you had hastened when I asked, we would be safely inside right now. If I had a pistol I would shoot you dead."

The horse, perhaps finally realizing that she had no weapons or even a crop, merely snorted and rubbed her up against the rough bark of a nearby tree, peppering her skirt with slivers of wood and smearing the fabric with crusty lichen.

Sensing that complete demoralization was at hand, Belle fought the wistful urge to fantasize about Stephan riding out of the woods at a full gallop as she had often seen him do as a boy, and this time—instead of riding on blithely—he would notice her watching him and gallantly stop to offer her rescue and a dry cloak.

However, it wasn't sensible to think that way. Stephan was not the proper party to rescue her. It would ruin everything if he did. Running away had been difficult; she didn't know if she would have the will to do it again.

Belle sniffed dolefully as rainwater trickled off her hat and down the back of her habit. She had to accept that all hands were against her, and that there was no one to liberate her except herself. She would simply have to be resourceful and brave, and pray that she did not contract an inflammation of the lung and die before she was discovered in this wretched condition.

Chapter Four

Stephan snarled at the sky. If someone yesterday suggested to him that he would be chasing a woman across the north shires of England—in the driving rain, no less—to abduct her and force her to marriage at Gretna Green, he would have proclaimed them mad. He would have said emphatically that such acts of giddy folly were foreign to his rational nature. He had learned from the mistakes of his youth, and he did *not* chase women like some actor in a bad play, let alone abduct them and force them to Scotland so that he could marry them.

Of course, *his conscience reminded him as he fingered the scar on his cheek*, he was not a habitual seducer of innocents either, and *that* had happened— or so nearly had happened that the difference did not matter in the eyes of the world.

A twinge of protest from his lower body suggested that it was aware of the difference between perception and deed, but Stephan ruthlessly ignored it while he continued his mental catalogue of recent behavioral aberrations, trying to understand what manner of changes had overtaken his mind.

There were several, all alarming because he had sworn to never again become involved in a scandal over a woman.

While enumerating his current strange experiences he also had to admit that he had never noticed himself being prescient in regards to the female sex. But most clearly he was omniscient as well as libidinous now. At least he was prescient as far as Belle Winston—*Lydgate,* he reminded himself—was concerned. Had he not suspected this morning that flight was on her mind?

For that matter, had he not taken one look at her the previous evening and known that his life was somehow to become attached to hers, altered for all time, *and he hoped for the best, even if the omens were not at the moment favorable*?

"Bloody hell." Stephan slashed a low-hanging branch with his riding crop, eliciting an extra shower of water to dampen his breeches.

Belle had run away from him! He still couldn't believe it. It was a fortunate thing for her that he had listened to his inner prompting and decided to return early to Ormstead Park.

Not that he had enjoyed his reception there. Instead of a hot meal and a shyly adoring Belle waiting to greet him, he had been met with disaster in the form of his epistle-bearing hostess. Lady Duncan had actually tittered behind her fan as she handed him Belle's short letter, whilst a grinning servant looked on.

Stephan hardly needed to read the note to know that all had not gone well in his absence. His addle-pated hostess's careless actions in front of the staff proclaimed that his situation—and Belle's flight—was now well known to the serving classes.

Stephan had quickly scanned Belle's brief letter to Quincy's aunt, trying to ignore Lady Duncan's chatter, the giggling serving wench who hadn't the tact to take herself off, and his uncomfortably damp feet, which were strangling in his rapidly tightening boots.

Belle's missive was a model of brevity. It was a relief that she had not said anything of a personal nature about either Quincy Marvelle or himself, though his actions would doubtlessly supply all of the context she had hoped to avoid by remaining silent on these matters.

But there was nothing for it. He was forced to go after her. He could not leave her traveling about without a chaperon and protector—especially not after learning what Lady Duncan believed was Belle's true history. The chit could be made the object of ribaldry by any man who heard this distorted tale and chose to pursue her for sport. Such things had happened before and there were members of the Hellfire club present at Ormstead Park.

He could only hope that the gossip stopped at the borders of the estate, at least for the next few days. If it did not, their hunters could be legion.

Perhaps a long spell of this cursed rain would contain the news while he marshaled his resources, he thought, looking up at the black sky. Once the gossipmongers of London scented the blood of fresh scandal it would be difficult to lead them off the trail. Measures had to be taken at once.

Fortunately, from her artless discourse, Stephan gathered that his hostess had a habit of reading the most deplorable sorts of fantastical, romantic fiction that scribblers could pen, and she had taken a page from this ghastly mind-rot and conceived of the notion of ordering the servants pack up both his and Belle's bags on the off chance that he chose to pursue the wench.

That he was suspected of being such a cork-brained—not to mention licentious—idiot was galling, but Lady Duncan's actions meant he was able to leave the house before the roisters returned and added their share to the perceived hilarity of the situation.

Or, worse still, tried to accompany him on the chase. That would be completely unacceptable. For one thing, Belle wouldn't like it. And he simply did not have the time to discourage the pack of rakehells by making an example of one of them by putting a bullet in someone's arm, much though he would enjoy shooting several of the arrogant jackasses on general principle!

Besides, shooting the flowers of the British nobility would remind everyone of what a bastard he was, and that would never do. Right now Belle needed a *gentleman* to offer her stepfather.

Stephan smiled without humor and ducked under another low limb.

At least he had remembered at the last moment to thank Lady Duncan for her kindness and hospitality, though it was done through grinding teeth. He had also thought to ask that she extend her charity to having a servant deliver their bags to Templeton's one and only inn where they would be taken up later.

Lady Duncan had looked at his tight face and misreading the cause, had suggested that if he did not wish to catch the chit that he delay for luncheon and allow her to board the stage alone. After all, pleasurable bits of muslin could be had any time, and the joke would teach the girl a lesson about being overly confident and putting herself above her betters.

Of course, knowing that Belle was not a light skirt and that he was at least partially responsible for this latest blow to her reputation, Stephan—though hungry—had declined the advice and then gone back out into the downpour to set off immediately after his errant fiancée. He might be a bastard by birth, but he was not one by nature, whatever the *ton* might say. This was one wrong that he could and would right.

However, he saw no need to inform Lady Duncan of his honorable intentions toward Belle Winston. Such a piece of news would indeed cause scandal among the *ton*. She was no longer just a trade-heiress traveling incognito, and while chasing a light skirt was cause for gossip, marrying one was the stuff of which infamous legends were made.

"Roi, *mon ami*, let us depart for less stupid climes. Surely it cannot be raining everywhere between here and the Scottish border." Stephan drew his cape around him and leaned forward in his saddle.

Roi, the son and grandson of great equines, sprang toward the park's gate with alacrity. He did not care at all about the bad weather or Stephan's dark mood.

It was so dark that dusk may as well have descended. Perhaps it had. The ride had seemed interminable, so perhaps many hours had actually elapsed since she'd departed Ormstead Park.

Belle was miserable. Chilled, possibly lost, soaked through every layer of clothing, and working on those predicted saddle boils. She was also feeling an urgent need for the comforts of civilization—a need that had increased for the last hour until she knew that she must either find the missing inn, or else risk dismounting and tending to things in some concealing stand of shrubbery.

Aside from finding this notion distasteful in the

extreme, there was also the chance that, weighted as her sodden skirts were, she might not be able to regain her seat on the slug's back. This was a choice that would have appealed on a fine day, but with the ground so mired, she knew from experience that every step would mean a heavier and heavier accumulation of mud upon the soles of her riding boots and dragging hem. She did not feel strong enough for such a burdensome hike with darkness and greater cold coming on.

Weaker now, she still cursed her horse for being an invertebrate, but he only walked her closer to a stand of brush whose harsh foliage was only minimally softened by the fact that it was at the height of bloom.

The cruel wind was also against her now, slapping at her face with cold, wet hands. It snatched her unkind words away and then further punished her by clawing at her wet skirts with cold fingers and forcing stinging rain down upon her flattened hat. Belle had never felt so alone and aware of her body's physical misery.

It was a tremendous relief when the lights of the gray village came swimming into view. She remembered that the inn was situated at the edge of town and urged her mount to one final bit of effort. Perhaps recalling that the hostelry's stable offered food and shelter, her horse finally achieved the gallop she had requested all day, and they arrived at the tavern in record time.

A boy ran out immediately to see to her horse, and kindly helped her to free her bandbox from the saddle's sagging strap.

"Here it be, mistress."

Belle smiled wanly and made a mental note to leave the lad a generous remuneration for his assistance when her hands thawed enough to manage her purse strings.

Feeling exhausted, and fighting the unladylike urge to sneeze, Belle turned from the groom and slogged for the inn door. She looked up from the rough cobbles only when the entrance opened, spilling out heat and light—and the delicious aroma of roasting meats—into the sodden afternoon.

"Landlord, I am afraid that there has been a mishap," she began, only to choke on her lie when she realized that it was Stephan standing in the doorway casting his long shadow over her. The single heated glance he gave her was as consuming as a kiss, though filled with quite different emotions than had been between them last night.

"Belle, my dear," he said, stepping down to the cobbles to take her arm and propel her firmly indoors. "*My pet, we have been worried. When Lady Duncan told me that you had requested a picnic to take out into the countryside—so foolish of you when the weather was closing in!*—and then when you did not return, I was given to the gravest of fears for your safety."

Belle didn't try to defend herself. She was too tired,

and the sight of the round-eyed and suspicious land-lord fluttering in the passageway was all by himself enough to stop her tongue. In any event, Stephan did not leave her much opening to do more than drip water upon the broad plank floor of the entry.

"How fortunate that I realized you would be making for the inn. Lady Duncan has kindly packed your bags so that you have something dry to wear." Stephan marched her toward the stairs and mounted them briskly. He had to tow her along as her damp skirts badly hampered her, but she didn't really notice, her whole focus being on the warm fingers clamped about her arm. "I bespoke a chamber for us and lodging for our beasts, so you may get out of those wet clothes immediately."

"Thank you. I will be forever in your debt," she said with earnest fervor, and gained a quick but searching look from Stephan. She blushed but did not explain about her physical distress.

"Are you hurt?" he asked with a degree less irritation, finally easing the grip on her arm. "Truly, I had expected you here some time ago, Belle. You said there was a mishap?"

"I shall let you know about my health when feeling returns to my legs. You do not by chance have a pistol upon you, do you? I should dearly love to shoot that thing that masquerades as a horse. He has done everything in his power to lame me. I have been pierced by branches, slapped with tree limbs and forced into hideous contortions just to stay atop the beast," she said bitterly.

Stephan's lips twitched once and his posture relaxed a fraction.

"I have a pistol, but I shall not shoot the beast. We have abused the Duncans' hospitality quite enough. In any event, sore limbs are what you deserve for being such a coward and running away from me," he accused softly.

Belle glanced back once at the rotund landlord who was still staring up at them with greedy eyes and then let go with a cavernous sneeze, which she caught in a sopping sleeve.

"I do not think our host cares for me messing up his floor, particularly as he doesn't believe your story about the picnic. No one takes a bandbox on a picnic."

"He is being well paid to believe whatever I tell him. Don't give the matter another thought." Stephan frowned and fished out a handkerchief. It was not an unpleasant scowl, or Belle did not find it so, since it was prompted by concern for her. "Here, blot off. I've seen wet cats look less miserable."

"Thank you."

"We'll talk about our affairs later." He hesitated. "I fear that there will be a great deal to discuss now as things have changed in the last few hours. I'll send up the abigail to you immediately. You get changed and then come down to the parlor where there is a nice fire. We have the room for ourselves tonight because of this storm, and you probably need to eat something after your day in the fresh air."

Belle suddenly realized that she was actually very hungry and forgave Stephan for his bullying and ruining her flight. A small part of her was even glad that she had been thwarted.

"Thank you," she said again, pulling off her sodden hat. "I find that I am quite famished."

Stephan shook his head, perhaps marveling at her calm, but managed a slightly bewildered smile in answer as he opened the bedchamber door and gestured her inside.

"This is the chamber. I hope you will be comfortable."

The room she was shown into was of generous size, though with an unfashionably low ceiling and withal was rather too *blue* in tone to pass for tasteful. This universal hue was due to the rugs, drapery and counterpane being sewn up in an overwhelming shade of ripe whortleberry, which the small fire's golden light completely failed to overcome.

Stephan hovered in the doorway, apparently waiting for some comment from her about the chamber, but Belle wasted no time on appreciating the architecture—though the windows were certainly fine and the carven fireplace mantel attractive with the blaze burning in the grate. She thrust the idling Stephan from the chamber with more haste than tact, then hurried to take care of the most pressing matter.

The promised abigail soon arrived, bearing a canister of hot water and some linens, and Belle gladly accepted her help in escaping her sodden and torn riding habit, and restoring order to her badly mussed hair.

Dry clothing and the chamberpot alleviated much of her distress, and Belle found herself able to appreciate the charm of the old building as she descended to the parlor. The wood of the stair was well preserved and carved with some precision and imagination as it spiraled about the central smokestack.

Belle sniffed and dabbed at her tender nose with Stephan's handkerchief. The aged stone of the chimney itself smelled slightly, and not unpleasantly, of roasted meats and soot, as though the memory of hundreds of years of fine dinners had loaded themselves into the stones.

As she drew closer to the kitchen passage, the old aromas were replaced with new ones, which were most enticing and caused her stomach to growl in a disconcertingly vulgar manner. She supposed it was just one more symptom of her fall from grace.

Stephan was waiting for her in the parlor doorway and drew her immediately to the fire where he urged her into a carven settle. He did not join her on the seat, but instead took up a vigil by the fire, resting one elbow on the mantel and propping a still-damp boot upon the grate. He stared, frowning in abstraction at an old clock ticking in plain view.

Feeling more brave than she had all day, and prepared to accept the situation with at least a show of equanimity, Belle courageously decided that she would herself bring up the subject of Stephan's appearance at the inn.

"I take it that Lady Duncan had my note," Belle said, aware of the fact that servants were about and keeping her voice low.

Stephan shook off his abstraction.

"That she did," he agreed, turning his head and smiling wryly. From the glitter of his eyes, Belle thought that perhaps he had been drinking. That or he was experiencing some unusually strong emotion. "Of course, that was after the maid had taken it to the housekeeper who doubtlessly read it out to everyone in the servants hall."

"Oh." Belle frowned. "I was afraid that might happen when I couldn't find any sealing wax."

"Were you afraid? How odd. I have seen no sign of any such emotion in you. Rash boldness there has been aplenty, but you have been remarkably calm about your circumstances from the moment I encountered you. I felicitate you on your iron spirit."

"Well, my stepfather never encouraged hysterics, or any other show of nerves," she explained, feeling slightly unfeminine and suspecting him of mockery. "Also, I think that I have not entirely comprehended the situation. It is so very enormous and awful that my brain keeps shying away from it when I try and think."

"That would explain everything," he said with a touch of irony. "I, on the other hand, have had no such hardy upbringing and am quite faint-hearted by nature, which makes me peevish when ambushed with disagreeable situations. I also tend to dwell upon unpleasantness with single-minded attention until the problem is resolved."

There was a pause.

"That is unfortunate," Belle finally said, trying to guess at Stephan's real mood.

"Indeed. However, given this fault of nature, you will forgive me when I say that I hope you had an afternoon that rivaled mine for alarm and unpleasantness—you wretched girl—for you certainly deserved it," Stephan added, but without real rancor.

"I am certain that it did. I have never passed a more unpleasant day," Belle assured him.

Stephan snorted. "I am not certain that such a thing is possible, for I am all but unmanned from my experiences, and you look in quite fine fettle except for your nose."

Belle folded her borrowed handkerchief, determined not to call any more attention to her reddened appendage.

"I am really quite sore and hungry," she offered.

"I wish that was my only woe," Stephan countered. "I have endured a most objectionable day of my life, and my nerves are shattered. First there was this morning's ride to the cavern with my head throbbing every step of the way. And then the rain, of course, which seems wetter and colder here than in any other corner of England. It has ruined my new riding boots.

They have shrunk so tight that I cannot wear them again until they are stretched."

"None of these things were my doing," Belle pointed out tiredly, propping her chin against her fist and pretending to study the indifferent painting of waterfowl that graced the wall. "Certainly you can't blame me for the unusually hard showers, or for the poor leather of your boots."

"No, that is quite true. But I think we may blame you for the presumptuous interview I had with our former hostess, Lady Duncan—conducted in front of sniggering servants, I might add."

Belle winced. "For that I am sorry. But surely she did not blame you for my leaving? After all, she knows that Quincy deserted me, and I said nothing about you in my note."

"Yes, she does know that. What she apparently did *not* know was that Quincy was your betrothed. Somehow, he neglected to mention this connection when he asked that you be invited for the weekend, and she is laboring under a large misapprehension about your role in his life. The only blessing is that she apparently does not know who your stepfather is either."

Belle's eyes grew wide. "But . . ." She trailed off, the horror of the implication setting in. "Then she thinks that I am a—?"

"Yes. And Lord Duncan's story about how we spent our yestereve has doubtlessly confirmed that notion." Stephan turned to face her.

Belle was appalled. She stared unblinking at Stephan, but no trace of matching distaste or anger could be seen on his firelit countenance. She wondered if his imbibing of spirits had shielded him from the full comprehension of the awfulness of the news he related.

"This is horrible. The gossip alone . . ."

"Yes, that thought occurred to me, too. Especially since, as we speak, the entire company of Ormstead Park is probably being regaled over supper with the tale of how I took our luggage and went to meet you at this inn. Being of the lowly sort of imaginations, they shall doubtlessly infer the worst and then embroider it before passing the tale along to their friends."

"You didn't tell them that you planned to marry me, did you?" she asked anxiously, feeling the room tip and then spin about her.

"No, I did not. Things were quite bad enough already. All that would be needed to fan the flames of gossip into a wildfire would be the news that I planned to marry a member of the *demimonde*. The only thing that might be worse is for them to discover who you really are."

"How can you stay so calm?" she asked, laying a hand over her eyes and shuddering.

"I am calm only because panic will serve neither of us. And because there is yet some reason for optimism."

"There is?" The room righted itself at these words,

and Belle lowered her hand, looking up hopefully. "Was this just a tale? Have you been teasing me all along to punish me for leaving?"

Stephan shook his head.

"No, what I have related has all been distressingly true. However, we have allies. One is the truth about your background, which shall eventually serve us. The other is the rain that looks to be of the sort that shall last a day or two. That will, with luck, keep the inhabitants of Ormstead Park confined. Which gives us a while to plan a counterdefense to their gossip and put some distance between us."

"Yes?" Belle prompted.

"At this point, we are closer to Scotland than the Archbishop of Canterbury, and the north is less inhabited. I think a trip into the wilds of Caledonia is perhaps the best solution. Then a honeymoon abroad. We cannot count on your identity remaining a secret for long in this district . . ."

Stephan broke off as two serving wenches brought in their dinner and began to lay covers on the table. "We shall discuss this more after we dine. Come, you look pale. We will both be the better for some food."

Belle rose shakily and took Stephan's proffered arm. Again, touching him was both pleasure and pain. Her stupid heart and its old infatuation for Stephan was determined to only recognize its own needs and would make no allowances for society's rules.

Apparently unaware of the havoc he wrought in her breast, Stephan saw her to her seat at one end of the table and then retreated calmly to the head.

The meal was a simple one and served all at once rather than in courses: some lamb with oysters, sauced chicken with a wedge of pigeon pie, gingerbread and greens. Belle found it all ambrosial, even the rather thick, sedimentatious wine that was all the house had to offer. Recovering more with every mouthful, Belle thought firmly about sensible things as she ate, trying to decide what would be best to do.

"I can see that your brain is again hard at work plotting stratagems," Stephan said when he observed her knitted brow. "But I sincerely hope that you do not execute any more plans without consulting me. Whether you care for the fact or not, we are bound up in this adventure together."

"Of course," Belle answered. But she did not look up from her plate. "I have been thinking, though, and I still feel that my first notion might be the best one. I can take refuge with my friend in York while the scandal dies down, which it surely will if given sufficient time. Why, have you not considered that if we wait long enough, the entire incident will likely be forgotten? You said yourself that no one actually knows who I am. If we part company immediately, perhaps no one will ever know we were here together."

Stephan put down his knife and frowned at her down the length of the table.

"I said that no one seems to know *yet*. But trust me about this, Belle, they will know soon, and they will delight in the situation." He took a swallow of wine and grimaced. He added: "You really have remarkably foul notions about my character, don't you? Do you really think that I would abandon you now? Alone in a strange country, without even a maid to lend you consequence?"

Belle winced, feeling ashamed.

"Stephan—"

"It doesn't matter, I suppose," he went on. "It is only that it would be nice if my wife held me in slightly higher regard than the general populace."

"But, Stephan, I do hold you in high regard—" Belle said, appalled at his interpretation of her words. "It is because of this that I—"

"Very well, then, let us say that I wish you to respect my intelligence and will." Stephan wasn't smiling as he again interrupted her. "We have not, in recent years, associated together. And I understand that you had no thought of ever compassing such a marriage as I have proposed. But make no mistake about this. You shall be my wife, Belle. You shall be ruined else, and I'll be made an object of infamy. I do not care to hear again about being the *bastard Kirton*, a seducer of innocents—particularly not Nabob Lydgate's stepdaughter!"

There was a pause and Stephan's angry phrase seemed to echo in the room.

"I see," Belle said slowly, meeting Stephan's dark gaze with one that was thoughtful. "You are proposing that I marry you so that *your* reputation, as well as mine—and my stepfather's—may be saved."

"Not saved, my dear; nothing can do that. Just not worsened by our encounter."

Belle lowered her gaze back to her plate. "I will have to think about this. And I feel I should warn you that my stepfather is not likely to thank you for *saving* his reputation in this manner."

Stephan finally smiled. It was only a slight flexing of his lips, but it improved his expression dramatically. "Think all you want, my dear, but you shall live with me as my wife. In fact, you will begin rehearsing the role tonight."

"What?" It was Belle's turn to drop her cutlery and gaze raptly down the table. "What do you mean I will be *rehearsing the role*?"

"I mean that in order to allay the landlord's suspicions and secure the last bedchamber, I gave him a false name and told him that we were man and wife." He said the outrageous with absolute calm. "We will be sharing the room."

Belle rubbed at the sudden sharp pain between her brows. It didn't seem possible, but every passing moment looked to make her situation worse. It was like being hounded by some monster from Greek myth.

"I don't suppose there is any possibility that you are jesting?" she asked without any real hope.

Stephan shook his head. "None. In any event, I want you where I can keep an eye on you. There will be no more flitting across the countryside when my back is turned. We haven't the time for any more foolishness."

Chapter Five

"So, you truly were not jesting," Belle said in a rather hollow voice as Stephan followed her into the violently blue bedchamber.

"No," Stephan agreed, casting her a quick glance as he shut the door that was perhaps slightly apologetic, and suggested that he was not without misgivings at this act of highhandedness.

The sound of the door's latch falling into place was loud in the silence and made Belle start nervously.

"Damnation, Belle," Stephan said in guilty exasperation. "You survived last night, did you not? You know good and well that I'm not some ravisher of innocents. You can stop looking like I am about to beat you."

"Perhaps fewer remonstrances and scoldings would improve my mood," Belle suggested, managing to smile and unfreeze her locked limbs. "I apologize if I look rather wan. Though I do not seem to possess the usual complement of female nerves, those which I do call my own have lately sustained a number of shocks."

Stephan exhaled slowly. "Aye, so they have. And a lesser woman would have been prostrated by them. For your calm and courage I am truly grateful." He crossed to Belle's side and took her hand. He pressed it gently as he looked down at her slightly averted head.

Belle returned the pressure fleetingly and then retreated to the fire. In the continuing lull in conversation, the endless spring shower could be heard pattering on the roof overhead.

"It is still raining. It seems it shall never end," she said inanely, stretching her fingers toward the small fire on the hearth. She still did not look at Stephan. "I do hate such dreary weather. I am quite unused to it now."

Stephan approached her. "Belle, you do see that marriage is the only thing that can extricate us from this mess?" he asked quietly, ignoring her suggested topic of conversation, and endeavoring one last time to persuade her to his logical position.

Belle shrugged helplessly. "Perhaps. But I also know that the impulse that prompts such chivalry will eventually die, and that there must be something else there to replace it or there will be enduring misery for both parties. And every misstep we have taken simply tightens the noose about our necks." She said earnestly: "I do believe that Fate is dogging us."

"A noose, is it? That is worse even than the shackles I was certain you were imagining. This trip shall rather tax my ingenuity, I fear." Stephan sighed after a moment, taking the other chair at the hearth. "Still, it will give you some time to know me better and grow accustomed to the idea of being my wife. You'll see that it isn't such a bad thing, Belle. We shall rub along tidily enough."

"Might we speak of something else for a while?" she asked. "Probably I am too weary for vapors, but it might be best not to test the limits of my nerves."

"You are not tired?" Stephan asked, studying the purple smudges beneath her eyes that spoke of the need for healing sleep.

She cast a fleeting glance at the single bed in the chamber and then she shook her head, causing Stephan to grimace.

"Well, then perhaps we might play cards for a while."

"Do you play cards?" Belle asked, surprised.

"Aye—and a sight better than I do chess, I might add. I have a pack in my valise." Stephan rose and went to the armoire. Their clothes were resting side by side within the cupboard, but both were careful not to comment on this intimacy.

"Do we leave in the morning?" Belle asked, as Stephan closed the armoire's door and went to fetch a small table for them to play upon.

"Aye, the Smythes will be departing and early, too. It will be best if from here forward our travels are attended by secrecy. In fact, we shall have to continue to assume other names until out of the district."

"We leave even if it is raining?" Belle asked again, surprised.

"Aye, the sooner we are away from Ormstead Park, the better it will be. Someone we know might venture into this inn. I do not trust life's vicissitudes."

"And I do not trust Lord Duncan," Belle muttered. "It would be like him to think up some nasty jest for his guests—perhaps even to write to Quincy and tell him of what has happened."

"My current feelings toward our host and hostess rather defy polite description, but Lord Duncan is not so careless of his skin that he will risk involving himself in our affairs. Nor will the coward Quincy," Stephan assured her. "And don't fear the weather. In this case, it truly is our ally. I've arranged for a private coach for the next leg of our journey."

"A judicious expenditure of funds if this foul weather holds," Belle agreed.

"Aye. It isn't pretty and shan't be the fastest mode of travel, but the roads are rough and mired. A curricle—and your saddle boils—would never survive them."

"And Roi?" Belle asked.

"I shall ride when the weather permits. Closed carriages are not my favorite mode of travel," he confessed.

"Travel sickness?" Belle asked sympathetically.

Stephan grunted an affirmative as he set the table midway between their chairs.

"Carriages always turned my mother's liver upside down," she confided.

"It isn't that so much as just not liking to spend a great deal of time in tight spaces," Stephan said honestly. "It has made sailing a bit of a challenge. I do not travel much in winter when one would often be forced below decks."

"Ah."

"As for Roi, though it will not suit his dignity, he shall have to endure being tied to the coach if the rain continues to be so heavy."

"He'll be lonely after being so much in your company," Belle teased, taking up the cards and fanning them out. She paused over one that had a bullet hole through the middle pip.

"A souvenir," Stephan explained. It was impossible to tell in the dim light, but Belle thought he blushed. "It was a fool's trick, but it was winning that wager that got me the money to buy my ship."

"Oh." Belle shuffled the cards. "So then your heart must be in Dover. Is that not the saying? *'Where your treasure is, there is your heart.'* "

Stephan shook his head and smiled slightly. "That would hold true only if my ship were my greatest treasure. But I can assure you that my heart is not in Dover, nor even in London where *The Kelpie Lass* currently docks."

93

Said with more heat, Belle might have taken his words as a compliment or even flirtation. As it was, she did not know how to interpret them.

"Roi will be relieved to hear this."

"Roi is not so jealous as you apparently imagine. And so, what shall we play—Commerce? All-Fours?" Stephan teased in return.

"You think to shock me, sir, but it will not serve. My stepfather is quite fond of all manner of vulgar games and for years has caused me to play with him. Frankly, I am not ashamed of my own skills." Belle relaxed some of her rigid posture.

"No?" Stephan also leaned back in his chair and stretched his legs out toward the hearth. He did not comment on this vulgar boast about a dubious achievement, nor volunteer any explanation of where he learned the disreputable game. "Well then, perhaps since we are to have a true contest of skills we should play for something more interesting than half-farthing points."

"As you wish. All-Fours is the game then, and we shall play to eleven points." Belle began to deal the cards, giving six to each of them. "What do you suggest as a wager? I have little with me that you might want. In fact, all I really have that you might want are my riding boots, and I do not think that you would fit in them."

"I believe that I saw some ink and parchment downstairs," Stephan said. "I could fetch it up for our use."

"You would accept a promissory note from me?" she asked, both flattered and charmed. She had never had a debt of honor and found that she rather liked the idea of someone accepting one from her.

"I should do so, of course," he assured her. "But that was not what I was intending."

"What, then, shall we stake?" Belle asked, intrigued.

"I propose that we handle our wager thusly. The paper will be quartered and we shall each take two pieces. On one, we shall write down what we would like to have from the other person—this may be anything that is not injurious or illegal. On the other we shall write down what we would give in wager—for instance, a bauble, a song . . ." Stephan looked a moment at Belle's lips and added: "Or a kiss."

"And then?" Belle asked, glad for the warm light of the fire that might cover any betraying blush that rose in her cheeks.

"And then we play. The one holding the winning hand may then select any one of the four pieces of paper and the loser must pay the forfeiture that is written there."

Belle considered for a moment. She very much wanted to play but sensed that there was some trap nearby. "And if the loser were to be repulsed by the wishes of the winner?" she asked.

Stephan shrugged, his face expressionless. "These are the terms, and that is how debts are. Honor demands that the loser pay up."

Belle looked at the cards waiting on the table, chewing thoughtfully on her lower lip. She truly was very skilled at All-Fours, and Stephan had been spectacularly bad at chess.

And, a voice inside added, *would you really mind being kissed again?*

"Very well then," she decided. "Fetch the ink and paper. We shall play the game for your stakes."

The satisfied gleam that came to Stephan's eye was not comforting, but Belle refused to be shaken from confidence. Instead of wasting her time in worry, she built up the tiny fire and brought a branch of candles to the table so that they might have adequate light.

The card with the missing pip had been put aside and Belle looked at it thoughtfully. It was another clue about a side of Stephan that she had never seen. First there was the small scar on his cheek as a reminder of a long-ago duel, and now there was this evidence of his being a master of pistols as well. Evidently his life had been filled with adventure since the year they parted.

Stephan returned swiftly and set about sundering the paper into fourths. He politely offered Belle the quill and well so that she might be the first to write down her wagers.

The old quill was poorly sharpened and the ink reduced to sludge, but it was still adequate for a short scribble.

Belle wished that she had longer to reflect on a prudent stake, but since she was convinced that she would emerge triumphant, she decided in the end to ask for what she wanted: a miniature portrait of Stephan, something that she was certain he did not have but which they might fairly easily acquire. *Belle did not stop to ask herself why she would want such a memento,* and for her forfeit she played fair and offered what Stephan wanted: a kiss.

Belle finished writing the last *s* of *kiss,* and then pushed the ink and quill toward Stephan with a deliberately calm hand. She blew lightly on her scraps of paper and, presently assured that they would not smear, folded them into quarters and waited politely for Stephan to do the same.

"You said eleven points?" he asked, taking up his cards and settling back in his chair.

"That is customary, I believe," Belle answered, arranging her hand and counting high and low trumps.

The game was not a long one where sober reflection might set in, and as they played out the hand, a slow fit of madness seemed to overtake Belle's tired brain. She'd had every intention of winning this game when she agreed to play, for she hated to lose and also very much wanted that miniature of Stephan. But as she stared at the lovely array of cards in her hand, which gave her the needed eleven points, she had a sudden, undeniable impulse to know what it was that Stephan had wagered. She did not have to ponder what it was that he wanted from her—or she did not believe that she needed to ponder this—but she was quite curious to know what he thought was a suitable forfeiture.

From there, it was only a small leap to the vexing question of which paper Stephan would choose if *he* were to win their game. At first, she had been certain that he would select his own paper and demand a kiss from her. But what if she was wrong in thinking that? A kiss he might acquire by some other means. What if he was actually as curious as she to see what was written on the other person's own folded scraps? Would the unknown prove more appealing than his most straightforward desire?

Stephan watched Belle worrying her lower lip and wondered what she was thinking. She had not lacked confidence at the beginning of the game. Indeed, she had set about playing her hand with relish, clearly intent on trouncing him. Even now, she did not seem so much concerned about losing as meditating deeply on some strategy.

The time came to lay their cards on the table. Stephan went first, watching not his own hand but Belle's face as he placed the cards in a row. He had only nine points.

"You've won," she said, without actually glancing at his offering. Her own cards were dropped face-down in a careless pile. Belle finally looked up, her expression schooled into guilelessness.

Stephan studied her face thoughtfully as he contemplated her lie.

"Have I?" He pondered for only a moment longer and decided not to call her on the obvious untruth. This was not the time to demand an explanation of why she had thrown the game.

"Yes, so you may choose a paper—any one." She suddenly looked nervous.

Stephan, whose hand had been hovering over one of his own scraps, acted on a sudden wise impulse and instead reached for one of hers.

"That paper is what I wished to win from you," Belle warned him.

"Is it?" Stephan looked at the burgeoning pleasure on her face and realized that he had made the right selection. He added lightly: "Well, this is the paper I wish most to see. Persistent curiosity has ever been my failing."

"Oh." Belle looked down as he unfolded the scrap and held it to the candlelight. When he said nothing of her request, her eyes were forced back up to his face.

"I think we can find an artist in York if you are impatient," he said, his eyes puzzling her out. "Or, if you are willing to wait, I am somewhat acquainted with Elisabeth Le Brun, and we might have her do one when we return to London after our honeymoon."

"I can wait," Belle assured him, giving him a blinding smile. Then, obviously recalling that he had said *after their honeymoon* she added: "You promise that you will have the miniature done for me, will you not, no matter what happens?"

"Of course. I shan't forget," he assured her. "I always pay my debts."

"Thank you. I shall hold you to that,"

Stephan nodded agreement. Her odd words probably portended something he should be worried about. But Belle was happy and smiling for the first time that day, and he was feeling rather cheerful, too. True, her smile wasn't the kiss he wanted, but somehow Stephan did not feel entirely deprived. He had been given another, more valuable gift. Belle cared enough to want a picture of him to carry on her person. That could only be taken as a propitious sign.

Curious, as he had honestly confessed to be, Stephan was still unwilling to risk Belle seeing what he had written on his own papers. Quickly, he gathered all four scraps and cast them into the fire. After her sweetly romantic request, his own demand for a kiss seemed somehow disappointing and mundane.

"You don't want to play another hand?" Belle asked, dissatisfaction in her voice as she watched the scraps burn. "I think that I should have a chance for revenge."

"Not tonight. We need to *'plough the deep,'* as the sailors say. Tomorrow morning is but a few hours away." Stephan rose. "I shall step out for a last breath of air and give you a while to prepare. Shall I send the abigail up to you?"

"No, I can manage on my own," Belle replied. Her

nervousness returned in a rush as she recalled that they would be sharing a bed.

And she would manage, too, Belle vowed. For the second night in a row she planned on sleeping fully clothed. Only this time, she was also leaving her hair in a tidy braid and burying herself beneath the shielding covers before Stephan came to bed. No matter what her silly heart wanted, there would be no repeat of what had happened the night before.

Chapter Six

Stephan returned to the bedchamber to find it lit only by the dying fire and Belle tucked beneath the covers, either in a deep swoon or feigning heavy sleep.

He walked quietly across the plank floor and took a seat in the chair near the hearth and prepared to get comfortable. A bootjack was needed to pry off his footwear, an abuse of leather that would have made him cringe except that these boots had already proven a disappointment and would be replaced at the first opportune moment.

Looking over at the unmoving lump beneath the covers, he shook his head. For an instant he considered being noble and passing the remainder of the night in his uncomfortable seat, but the day had been a long one and the morrow promised to be longer yet, so he would once again share Belle's pallet and hope to find rest for his body if not for his churning mind.

Walking quietly to the bedside, he looked down at his reluctant fiancée and saw, not without some amusement, that she had decided to remain dressed in the gown she'd worn to dinner. Perhaps she thought her numerous petticoats would be sufficient armor to ward off any libidinous impulses that might come over him in the night.

Stephan smiled wryly.

Had there ever been a less enthusiastic seduction and affair? He had never heard of one. Of course, what man would ever admit to such a farrago? What poet would look to such a situation for inspiration?

He laid down atop the covers and cast a pillow over his bootless feet so they would not take a chill. It wasn't easy to ignore his body's disappointment at its lonely state on the one side of the cloth barricade, but he was a man who understood the value of patience. He was no longer out to find triumph in a single battle, but was determined to win this entire campaign—and through as honorable tactics as he could manage.

He had been drunk—and perhaps even a little mad—when starting this enterprise, but he was sober and sane now, and ready to face the consequences of his action.

It was his wish that Belle also become accepting of what must be done. It was perhaps unreasonable to desire it, but he truly wanted Belle to surrender willingly to this marriage and not be defeated by force or coercion.

He grinned briefly. Seduction was another matter, of course. He would happily use passion to bind her to him. He had seen the shy desire in her eyes last night. The girl was not cold.

But she *was* stubborn and reckless. And without the suborning influence of brandy, it might be that she would be able to fight off her desires.

This thought removed the smile from his face and replaced it with a scowl.

Whatever her mind, the venture of marriage still had to be undertaken. He understood this fact even if she did not. Somehow he had to convey the wisdom of this solution. He had to find a way past her shields and get to the headstrong mind that lurked behind her pretty face. He needed to win her agreement so that there would be no more surprises like he'd had today.

The first step in this campaign would be to gain her confidence and trust. The *how* of the matter evaded him, but he would think on it . . . while his body struggled with realization that it would not be having Belle tonight, nor any other in the near future.

Belle exhaled slowly. Stephan had brought with him into their chamber the smell of rain and unsettled wind, making her very aware of him and disturbing her new, but precarious, peace. It was true that this was not the first night that she had passed with Stephan in her bed, but the previous evening could hardly count as true experience. She—and he—had been largely insensible through most of it.

Restlessness infused her limbs and made her nose itch. The urge to get up and pace was terribly strong. It was difficult, but she gritted her teeth and forced herself to remain still while he removed his boots and checked the dying fire. Her very breath was suspended while he walked over to the bed and looked down at her.

Once Stephan settled onto the mattress and appeared to compose himself for sleep, Belle finally allowed her eyes to open and entertain themselves by watching the gold and red shadows dance on the plastered ceiling. She meditated on the day's events while waiting for sleep to overcome her.

Not being of spiritual inclination, she did not bother with prayers for guidance, but rather made an effort to sort out her tangled thoughts and impressions by the old device of her childhood where she pretended to compose a letter to her mother. Where this habit first came from, she did not know, but in pastimes, when she was distressed or confused, she had found a measure of peace in creating these counterfeit missives to her parent.

At first her emotions so baffled description that she could not think where to begin her woeful tale. It was the first time that her character had been traduced, and she faced public humiliation. Her original impulse had been to indulge in a bout of angry—if futile—tears. Fortunately, Stephan's calm presence held off her incipient hysteria and demanded that she think and act reasonably.

Eventually she shook off the feeling that Nemesis stalked her; and she remembered her first sight of the beautiful Hyde Park in London. She had glimpsed it on the day after her arrival in England, and she found in the memory of its gardens a calm place to start her tale of affliction and Marvelle treachery. And from that beginning she was able to at last relate the events that had overtaken her in the last two days in a coherent manner. In this quiet, mental recitation she discovered that she was—quite oddly—still aided by Stephan's presence, for she found his warmth and regular breathing to supply a strangely soothing effect on her ruffled nerves. Little by little her feelings of anxiety died away and she relaxed her tense muscles, surrendering to the mattress's blandishments, which called her to dreams.

So you see, Mama, it has finally happened. If you were still here you would have to see your daughter wearing the willow. Actually, more than wearing them . . . I am considering cutting some willow branches to beat myself with. Of course, I am in no rush to begin the self-flagellation. I suspect that there will be ample time to rue this day's work in the weeks to come.

And this whole imbroglio comes about because I was indulging in the pleasant but foolish trick of thinking that all would be well if I made just a simple push to set things right. I hadn't remembered that Stephan is bloody crafty and stubborn when he's set his mind upon some goal.

The whole situation is as ridiculous as it is painful, and he quite refuses to see the difficulties. Perhaps he doesn't understand the sort of notoriety that will come with open scandal. I can hardly imagine it myself . . . but what I have thought of is sufficiently harrowing to make me think that I had best remain resolute and stay with my plan to depart from him.

I suppose that I should be grateful that this hasn't turned out to actually be "worse than death" instead of mere disgrace. But I suspect that it is only a matter of time before it becomes "worse than." The poets made it all seem rather tepid, but the flesh-and-blood reality of the situation is most bloody distracting. I hope that I can remain firm and do what is right. I am sure that this is what you would want me to do.

Missive finally complete, Belle decided that it was time to cease worrying about the disasters of the day and give herself to slumber. Yet, try as she did, entrance to Morpheus' realm still evaded her. However weary her body and comfortable the bed, her mind was yet too restless to retire.

And that was Stephan's fault.

Rolling onto her side by stealthy increments, she was finally able to see half of Stephan's profile. It was a handsome one, if perhaps a little harsh and rugged by the standards of male beauty currently in fashion.

Inch by cautious inch, she eased the stifling linens

down from her face and looked more fully upon his ruthless features.

She found it extraordinary that he showed none of the vulnerability that sleeping people usually evidenced. When he smiled, she could see bits of the sweet boy she had known and was misled into believing him compliant of nature. Perhaps because he did not rant and bellow as her stepfather did, it was easy to dismiss his temper. But at that moment, without a distracting smile on his lips, he looked resolved and even implacable.

A lesser woman might be discouraged by such apparent resolution even in slumber, but Belle had devised her own defenses against male stubbornness and did not fear that her will would be suborned. It was simply a matter of remaining resolved upon the most sensible course.

And not letting him touch her. Or wear down her defenses with sweet words or smiles.

Intrigued by a dark lock of Stephan's hair, which had escaped from confinement and strayed over to her pillow, Belle wrapped the black silk about her finger and savored the feel as it slid over her skin.

"Oh, dear," she breathed, lifting it to her lips. So, she had not imagined last night's pleasure of running her hands through his hair!

She had probably enjoyed kissing him as much as she recalled, too.

Unhappily, Belle concluded that her time with Stephan was not going to be easily forgotten. If only the circumstances of their reunion had been different! Aside from his face, there was so much about him that she admired: his wit and quickness of apprehension, his success at building a better life than the one that had been allotted to him by birth.

But Fate obviously had other plans for them, or she would not have thrown them together in circumstances that absolutely forbade their marriage. Whatever her own inclinations, Belle knew that she could not marry Stephan when such a union would cause a scandal so large that he would likely be rejected by the society, which he had wooed so diligently, and which had finally accepted him in spite of his birth. It was overindulging optimism to suppose that the case would somehow be otherwise. The hypocritical moralists in the *haut ton* would revel in the scandal of Stephan Kirton marrying a ruined female from the shops. Everyone would say that he wed her because her stepfather was rich beyond all dreams of avarice, and not because of a sincere attachment. That such avaricious behavior was encouraged among the well-born would not matter; it was different for bastards.

No, in some manner, by some means, she had to convince him of this fact before it was too late.

The thought of succeeding was nearly enough to oppress her spirits, and it did make her heart feel heavy.

"It's all quite impossible, but good night, Stephan," she breathed, leaning close enough to brush the lightest of kisses over his marred cheek. Then, surprised by her boldness, she retreated to her own pillow and forced herself to close her eyes and ignore her newly agitated reflections.

The fire settled in the grate with a soft clatter that could barely be heard above the rain, which continued to hurl itself at the window, and then Stephan said: "Good night, Belle. And you will find in time that it is all quite possible. It simply requires some courage and planning."

Belle managed to stifle an embarrassed groan by pulling the covers over her head.

Beside her, Stephan smiled in satisfaction, and finally allowed himself to sleep.

The exigencies of fashion made it necessary for a lady to have support when dressing and arranging her hair. The abigail at the inn was not entirely without experience at assisting guests who sometimes traveled without maids, and was fortunately able to achieve a suitable coiffure in a very short time—and with little extraneous conversation.

Belle glanced quickly at the offered looking glass and then gave it to the girl to pack away. Her reflection should have assured her that she was in her best looks that morning, but she still wore an air of anxious distraction as she joined Stephan in the breakfast parlor.

"You are frowning, my sweet," he said, pouring her a cup of coffee. He looked very tidy for not having had any assistance into his clothing. It made Belle wonder if he had a valet at home, and where home was these days. With all the intimate things they had spoken of, there had been no talk of domestic details beyond the fact that he kept two houses.

"Surely it is too early for you to be vexed at the day," he said. "Unless you are regretting our game from last night?"

"I am not vexed, precisely," Belle temporized, accepting the warm cup. About the game she made no comment. "I see that it is still raining."

"Aye, but we will press on regardless. Sit down and break your fast. You shall feel better for getting something in you. It is hard to be cheerful when your liver is turned upside down."

"My liver is in its proper place, thank you."

"Then perhaps it is the neighborhood that is affecting you. I find that I have no love for this place outside of the summer. It is to be hoped that the north will not be so uniformly bleak. Kent, I swear, is never half so gloomy. Nor London either. We shall travel as quickly as we may to escape this horrid clime."

Belle assented, pleased but also slightly saddened to have one question answered. *London* and *Kent.* She had heard that Kent was very pretty. She was quite certain that she would have enjoyed living there.

They were on their way only a short time later. In spite of the drizzle, Stephan elected to ride so Belle was allowed some more time to think in the privacy of the dark carriage.

Unfortunately, she found very little that was useful or cheering to think about. She still planned on parting company with Stephan when they reached the safety of Ashlars. Yesterday's misadventures had discouraged her from attempting any more travel on her own, so she and Stephan would have to remain together for a time. Which meant that, until she reached Becky's home, there was little she could do to advance her plans except be an agreeable, docile companion, and not fire Stephan's ever-ready suspicions by being too willful.

Perhaps she might even enjoy having this time with Stephan. It would likely be her only chance to visit with him, as it seemed improbable that she would see him once she returned home. She should count the moments as a blessing.

Bored with her own unhappy company and the swaying of the coach, Belle pushed aside the carriage shutter and stared out at the damp scenery.

The outside view was not encouraging. They were traveling by lesser-known routes that led into the country, and the world grew darker with every mile. It was a curious atmospheric effect that the dull landscape, which should have been tempered by the spots of spring florals was instead made drained and bleak by the washed-out colors of the closed-up blooms that had gone against nature and furled inward in oppositional protest of the unseasonable cold and rain.

It did not relieve the tedium either that in their effort to avoid detection, they seemed to have left behind the inhabited world and all man-made diversions that might amuse the eye. Everything was desolate and barren in this monotonous, tenantless realm.

It was early afternoon when they reached the small and ill-named village of Buckswood. It was little more than a huddle of lonely gray buildings amid the grasses and brambles that were the only vegetation at that end of the moor. There was no sign of life in the few mean cottages that lined the road, not even a light or twitching curtain, and not so much as sheep or stray cat idling along the narrow lane.

Fortunately, there was an inn. Caskers' Chance, though surrounded with an air of dilapidation, at least had a lantern hung out next to the door. It shone like a beacon in the late-afternoon murk.

As Stephan alighted from Roi and came to assist her down from the carriage, a solitary figure stepped out onto the sloped step at the front of the inn and looked at them assessingly.

Belle, once again on the ground, viewed the building with a dubious eye, disliking it instinctively. There was something slightly wrong with the architecture—the angles and heights were not harmonious. Nor did she care for the color of the building, which seemed a gray of desolation and despair.

113

The landlord, Casker, was next to be scrutinized, and Belle found that she liked him even less than the building. Something in his face was very ill-made, and he was too tall and large to look entirely normal.

Stephan, having made his own assessment of the remoteness of the village and their accommodations, finally turned to the landlord and said: "My wife and I would like rooms for the night, and our coachman will also need a place to sleep."

"Yer wife, is she?" The man's voice was gruff and somehow more unpleasant than any other she had ever heard. "Then ye'll have tae share a chamber or make do with the loft. We have another gentleman here who has already bespoken my other room. Yer coachman may sleep in the stables. 'Tis warm enough there."

Belle was surprisingly relieved when she heard Stephan agree to sharing a bedchamber. It did not please her to feel so unnerved by her surroundings, and she could not ignore the chills that were creeping down her nape. Even disgrace was preferable to whatever ills might accompany this place.

They separated in the entry. Belle followed the landlord to their room and dismissed him quickly. She made only a short stop in their assigned bedchamber and saw to her own needs as she was informed that there was no chambermaid to be had. The room was filled with commonplace furniture and was rather dusty, though a quick inspection of the sheets showed that they were not obviously soiled.

There was a fire in the grate and a latch on the window. . . .

Still, Belle was nervous and wished to be away from the chamber. Personal ablutions seen to, she hurried down the dark stair, lit only by an oil lamp, which, because it was turned too low, completely failed to shed any light on the dark man-sized niches of the stair's turnings. These turnings were most disturbing for they were made up of the kind of dark and seemingly purposeless recesses where any sort of monster might lurk in the gloom.

Completely intimidated by her imagination and the dark, Belle hurried on, preceded by her timid, wavering shadow. She was more than anxious to rejoin Stephan in the inn's only parlor and profoundly grateful that she had not come to this place alone.

Belle did not in the least mind when she discovered that the inn's other guest was also sharing their smoldering hearth and would be partaking of his dinner at the same table. A dozen guests would have been welcome, even had they all worn hideous catskin coats and smelled of onions as this specimen did.

They had time only for desultory introductions, though those were somewhat diverting as Stephan followed his plan to use another name, and Belle was amused to hear herself called *Missus Smythe*. The landlord and a sullen woman, whom Belle was not too surprised to learn was his sister, brought in some rude platters and set about distributing smudged crockery with a careless hand.

Their fare was to be mutton and wilted salad, and as Belle had feared, the meat was ancient—gray, greasy, and tough enough to resist the dull knives provided. The greens, too, were rather aged and looked as anemic as all the other vegetation they had seen about the unhealthy town.

Even the porter they were offered was foul stuff; in spite of being sweetened with some kind of treacle, the brown beer was too thick to be enjoyed. She, Stephan, and the inn's other guest each took but a single mouthful, then by common consent put their cups aside, the latter even going so far as to spit the drink back.

When the landlord and his sister at last withdrew, Mister Oliver Frye, as the other diner liked to refer to himself, finally grew somewhat loquacious and proceeded to regale them with a gruesome history of the inn and its supposedly haunted locale.

It did not improve either Belle's appetite or her nerves to discover that that Casker's Chance, named after the present owner, had at one time been an undertaker's establishment. It was built by the town's casket maker at a time when the village population was aging and he had a great deal of business, which demanded an expansion of his premises. Those dark niches on the stair's landing, she learned, were there to accommodate the coffins at the turning so that the body would not be upset by being righted on end in its transport up and down the stairs.

She also had the unpleasant feeling, though Mister

Frye never said so, that the bedchambers had been used for other purposes than housing the living.

"But then plague came to the town and there was too much custom for a time—and then none at all. Casker's son changed professions to innkeeping."

"How enterprising of him," Belle said hollowly. "It is a pity that he did not change buildings as well."

"Aye, but that takes some brass, and he likely knew that he was not much of a businessman. I can't say that he is making much of a go of things here. This beer is a disgrace. I'm as fond of the home brewed as the next man, but I'd not drink any of the pish that's offered here," Mister Frye complained. "I've traveled the length of the land and I've never known the like! You have to watch these out-of-the-way places. Why, I've seen some travelers who ended up with piper's cheeks, so swollen were they that their own ma wouldn't know 'em. And once sotted, they could be sold like bullocks and be none the wiser."

Mister Frye shook his head sadly.

"Sold like bullocks?" Belle repeated, baffled by the expression.

"Cheated, ma'am. Not but what most of these wasters wouldn't spend the Michaelmas rent in midsummer's noon anyway. Still, it's dishonest industry, and Mister Oliver Frye doesn't stand for any but pound dealing!"

"I see." Belle looked over at Stephan who was studying their companion with a fascinated eye. She had never seen him wear such an unpleasant and suspicious expression, and had to wonder at its cause. Mister Frye seemed harmless if rather too colorful for respectability.

" 'Course others just died. They sent for the vein-opener at this one place I was at, but there was naught to do when a buffle-head has drunk that much poison. He was dead as mell by morning. Ah, the evils of drink are many!" Mister Frye sighed heavily.

"I shall certainly heed your advice and not drink anything," Belle promised, glancing again at Stephan, who now wore a rather arrested expression as well as being very still. She wondered what was in Mister Frye's last narrative that had so particularly riveted his attention. She did not think that it was haughty condescension of a social inferior that froze him in place.

"Then a wise woman ye are, Missus Smythe."

Belle tried not to blush at the undeserved title as Frye went on: "I like to meet a lady with a brain built well to the fore."

"Thank you."

He beamed at her. "Now, if it would not be too personal a question to ask, what has brought ye here? It isn't often we get the folks living on velvet in this part of the country, for there's no quality about that you might be visiting, leastwise, none that I know of."

"We are going to visit a friend at Ash—"

"In Northumbria," Stephan interrupted, finally taking a hand in the conversation. "This seemed to be the most direct route to our destination, but I think we may have been misled about the roads."

"Aye, I believe you were," Mister Frye agreed with a sapient nod. "These country turnips are all the same—no notion of distances at all. The fact is, there is no short path from here to anywhere in Northumbria. Ah well, perhaps tomorrow the sun will be out and you can be safely on your way back to a main road. 'Tis a much safer place. Especially with a lady along. Too many dishonest men about these days."

He and Stephan exchanged a glance that left Belle feeling wholly excluded.

"We shall be on our way in the morning, with or without the sun," Stephan said a trifle grimly.

The landlord came slinking back into the room, this time bearing a tray that had the makings for rum punch. He set it smack in the middle of the table, and after a glance that contained obvious annoyance, he noisily gathered the glasses of untouched porter and retreated from the room.

"I wonder what ails that creature," Belle muttered. "Surely he is not offended that we did not drink his horrid beer. Certainly this is the most ill-run establishment I have ever stayed in—no chambermaid, no groom. And I am sure no cook. It is most abnormal."

Catching the second look that passed between Stephan and Mister Frye, Belle scowled and demanded: "But why would that anger him? We have paid for the beer. What we do with it is our own affair."

"He's a queer one, right enough," Mister Frye said cryptically, casting Stephan a last quick glance before leaning back in his chair and picking at his teeth with his knife's point.

"I think that we had best pass on the punch," Stephan said. "It is high time that my wife and I retired, as we plan to make an early start."

"Very sound notion," Mister Frye agreed, putting aside his knife and rising up politely as Stephan assisted Belle from her chair.

Sensing that something of import was in the air, Belle did not argue, but instead said a smiling good night and allowed Stephan to guide her from the room.

She looked back once when they reached the stairs and was not entirely surprised to see that Mister Frye had pried open a window and was pouring the rum out into the rain.

"Stephan," she began firmly, "I want an explanation of what is going on here."

"Not yet, Belle," he said softly. "Let us regain our chamber."

Beginning to feel alarmed, Belle remained silent, being careful to stay away from the dark niche on the landing even though Stephan was with her.

Stephan was apparently unimpressed with their accommodations, especially when he noted the faulty latch on the door. His first action was to thrust a chair against the thin panel and then to make up the fire and light the meager lamps that had been provided.

"What is wrong?" Belle whispered, so caught up

in Stephan's mood, she checked the window shutters to see that they were secure.

"I believe that our Mister Frye is from Bow Street."

"Bow Street? Oh!" Belle spun about. "You mean that he is a *runner*?"

"Aye. That is exactly what I mean."

"But why on earth would he be here?" Belle asked, coming to the hearth where Stephan waited.

"I have a notion or two," he answered. "None of them pleasant."

"He can't know about us," Belle insisted.

Stephan's lips twitched, easing some of the grimness from his face. "No, I don't think he is after us. There simply hasn't been enough time for anyone to send a runner after us. It would need one more day at least for the news to get to London. And in any event, there is nothing that a runner could do as we are both of age. No, our Mister Frye is out to catch a bigger fish."

"Then what—oh, smuggling." Belle sank into the hard wood chair. "It must be that. Why else would he talk so much about the evils of drink?"

Stephan stared at her for a moment and then agreed: "Why else?"

"Do you think that they shall arrest someone tonight?" Belle asked. "After all, I saw no evidence of French wine or brandy in this inn. Quite the opposite. But perhaps that was to delude Mister Frye into thinking that there is none here?"

"Perhaps. Certainly they'll arrest someone on the

morrow. With any luck, we shall be well away before anything happens. I fear that you shall have to miss your breakfast, Belle. We will stop at some other Inn later in the day."

"That is not a hardship," she assured him. "I do not believe that I have ever eaten so ill prepared a meal. In fact, I spit out my mutton into my napkin. It was too foul to swallow."

"That was probably wise." Stephan rose and went to his valise. He seemed distracted.

"But could it really be smuggling that brings a runner here? Isn't stopping free-traders the job of the navy and inland coast guard?" Belle asked. She thought a moment more. "And we are miles from any coast. He could not be after free-traders."

"There are land smugglers," Stephan said, shutting his bag. "And those who receive smuggled goods. However, I don't propose to waste a great deal of time worrying about it. My only concern is to get you away from here as speedily as possible. We do not need to be caught up in events and summoned as witnesses for an inquest."

Belle yawned abruptly. "My apologies, Stephan. I find that I am suddenly very tired."

"Too tired for a game of cards?" he asked, holding up a deck and a small silver flask.

Belle's eyes widened, her sleepiness temporarily held at bay. "No, I am not that tired. We could play for a while. What shall it be? Whist?"

Stephan shook his head. "Nay. I want revenge for last night."

"Revenge? But why? You won after all."

"I did not win," he answered, dragging a table closer to the hearth. He handed her the flask. After a moment, Belle uncapped it and took a small sip. "You cheated and let me have that victory. There'll be none of that tonight, however. I plan on defeating you at All-Fours."

"Hmph!" Abashed, Belle looked down, being careful to secure the flask's lid.

"I understand why you did it, Belle. Being curious is a trait we have in common, and it probably told you a great deal about me. Nevertheless, we shall play honestly tonight."

Belle looked up and was relieved to see that Stephan was smiling at her. She returned his flask to him. "We haven't any paper for our wagers," she pointed out.

"Then we shall simply have to name our stakes this time." He returned the flask to his pocket without drinking.

Belle's eyes went back to her lap as she considered this. "And what do *you* want this time?" she asked, studying her hands.

"Why a kiss, of course," he answered matter-of-factly. "And what would you like of me?"

Belle was silent a moment as she studied her fingers. Then she said carelessly: "Oh, I should like a chance to ride Roi."

"Fair enough," Stephan agreed, shuffling the cards. "Shall we begin?"

Belle took a deep breath and, glancing about uneasily at the shadowy room, she finally answered: "Yes. Let's have a game."

Chapter Seven

Belle's hair had responded to the prolonged exposure to damp air by becoming daily more wayward and curly until that evening, escaping from its bands, it reached the circumference and color of an angel's halo. Much to Stephan's delight, she seemed disinclined to restore it to order and it was left to stray where it would, painted red and gold by the light of the lamp and small fire, which smoldered sullenly on the hearth.

Annoyed at the interruption to his reverie by the smoky, twisting plumes, Stephan frowned at the inadequate blaze. He hoped that there would be sufficient coal to keep he and Belle warm until morning, but was pessimistic as the coal shuttle was nearly empty. It also seemed unlikely that there was a lad available to fetch more to the rooms. Casker's

Chance wasn't the sort of establishment that catered to quality.

"We had best hope the wind doesn't switch 'round to the northwest, or this chamber will be a smoke-house," he commented, eyeing the hearth with misgiving. The rain, which had come and gone in violent fits and starts, was again patting at their window, asking admittance like a timid but persistent cat.

Belle agreed uneasily and began arranging her cards with fidgeting fingers. "Stephan," she said, pretending to examine her hand. "I cannot escape the feeling that this room was never designed with the living's comfort in mind. As you noticed, the inglenook is so shallow, and you can see that it has hardly been blackened. I think it was intended only to present the appearance of comfort. After all, if Mister Frye was correct and this was an undertaker's, it is hardly likely that they would have burned fires—"

"Don't think about it, Belle," he replied, making his first discard. "Mister Frye was simply trying to frighten us into leaving before he started his work. This story of an undertaker's abode is likely only a fanciful invention. And if it was not, then these were the family's chambers. There would be no reason to put in fireplaces otherwise. Don't be so morbid."

"I am not morbid," she countered. "Merely making an observation about the architecture."

"In any event, there is nothing we can do about the building, whatever it was previously. And you shall surrender the game to me immediately if you do not concentrate."

"That is most unlikely. I am not the one who always loses at chess," she answered with a disdainful sniff, then discarded. However, a moment later she demonstrated that her thoughts had not truly turned to her game when she asked: "But, Stephan, even if Mister Frye was wrong about this house's history, do you not think that it is possible for some places to be haunted by past events? I had never believed in ghosts before, but this place is different. Can you not feel the unwholesomeness of the air here? The entire town seems to me most unhealthy. It is so unnaturally silent. We didn't see a single person on the road."

"It was raining, Belle. They would hardly be out to stroll around the muddy streets. Now be sensible. The only thing haunting this place is the smell of ill-cooked meals and unwashed travelers." Stephan looked up, eyes gleaming. He laid down his hand and the corners of his mouth lifted. "Ah! Your luck is out tonight, my sweet. My point is good, is it not?"

"Yes," Belle conceded, feeling annoyed with herself for her lapse in concentration. "That is to say, your point is good. Luck is not a factor. It is skill and experience that shall carry the day."

"And you are a Captain Sharpe?" he teased, eyes twinkling as he gathered in the cards. "That could prove useful to a man in business who has periods of quiet. Of course, it would be shameful to live off a wife's wits, but I am a most adaptable man."

"Well, I am not precisely a gamester, but I spent a deal more time playing cards than the pianoforte." Belle gathered her disappointing hand. In an effort to forget her foreboding she changed the subject. "I take it from your comments about business that you are a *Whig*, and supported the Reform Acts that are now causing such fervor in London?"

"Absolutely. Aren't you?"

"In sympathy—of course. My stepfather would have disowned me else. But, of course, in all practical ways my opinion does not matter. Women have no power in parliament."

Stephan snorted. "The politicians like to think that, but believe me, I have met some of those politicians' wives, and they are formidable creatures. Trust me, they have a great deal to say about affairs of parliament and how this nation is run."

Belle snorted back. "That is not real power. 'Tis borrowed strength at best."

"It's real enough, sweet. It simply isn't the naked power that men use. Women are more subtle than direct. Now, *en garde, ma belle*. Beware the agitating talk of politics or I shall have this hand from you, too."

"Well, I suppose that I must content myself with the knowledge that slavery has been abolished all over the empire. It is the first small step toward minor power for all living beings." Belle's tone was complaining, but her eyes gleamed.

"God help the man who ever attempts to enslave you," he muttered.

"Indeed, for he shall need it."

"Don't glare at me, my sweet. I only want to be your husband, not your master." Stephan handed her the flask. "Here, take a nip. Just in case your skill should momentarily falter, have a little something to take the sting away."

"Thank you, but I shall not drink while I play. I prefer to keep my wits about me." Belle yawned again, her insubordinate body betraying her. She said with a touch of pique: "That loss was simply momentary carelessness. This hand shall be mine."

"Of course," Stephan agreed with infuriating blandness as Belle bent her head over her cards.

"And you shall not succeed in distracting me again, so there is no point in inaugurating any more annoying discussions about politics."

A few minutes into earnest play and Belle had completely forgotten her newfound fear of ghosts. She was disconcerted to find that Stephan was actually a gifted player and well able to calculate the odds of their game. He also had a disconcerting trick of looking into her eyes and fathoming what cards she held and which ones she most needed to possess. And the fiend carefully kept them back from her. It was far too late for prudence in her wager, and concern at the course of events had her nibbling at her lip and her foot tapping restlessly on the floor as she redoubled her efforts to win.

They played on, absorbed in the game until the fire began to die and there were no other sounds from the inn's lower floors.

"You kept that heart most well-guarded." Belle conceded her loss at last as Stephan laid his hand on the table. She was more than a little stunned at the turning of her fortunes and could only stare at the array of powerful cards that faced her across the table.

"I have finally learned how to judge your more reckless style of play," Stephan answered, putting the table aside. He rose lazily to his feet. "Come, my sweet. It is quite late. Time to pay up. Then we must go to bed. We make an early start again tomorrow."

Belle blinked and then stood. Her heart was thudding in a most disconcerting manner and her knees were unsteady. It was all she could do to make the two steps toward Stephan without faltering. She had tried very hard not to let this happen.

Of course, that annoying but truthful voice in her head said, *if you had really not wanted this to happen, you wouldn't have played at all*.

"Will you give me your hand, Belle?" Stephan asked gently, extending his own.

It was a long moment before Belle could raise her eyes from Stephan's vest and meet his bright gaze, and another minute beyond that before she could bring herself to place her hands in his outstretched palms.

"Such tightly clenched fists," he remarked lightly,

urging her fingers open with the stroke of his thumbs. "One would think that you did not trust me to deal honestly with you, Belle. 'Tis only a kiss. I promise that this will not be so bad. You must trust me to keep you safe—even from myself."

"I do trust you, more or less," she answered, her voice a little breathless. Her knees were still infuriatingly weak.

"Good." Stephan urged her closer, putting one hand about her waist and drawing her near. His touch was warm and gentle.

Belle's head tilted and her eyes fluttered closed. Stephan stared down at the upturned countenance. It was delightful, painted with a slight blush, her lips slightly reddened from her worrying them during play. Even her hair begged to be touched. The temptation was almost enough to make him abandon caution and swoop down upon her like a raptor.

But that way lay madness. One step on that slippery slope, and he might never regain control. He could not risk it. He would have to postpone collecting his winnings until after their wedding.

With a suppressed groan, Stephan brought his lips down on her forehead instead of her mouth. He allowed himself a brief caress and then released his captive without once touching those reddened lips or pulling her tight against his protesting body.

"There! Was that so awful?" he asked, when her eyes opened and she stared at him in mild shock—and perhaps the smallest amount of disappointment.

"I'll leave you now for a minute or two so you may prepare for bed. I shan't be gone long, but while I am away I want you to prop that chair against the door."

"Wait!" Belle reached for his sleeve as he turned away. Her skirts brushed his empty hands. Stephan found the inanimate cloth was cold after the warmth of her fingers curled against his own.

"What is it?" he asked, facing her again. "I promise that I shall not go far. No ghosts shall get you in so short a time."

"It isn't that," Belle said, rising onto her tiptoes and resting her hands on his shoulders. She looked deeply into his eyes and said earnestly: "That was very sweet of you, Stephan. It was the act of a true gentleman. But I believe in paying my debts."

"Belle—" he began, but he was interrupted when she pressed her lips against his.

It was a fleeting kiss, a bare instant in duration. Yet that brushing of lips had within it all the latent fire that he had remembered from that first night of desire. One moment of contact and his body quickened. Reason and will fled.

"I think we have discovered the true motto of your family," he said through clenched teeth, backing away from her innocent but incendiary touch. "*Reckon not*. That has to be it."

"Stephan?" she asked, brow knitting as he hurried for the door. "What is wrong with you?"

"I'll be back shortly. Go to bed, Belle. Perhaps

once out of sight you shall be more out of mind. I can only pray so since I am not a plaster saint to withstand any amount of torment." His voice was as frustrated as she had ever heard it.

"Oh," she looked down and caught sight of his changing body as it reshaped his clothes. She colored and then muttered: "I see. That wasn't intentional. You *asked* for a kiss. I was just playing fair."

"Yes, my mind is aware of that, but my stupid body is rather slow to realize. It does not seem to grasp the distinction of your intent. I shall have to take it away while it regains its equilibrium. I'll be back in a while. Do not wait for me, Belle." Exasperated with himself, Stephan picked up one of the lanterns and fled the room.

A long walk through the cold fog was clearly indicated.

Belle began preparing for bed and, agitated, once again found herself spinning out her tale of woe for her absent mother.

Mama, you were quite right in warning me about the disastrous effects of reading horrid novels. I have quite succeeded in turning this inn into the Castle of Ortranto, and I've even peopled it with fiends.

I fear that the exhilaration of near-sin is rapidly leaving me, too, and I again feel cold and frightened. It's quite wrong of me, I know, but I do wish that Stephan would hurry back. I am likely to dream of ghouls and winding sheets if he does not return be-

fore I fall asleep. Yet, given his present humor, if he does return before I am asleep . . .

Belle looked toward the wardrobe.

Shall I perhaps try and save myself—and Stephan—from sin by changing into some drab merino and putting my hair up neatly beneath a cap? I should think that a gloomy enough costume to dampen any lover's feelings of ardor.

Ah! But I have just recalled that I do not have any itchy gray woolens with me. At this moment I can dress neither to invite or repel . . . How I hate being without all my luggage now that it has come so near winter again!

With this discouraging, but entirely prosaic thought, Belle laid herself down upon the bed and tried to go to sleep.

Belle woke to the soft snap of a door latch and the faint sound of retreating footsteps.

"Stephan?" she asked, sitting up with difficulty as the thick feather mattress had her trapped in its smothering folds.

Uncertain that she was not dreaming, Belle looked quickly about the empty bedchamber, which was still faintly lit by the last embers of the smoky hearth.

Had he left her again, this time without urging her to secure the door? Surely not! She could have sworn that he had only just returned from his walk and settled in to sleep a moment ago.

Belle waited, breath held, for a count of ten. No

footsteps returned to her door. Around her the shadows thickened and the wicked old house began to mutter threateningly in its joints and sigh through its eaves.

Or perhaps there was someone lurking in the passage outside her door! Maybe the person was on his knees with an eye to the keyhole, and she could hear their breathing!

"Stephan?" she whispered again.

A timber creaked loudly.

Alarmed, and trying not to be angry at his abandonment—there could be many things that would exculpate Stephan for leaving her alone in that horrid room, though at the moment she couldn't think of one that was forgivable—Belle quickly rose from the cot and pulled on her shoes, resolved to follow rather than stay another moment alone in that horrid chamber.

Fear rapidly overshadowed her mind, darkening her thoughts more with every passing moment. The longer she dwelled on the building's oddities, the more convinced she became that it wasn't an inn at all. Where were all the murmurs of servants or other visitors going to their beds? Or the sounds of the mail coach, or horses being changed in the yard? She had never visited a place so silent.

Alarmed to the point of panic, though unsure why except for the unusually intense silence, she could not entirely fight off the ridiculous conviction that something dreadful had happened to every living person in the building and she was abandoned in this awful place with the ghosts of all those who had died in the last epidemic.

"I should trust you, should I, *Stephan Smythe*? You'll take care of me—*Ha!* Clearly I am going to have to take care of you." Belle spoke aloud in the hope that it would give her courage.

In spite of the urge to hurry, it took her an additional precious minute to light the room's remaining lamp. It should have been unnecessary for her to do so, of course, but as there had been no indication of any lanterns left burning in the hall earlier that evening, Belle was taking no chances with wandering about in the dark in that horrid abode.

She moved stealthily across the room and stood for a moment at the door, listening carefully to see if there truly were voices in the corridor. But whatever she had heard earlier, all was silent now. Not even the floor creaked. She knelt quickly and peeked through the keyhole.

No eye looked back. The hall appeared empty.

Belle rose and pulled open her door. Stepping from the relative warmth and security of their room, she was immediately grateful for the lantern's temperate light and minor heat. Casker's Chance was not tightly built and she was dismayed to find that the solid fog from outside had invaded its halls through the ill-fitting casements and doors, filling up the dark corridor with fingers of thick white vapor that smelled most noxious.

Belle hesitated in the doorway, considering where first to go. To the right was a staircase that went upward, as yet empty of fog. That seemed the least objectionable route, but it was unlikely that Stephan had continued up to the vacant loft at the top of the house.

And, unfortunately, that was not the only place where he might go.

She turned to stare at the foggy corridor.

"Where are you?" she whispered.

In answer, there was a whisper of sound like a sleeve brushing against a door.

Mister Frye! Belle recalled with annoyance the strange looks that had passed between the men over dinner when she had complained about the inn's service. It seemed entirely possible that Stephan had gone along to Mister Frye's chamber to discuss some secret matter once he thought her safely asleep.

Belle swallowed her trepidation and prepared to pay a call on the runner. There was no light showing under Mister Frye's door, and no sound of voices there either, but it was the next most reasonable place to seek Stephan, so Belle forced herself to step into the pooling fog in the hall and to keep walking through the mist until the runner's chamber was reached.

She leaned forward cautiously to lay an ear against the door and was disconcerted when it gave way beneath her cheek. The room beyond was wholly dark

and cold. It hadn't even the scent of occupation clinging to its frozen interior.

Repelled by the dark, Belle stepped back hurriedly.
"Bloody hell." It seemed doubtful that Mister Frye
had returned to his chamber after dining. Which
meant that he was still in the common rooms, or else
outdoors. She would either have to abandon her
quest and return to bed, or she would have to go
downstairs.

Belle looked at the mist churning up from the floor
below. It seemed alive in a way that no ordinary fog
could be and threatened to enshroud both her and
the feeble lamp in its long, white fingers. If she went
that way, the mist might well cover her head. It could
touch her face and slip into her lungs.

"But it *is* only mist and an unfortunate current of
air," she told herself. "It is a draft, nothing more.
That is all it could be. You must go on."

Belle was aware that her speech contained some
inaccuracies, as any number of persons or animals
could be lurking down in the dark and fog, not to
mention less corporeal beings. But though unable to
adequately explain her growing unease, Belle still felt
that she needed to find Stephan—and before something dreadful befell him. There was a sickening tension mounting in her gut that demanded she descend
those dark stairs no matter how terrifying the mist.
Self-delusion, though not admirable, was necessary
at that moment to bolster her courage.

"Stephan, where are you? Why do you not return?" She breathed, her words turning to vapor when they met the chill air and mingled with the awful fog.

Recalling her stepfather's adage that rough ground was best gotten over with a light step and great speed, Belle turned about quickly and, thrusting the lamp ahead of her, she plunged into the fog, heading downstairs before her resolve failed.

With every step closer to the ground floor, the greasy fog grew thicker, as did the unpleasant stench that had hung in the air all evening.

The inn's common rooms were found empty except for the yellow mist, which hovered at the height of her breasts, and as quiet as a churchyard at midnight—an hour that she was certain had long since come and gone, though she could not be certain for the irregular inn had no clocks. The silence was absolute.

Making a patrol of the premises, Belle finally reached the dining parlor and could see even through the mist that it was empty as all the other rooms had been. And it was the last of the public spaces.

However, she could not fail to notice that an especially cold breeze was wending its way across the parlor from what she guessed was the kitchen, and since an examination had revealed that the front door was firmly secured against the night, she had to assume that this was the direction that Stephan and Mister Frye had gone, perhaps carelessly leaving some other door open behind them.

Doubtlessly they had gone to the stables, probably to speak to the coachman about what he might have seen of brandy kegs. Groaning at the thought of venturing into the wet night, but relieved at such a mundane answer to where Stephan might have gone, Belle started bravely for the back of the house.

The awful stench grew stronger. She did not doubt that mold and fungus abounded in the ill-run kitchens, but there was something else beneath the smell of uncleanliness and age—a half-familiar odor that had the silvery hairs of her arms standing erect and her nerves crying alarm at the thought of invading the rear of the house with only a lantern for company.

"Stephan?" she whispered into the gloom. "Are you there?"

She was answered by a soft creak and the stealthy latching of a door. Emboldened by the sound of human occupation and anxious for company, whomever it might be, Belle hurried after the men.

She paused again at the entryway. The kitchen was bare and empty, denuded of any civilizing comfort, and deathly still except for Belle's lurching shadow, which swayed behind her. A room that usually brought reassurance with its fires, and pleasant thoughts with its rich smells and the promise of grand meals, now terrified her. It was all she could do to force her feet toward the small door in the back wall and to open the latch.

The wood beneath her hand was greasy, and Belle had to fight the bile that rose at the back of her throat. She pulled the door open by inches, being careful not to let the hinges squeal.

Confronted with another stair instead of the expected outdoors, Belle held her lantern aloft and peered timidly into the gloom. The treads in front of her, old and worn, were stained dark as though an army of men with dirty shoes had tramped up and down them. The smell floating upward was also horrible enough that she lifted her skirt with her free hand to hold over her mouth and nose.

"Stephan?" she called again, but softly; her voice was muffled by the fabric of her gown.

There was no answer to her plea.

Summoning courage that she had never suspected resided within her, Belle stepped onto the dark stair and began to descend. The strange fog followed her, clinging stubbornly to her gown and hair until it met an invisible wall of heat. There it recoiled.

The stairs were sticky beneath her slippers and the stench grew until it was nearly gagging, in spite of the filter of her dress. She kept her limbs well away from the bare stone walls and her skirts lifted high off the filthy floor.

This wasn't a larder they kept in the basement. It had to be an actual butchery.

Carrion. The unpleasant word popped into her head, and Belle coughed as the invisible but stagnant vapors stole around her skirts and filled her mouth and lungs.

She finally reached the small chamber at the bottom of the stairs. It was empty, save for a bulging tarp laid in the corner. The bundle, about the length and breadth of a rolled rug, so terrified her, that Belle was unable to look beneath it or even come close enough to touch it.

She edged her way around the room until she came to a second small door. Not taking her eyes off the unmoving tarp, she fumbled about for the door's latch.

There came a sudden shout from beyond, a loud crash and then several thuds.

"Stephan!" Belle screamed, throwing open the door and rushing heedlessly into the room.

It took a moment for the dark images to sort themselves out. The heat and dim light in the basement room were as hellish as anything Dante imagined. A large pot was bubbling away on an iron stove whose careless welds allowed red light to escape into the room.

Before her on the filthy floor was Stephan, wrestling with the landlord who clutched a wicked-looking dagger in his right fist. He seemed intent on using it.

Beside them was the landlord's sister, lying beneath a gasping Oliver Frye. They were both bloody and swearing, but Belle could see no weapons between them.

All about the basement were a jumble of broken bones—ribs mainly, and some skulls that did not look bovine—and a stench so fierce that it was all

Belle could do not to surrender to paroxysms of gagging.

What Mister Frye's intentions were, Belle could not immediately decide, but it seemed apparent that Stephan wished to subdue the burly landlord before he was stabbed, so her duty was clear.

She cast about quickly for some weapon to use, deciding with a shudder against the cleaver and axe, which were sunk into the wooden block on the floor. Not even the dire circumstance that faced her could make her use a hatchet on someone.

The block itself was another matter, and Belle put her lantern aside in favor of the heavy wood. She had to loose her hold on her skirt and hold her breath against the poisonous air, but she did so, staggering over to where Stephan was attempting to throttle the larger man with one hand. Stephan was strong, but she immediately saw why he was having difficulty with the task. Casker's neck was huge.

She commanded in a clear voice: "Move aside now, Stephan!"

He looked up in surprise, clearly not expecting to see her. But, perceiving the burden in her arms and divining her intent, he threw himself out of the way, allowing her to drop the block onto the landlord's oversized head.

There was a sickening crunch as the wood met skull. The burly man grunted and then went still, the knife dropping from his limp hand.

"Murdering harpy," Mister Frye gasped, pulling himself up off the landlord's sister.

In the red light, Belle could see the deep scratches that scored his face and assumed that he was addressing Casker's sister. The woman was now also silent.

"Belle!" Stephan pulled her into his arms and wrapped a hand over her eyes. "Do not look at this awful place."

Beneath her cheek, his damp chest heaved, and she could feel his heart thundering. She did not mention that the gallant gesture came too late. She had seen the chamber's horrors, and they were burned into her memory.

"I'll check on John Coachman. I don't think they had time to do him in," she thought she heard Mister Frye say as Stephan hurried them toward the door and up the awful stair.

"It isn't the coachman under that tarp?" she asked, pulling her dress back up over her nose and mouth with shaking hands.

"No." His answer was short as he picked up her lantern and took her arm.

"Thank heavens. I was ridiculously certain that it was a body."

"What are you doing here?" Stephan demanded as he half-carried her up the stairs and then out into the kitchen.

"Following you," she admitted, beginning to tremble and feeling the world start to spin. She could hear the sound of cracking bone ringing in her ears. Unable to help herself, she asked: "Stephan, was that— were those—?"

"Don't think about it, Belle. I shall have us away from here at first light. Mister Frye's partner will be here then, and we can leave the two of them to deal with this nightmare. Mister and Missus Smythe are about to disappear."

Belle shuddered and wondered that she could feel both feverish and clammy with cold. "Is he dead? Casker?" she asked in a slightly slurred voice, fighting the blackness that crowded the edge of her vision.

"I hope not," Stephan answered coldly, setting down the lamp to swing her up into his arms. "That would be far too easy an end for him. They have been murdering and robbing travelers for years. I want to see that bastard and his sister hang."

"I don't," Belle whispered. Then, for the first time in her life, she fainted dead away. The last sound she heard from the end of the long black tunnel was a worried Stephan calling her name.

Chapter Eight

"I am glad that we did not have to leave John Coachman behind at that dreadful place. The poor man has had a most disagreeable adventure."

"And is being compensated beyond his wildest imaginings for getting a small knock on the head," Stephan reminded Belle from his seat near the window.

"Nevertheless, he will be glad to be rid of us." Belle glanced at the carriage ceiling, as though to confirm that the wounded man was in fact still with them. She added absently: "Of course, there was no need to overpay him if money is a present concern. I could have driven the coach if I had been called upon to do so. However, I must say that a curricle will be ever so much more fun, as well as faster. We shall be able to get one in York, yes?"

"Of course you can drive a coach," Stephan murmured, shaking his head once. "And a curricle, too."

"Does this displease you?" Belle asked curiously. She was very glad to have Stephan's company that morning and knew that it was a sacrifice for him to remain in the coach with her when the day was so beautiful. "I suppose it is yet another proof of my strange upbringing that my first stepfather taught me to drive."

"Not at all. I am in a constant admiration of your accomplishments. Any woman can paint watercolors. It is most unusual to meet one who can play cards with any skill or drive a coach." Stephan smiled suddenly. "In any event, the one time I saw you atop a horse has convinced me that you would do better to always travel in wheeled vehicles."

Belle snorted. "That wasn't a horse. It was some manner of cow. Lend me Roi and we shall see about correcting these gross aspersions you cast upon my riding skills."

"In due time," Stephan answered. "You must win that privilege first."

He reached over and tucked the lap robe more securely about her. He had been most solicitous of her all morning. Doubtless her swoon of the night before had convinced him that she was, after all, feminine enough to need to be treated gently. Belle was uncertain if this new assumption entirely suited her as it made her feel less of an equal partner in this venture.

She was also uncertain about how to react to waking up that morning and finding herself curled up in Stephan's arms, fingers fisted in his hair.

"And so I shall. That game yestereve was complete mischance. You shall have no more easy victories," she told him, forcing her tone to remain light even though her strongest memories of the previous night were of things much more grim. "I swear I was faint with fatigue and hunger."

"That was evident. Well, we shall see. At the moment I feel most fortunate," Stephan answered again, drawing back the curtain to look outside at the improving view. "Come, see what the new day has brought us."

Belle leaned forward, until their cheeks touched. Her gaze was eager.

The weather finally smiled upon them and the sun returned late in the morning showing them a vale of prostrated snowbells and moorland heather where sheep and birds grazed in quiet contentedness. The towns they passed through looked prosperous. The roads were not even too deeply mired, in spite of the recent rain.

Presently in their sight was a small hill covered in bowed-down daffodils, which were struggling back erect after the night's deluge. The splashes of cheery yellow served to entertain their eyes until the roofs of a village appeared in the distance. The town was obviously charming, with the houses' mossy green hats looking gay in the brightening light. Nothing could be more different from the bleakness of Casker's Chance.

It was a relief, *she told herself,* to know that this leg of their journey was drawing to a close and their masquerade as Mister and Missus Smythe could end. That poor couple had known little beyond unhappiness and misfortune.

Ashlars lay but a small distance beyond the village of Hotten and at the outskirts of the city. Belle was able to recognize it even from a distance by Becky's colorful description of its odd, perpendicular exterior and scabrous appearance.

Belle and Stephan continued to peer with vulgar curiosity as the house grew in the window's frame. Beyond the well-kept drive of pale yews, ridiculous, elongated turrets, attached after the main house was built, spiked into the air at irregular intervals. Their slate roofs went so high that they could be lost in the clouds on winter days when the sky lowered. There were a collection of fanciful and overly large gargoyles clinging to the overwrought parapets, and a most fashionable and carefully constructed ruin to the side, which hid the greenhouse where violets and orange trees grew.

Below the turrets were a plethora of pedimented windows, crow-stepped gables, flying buttresses, and arched doorways. The gothic revival, in all its ridiculous splendor had come to Ashlars, and being too expensive to remove once cemented into place, it was likely to remain there until the house itself was felled by time.

Stephan whistled appreciatively as they drew up outside the residence and the true awfulness of the place burst upon him. "Someone spent a great deal of money to do this," he said, awed.

"Not the most judicious of investments," Belle murmured. "The house is not large enough to entertain such foreign nonsense and looks all out of proportion. I can't imagine that anyone would wish to buy it."

"It is not an investment that I would make," Stephan agreed. They passed over a small bridge, which spanned a shallow green moat, filled now with a few inches of rainwater, but already draining enough to reveal the daisy-strewn lawn beneath it.

"Nor I. Fortunately, there is some nephew who will inherit it after Becky is gone. I must say that this hedge is rather nice," she allowed, looking happily at the stately promenade of ancient shrubs that ringed the moat. "It reminds me of some fairy story about a magical creature who lived in a stand of shrubbery."

"A troll, no doubt."

They soon discovered one practical note that spoiled all the dark whimsy of the tableau, and could only wonder at the worn oaken windlass, which surmounted an old well in the middle of the front courtyard.

"Becky said in her letter that it was ugly," Belle

muttered. "I wonder why they do not put another gargoyle on it."

"I apprehend that your friend is most candid with her opinions?"

"Well, it isn't her house, you see, and she feels no need to take responsibility for its oddness."

Belle was familiar with the story of the windlass, as her friend had written of the unsightly well soon after her arrival at Ashlars. Legend had it that a visiting Spanish monk had instructed Ashlars' builder to put the well there or risk disaster to his project. The owner, a man both pious and all-consumed with superstitious dread, had agreed to the monk's suggestion and the well was placed in its inconvenient and unaesthetic location, with instructions left in the entail forbidding its removal by his spendthrift heir.

Though the entail had eventually been broken, the succession of heirs had remained superstitious and the well was left unmolested, along with the collection of gargoyles, though an attempt to hide it had been made by facing the stone wall with a number of classical sculptures. The marble statues were an inadequate screen and rather impeded the carriage way, where it could be seen that a number of them were missing limbs and had badly chipped bases where some coachman had misjudged the distances.

"How very extraordinary," Stephan murmured, as Belle related the tale. "It is amazing what superstition will drive a man to do."

"A complete abortion of taste and it may all be

blamed on a monk who doubtlessly was having a jest at his host's expense," Belle agreed cheerfully. "Becky is aware of the ugliness, too, as I said, but is rather sensitive about this subject. She does not feel that she can spare the funds to remove the thing. Should she ask your opinion . . ."

"I shall lie with aplomb," Stephan promised.

"No, don't do that. She'll think you are a zany. Just tell her how much you admire the gardens. They are her great passion, and she has put forth enormous effort in improving them."

"Your every wish, my sweet," he agreed with a smile. "The gardens shall incite my admiration."

Belle decided that she liked Stephan very much when he was being solicitous and agreeable.

The great doors to Ashlars opened at that point and their hostess, clad all in black and assisted by her housekeeper and butler, emerged into the morning. As the carriage rolled to a stop, Belle flung open the coach door and alighted without assistance.

"Becky!"

"Belle Lydgate," the young woman squeaked, jaw dropping in surprise. Her gray-clad body rushed forward. "Is it truly you? I saw your carriage from the parlor window and wondered who my modish visitor could be. I haven't seen such a coach since my grandparents' time."

Belle laughed and waited for her friend to hurry down the stairs.

"Nor have I. But it has been wonderful at keeping out the rain so I forgive its ugliness."

"Do come in! Let Michaels pay off the coachman," Becky said as she fetched up on the bottom step. "I have been so dull since my husband died, and the winter will *not* end. And I obviously have not been keeping up with the new fashions," she added, eyeing Belle's gown.

"Oh, Becky! Dearest, do not jest so. These clothes are a fright and the carriage the ugliest thing made by man, but I couldn't help it—truly! We've been having an adventure."

The two friends laughed and finally fell into each other's arms where they embraced warmly.

"Only you, Belle, would do anything so wild as to come visiting without a word of warning. Tell me about this adventure."

"Becky, dearest, forgive me for arriving without any notice, but Stephan and I have had the most ghastly journey—" Belle stopped as she saw her friend's eyes go round.

"Stephan?"

Recalled to the fact that they were not alone by the sound of Stephan paying off the coachman and sending him away, Belle strove to find some explanation for a man's presence in closed coach where she had obviously been traveling without a chaperone. There were not many that would be acceptable.

"You are not alone," Becky said in an odd voice, then added the obvious: "There is a *man* with you."

Belle, seeing her friend's dismay, hastily made introductions and started inventing spontaneous and airy explanations for their travels north. Never had she been so sorry to be known for an only child, for a brother would be a most convenient and respectable thing to have at that moment.

"But I don't precisely understand," Becky began, casting a worried glance at the servants who wore the pickled faces and bodies of persons confirmed in their bourgeoise habits and thoughts. Plainly they were not given to broad opinions about modern manners.

Seeing her friend's anxiety in their presence, Belle promptly abandoned her first inventions of a distant cousin and told the annoying lie that seemed to make everyone happy.

"We are on our wedding trip—to see Stephan's family in Scotland," Belle forced enthusiasm into her voice. "But since we were so close and needed to change vehicles, Stephan said that we might stop in to see you for a time, and so, here we are. I am so sorry, dear, about your husband's passing. I wish that I might have been here sooner to console you."

Both Stephan and Becky stared at this mixed speech, one astonished and the other suddenly inscrutable. Belle found Stephan's considering expression a bit unnerving, though what there was in the speech that might have aroused his suspicions she could not guess. She was only telling the same tale he had told at several inns.

GET UP TO 4 FREE BOOKS!

You can have the best romance delivered to your door for less than what you'd pay in a bookstore or online. Sign up for one of our book clubs today, and we'll send you **FREE* BOOKS** just for trying it out...**with no obligation to buy, ever!**

HISTORICAL ROMANCE BOOK CLUB

Travel from the Scottish Highlands to the American West, the decadent ballrooms of Regency England to Viking ships. Your shipments will include authors such as CONNIE MASON, SANDRA HILL, CASSIE EDWARDS, JENNIFER ASHLEY, LEIGH GREENWOOD, and many, many more.

LOVE SPELL BOOK CLUB

Bring a little magic into your life with the romances of Love Spell—fun contemporaries, paranormals, time-travels, futuristics, and more. Your shipments will include authors such as LYNSAY SANDS, CJ BARRY, COLLEEN THOMPSON, NINA BANGS, MARJORIE LIU and more.

As a book club member you also receive the following special benefits:

- **30% OFF all orders through our website & telecenter!**
- **Exclusive access to special discounts!**
- **Convenient home delivery and 10 day examination period to return any books you don't want to keep.**

There is no minimum number of books to buy, and you may cancel membership at any time. See back to sign up!

*Please include $2.00 for shipping and handling.

YES! ☐

Sign me up for the **Historical Romance Book Club** and send my TWO FREE BOOKS! If I choose to stay in the club, I will pay only $8.50* each month, a savings of $5.48!

YES! ☐

Sign me up for the **Love Spell Book Club** and send my TWO FREE BOOKS! If I choose to stay in the club, I will pay only $8.50* each month, a savings of $5.48!

NAME: _____

ADDRESS: _____

_____

TELEPHONE: _____

E-MAIL: _____

☐ **I WANT TO PAY BY CREDIT CARD.**

☐ VISA   ☐ MasterCard.   ☐ DISC**OVER**

ACCOUNT #: _____

EXPIRATION DATE: _____

SIGNATURE: _____

Send this card along with $2.00 shipping & handling for each club you wish to join, to:

Romance Book Clubs
20 Academy Street
Norwalk, CT 06850-4032

Or fax (must include credit card information!) to: 610.995.9274.
You can also sign up online at www.dorchesterpub.com.

*Plus $2.00 for shipping. Offer open to residents of the U.S. and Canada only.
Canadian residents please call 1.800.481.9191 for pricing information.
If under 18, a parent or guardian must sign. Terms, prices and conditions subject to change. Subscription subject
to acceptance. Dorchester Publishing reserves the right to reject any order or cancel any subscription.

JOIN NOW!

"Becky, this is Stephan Kirton. Stephan, my good friend, Becky Claremont."

"But surely you were engaged to Quin—however, this is nothing of import. I am always confusing things," Becky said hastily, forgetting to comment on her own widowhood. "Congratulations to both of you. Please, come inside out of the wind—I declare I am so slatter-brained these days! What am I thinking keeping you outside?"

Leaving the servants to oversee the disposal of their luggage, Stephan and Belle followed their agitated hostess into the great hall.

The touches of bizarre fancy did not end with the house's exterior. There was a serpentine stair graced with a banister of green wood turned in a fantastic spiral and carved all over with scales, which ended below stairs in the mouth of a gaping dragon.

The walls were done in the Spanish style with panels of gilded leather. The effect of so much magnificence should have been overwhelming, but on that morning, with sun shining in through the paned glass, seemed to her rather charming.

Stephan felt that way, too, Belle guessed, as she was watching carefully for that betraying twitch of lips that meant he was suppressing a smile.

"I shall give you a tour later so that you will not get lost in this vast pile," Becky said. "As you can guess, this used to be the great hall."

Belle was a little startled to see that the hall's fireplace had been taken up with a giant bin whose purpose was, Becky explained when she saw her horrified amusement, to house such bulbs and tubers that could not withstand the wet of winter without rotting, but that were also inclined to early growth if left in storage in the greenhouse.

"Besides, it cuts down on the draft from the fireplace and makes everything snug and tidy. The upkeep was ruinous when we had to have daily fires," Becky explained happily, ignoring the frowning housekeeper as she personally led them up the stairs. "I also hired some men to install a new water-closet—and it was a most agreeable convenience this winter past!"

Belle blinked and wondered what the servants made of their unusual, outspoken mistress.

"So, what can I get for you, dear?" Becky asked. "Tea? Or perhaps you would like to rest, as soon as Mrs. Ratham prepares you a chamber? She is very efficient and shall have rooms made up in a trice."

Belle, who mainly wanted an opportunity to speak privately with her friend, instead took the prudent course and pleaded a need for titivation: "My most pressing consideration for the morrow is replacing my wardrobe," she said, braving Stephan's increasingly suspicious glances. "Most of my luggage has not caught up with us and I need shoes, stockings, a new reticule. . . ."

"We shall make a trip into the city then," Becky said happily. "We shall have you fixed up in a trice.

My! You have been on a most uncomfortable journey!"

From the corner of her eye Belle saw Stephan's face relax, and she went on ruthlessly: "And I must have some gowns made as well. I have only the one traveling gown and a badly stained riding habit, which is in need of mending. And a wedding dress, but I shall never wear *that* again."

"That is not a difficulty. I have an excellent dressmaker," Becky assured her, tucking a friendly hand into her arm. "Madame Dubois just this past week showed me a truly fine-figured French muslin—and also a ravishing Berlin silk, which I cannot yet wear as I am still in mourning."

"Then we shall visit her tomorrow. I am not traveling another league until I have replenished my wardrobe."

Belle glanced back at Stephan and waited for contradiction to this statement, but he remained silent and thoughtful as he followed them up the stairs.

"Let us go to my private parlor and have some tea. You must tell me all about how you two met and when you were wed—and, well, everything! I have been living so retired that no word of this event has reached me, and I am certain that it must all be very exciting."

"Oh, it has certainly been that," Belle agreed, looking over her shoulder again. "Wouldn't you say that it has been exciting, Stephan?"

"Among other things," he answered blandly.

Chapter Nine

A duck, large with eggs, wallowed lazily in the stream, seemingly too sleepy to bother eating any of the fat snails that had ventured out recklessly near the slowly eddying waters to nibble at the defenseless bluebells that grew there. The bees, too, were moving unhurriedly from flower to flower, their low drones soporific on the warm afternoon.

The remains of their alfresco meal had been stowed in the hamper, and Belle could find no other occupation but to watch the play of soft leaf shadows dancing over Stephan's face as he lay resting on their blanket.

Their stay at Ashlars was proving to be peaceful. Stephan was apparently content to remain here for a few days, while Belle awaited her new clothing, playing politely at being the attentive bridegroom.

They were assigned separate but connected chambers. Belle had not opened the door between them, and Stephan had made no protest to the arrangement or the barrier, apparently satisfied that Belle was no longer intending to run from him. Belle decided that she was more piqued than pleased that this should be so, for the nights often brought a superfluity of unproductive thought, which had not been there when she and Stephan shared a bed.

Surprisingly, given the circumstances, Belle had also found an unexpected pleasure in York, visiting the dressmaker and shops with her old friend. Their outings had returned her to her days of giddy girlhood, and she had to admit that was easy to put aside her worries about scandal while being fitted for new and flattering gowns.

When she thought at all about their dilemma it was with frustration and more than a little anger at the situation that had brought her to England. Fate had reunited her with Stephan after many years, but had also made their union—at least in the foreseeable future—impossible. She had also most unkindly bequeathed to Belle what was surely an undying memory of how Stephan felt when she snuggled against him in sleep, and this, too, made her nights alone seem very lonely.

It was so unfair that they should be thrown together thus, giving her time to store up longing, and making the day when she had to leave Stephan behind seem all the more unbearable.

She found herself wondering ridiculous things: Did love come into the heart with the eye when it beheld the right man? Or through the ear with his voice? Or with a breath when one kissed?

However it had come, it felt large, like a soul, filling her up. And she knew that when she left Stephan it would drain from her heart, leaving her empty again.

Yet, leave him she must. At least for a time, giving him the chance to decide what he wanted without the weight of obligation pressing upon him. And with that fact in mind she had made a plan and visited a chemist where she requested some sleeping powders.

She would selfishly leave the moment of parting for as long as she could but, on the night before they left for Scotland, she planned to drug Stephan and return to her father's people in London. From there she would arrange passage on the first ship back to India.

Belle exhaled slowly, fighting the urge to cry. It was too beautiful a day—and a chance to make too beautiful a memory—to spend it in futile tears. She had thought about it carefully and knew how she wished to say farewell to Stephan. It was not with weeping.

Looking at him with love-softened eyes, she could find no fault with his figure, face, manners or mind. It was only his stubborn intentions to ruin his life by marrying her that caused her dismay.

That, and the thought of their final parting.

Staring at him with a longing that she could no

longer conceal, Belle made the final step into degradation and admitted that she wished she and Stephan had become lovers that first night at Lord Duncan's ball. She wished that they were lovers right now.

You could be, her heart whispered, *if you were not afraid.*

"Are you bored, Belle? Or plotting something?" Stephan rolled onto an elbow and studied her with knowing eyes. "Shall we perhaps have a game? I have brought a deck of cards."

Caught up in her unprecedented thoughts, Belle assented without thinking.

"And what shall you play for this time, my sweet?" Stephan asked. "Not a gown, I think, as you have a great many new ones coming already."

"True, but there is this ravishing bonnet at a shop in town," Belle answered promptly, though she did not in fact care whether she owned the bonnet. All she wanted was Stephan.

"Ah! Very well, if you win you shall have your ravishing bonnet."

"And what do *you* want this time, Stephan?" she asked.

He looked once at her lips and then her face, watching as she colored beneath his scrutiny. "Do you know what I really want, Belle?" he asked at last.

Belle could guess, but not trusting herself to answer, she wisely remained mute while shaking her head.

"I want you to trust me."

Belle blinked at Stephan's request, and he added gently: "Do you not think that I have earned it?"

Belle mulled his question over for a moment and then nodded. "Yes, you have. And I do trust you, Stephan. But I do not understand the wager. How am I to show that I trust you? What are you asking me to do?"

"Nothing," he said, rummaging for the cards.

"But then that is a silly wager," she protested, feeling suddenly guilty as she remembered the packet of sleeping powders in her reticule. "How shall you ever know if you have won."

"Time will show me that you have honored your word," he answered, causing Belle to wince. "And, more importantly, there may come a difficult moment at some time in the future when you will have to make a decision, and then you will recall that you have given your word to trust me and will do the right thing."

"Very well," Belle answered with an assumption of ease, though she felt far from calm at his words. She said dartingly: "In any event, you shall not win this game, so the matter is an inconsequential one."

"Very likely true," Stephan answered meekly. But Belle, coming to know his mind and manner, was not deceived by the docile reply. She would have to play very well, for Stephan had no intention of losing this wager. The stakes, she could tell, were too important.

Which was unfortunate because all she could think

about was being back in his arms and spending their last days as lovers.

Stephan watched Belle's face, trying to understand which emotions were rioting there in her pinkening cheeks. That she was moved by something, he did not doubt. That she was planning something of which he would not approve was also not beyond probability. It was to address that possibility that he'd suggested this less than spontaneous game of cards.

He was bloody fortunate that she had not named his own stakes as her heart's desire, for most unfairly, he would not have been able to give Belle the same trust that he had asked of her. Some part of him had given up trusting anyone many years ago. The fairer sex, he had learned, could be especially fickle.

Still, fair or not, he was taking out some insurance to guarantee Belle's good behavior. If trust could be had no other way, he would win it at cards.

Stephan dealt their hands slowly, watching Belle's face as she arranged her cards. She masked it well, but he could tell that she was dismayed, probably at her unlucky selection. Stephan could well understand this reaction as he had been at great pains to see that she was not given any useful cards. It was base of him to cheat this way, but he wanted Belle's agreement of trust and was willing to defraud her in order to have it.

"Are you ready, my sweet?" he asked.

Belle worried her cards a moment more, clearly in turmoil. "Yes, I believe I am . . . Stephan," she said, not looking up from her fidgeting fingers. She was breathing quickly, appearing on the edge of some form of panic. "I believe that I am ready. But I have changed my mind about what I want."

"That is rather unusual, Belle," Stephan said slowly. "But I am willing to modify the wager, if the stakes are reasonable."

Her fingers tightened and she swallowed. "I am not sure that you could call this reasonable exactly," she said diffidently. "But I have given the matter some thought and it *is* what I truly want."

Intrigued, Stephan lowered his winning hand and asked: "What then do you wish, Belle? A hat shop instead of a hat?"

"No." Belle laid her cards down, and with a face that was both flushed but also determined, she leaned over to him. Their eyes locked. Her hand lifted slowly to his cheek and then caught up his hair. "I want you."

Stunned at her words, Stephan sat immobile while Belle came closer, brushing her lips against his own. Embers that had smoldered low regained strength and then blazed. He nearly dropped his cards in the first shock of reaction.

"It is customary to play out the hand first before—" he started to say, but was silenced as Belle pressed first her lips and then her body against him.

"I don't want to play cards just now," she murmured.

"Belle," Stephan began, basely suspecting that she was simply trying to distract him with kisses and succeeding all too well.

"The day is beautiful and we are alone. I cannot think that we will ever improve upon the place or the hour."

Stephan could actually feel the flush of heat that rolled up her bosom and neck and into her face as she said this. Her next words astounded him: "Since you wish to be my husband, would it be so wrong to become lovers?"

"Belle," he tried again, shaking his head in a hopeless effort to clear it. He did not like being confused.

"Please, don't fight this," she whispered, taking his cards and casting them aside. "My courage is not limitless and you may well defeat me if you resist. Surely that isn't what you really want."

She pushed against his chest, and Stephan allowed himself to be overpowered, catching her in his arms as he fell back onto their blanket. The scent of crushed hyacinth exploded around them.

"This is madness, Belle. Why now? I don't understand." He made an effort to hold her back so that he could study her face.

"Aye, that it is. Madness—and has been from the start. But still it is what I want. Please. Let me do this now, while I may."

Thinking that modesty would soon force her to

abandon her distracting pursuits, he did not again try to stop her as she pulled at his cravat and then unfastened his shirt. Nor did he utter a single protest as she loosed her hair and let it rain down between them, though this was rather hard not to react to as the soft tresses licked at his skin with amorous nippings.

Belle lifted his hand and brushed a kiss into his palm, then laid it against her chest. Beneath his hand her heart thundered. It didn't seem possible, but he could feel new warmth steal over her skin. The blush proclaimed her innocence and her bold act her determination.

Belle wanted him! The idea was amazing. Perhaps too amazing to be true.

Unable to resist the invitation, however much he suspected the motive behind it, he caressed her lightly. "Belle, this is most unwise. I do not think that you want to do this. Let us simply play the game and delay this for a better time," he began, but stopped when he looked into her eyes, which were luminous and steady.

She shook her head once. He could not read the odd smile that briefly crossed her lips, and she said nothing more to entice him, though her eyes spoke volumes of some romantic verse.

His body demanded that he answer her in kind.

Conceding that her ruse—if such it was—had worked, Stephan ran a finger over her collarbone. The touch was gentle but apparently far from soothing as her pulse redoubled under his touch. He could see her nipples tighten against the fine lawn of her dress. The reaction fascinated him.

"Am I being a fool?" he asked himself, resisting the urge to take the weight of her breasts into his hands. "Am I allowing you to distract me from my purpose and rush us to regret?"

"Probably, but I already feel unmade every time we touch. Surely this cannot hurt us more," Belle whispered, slowly running her hands down his torso.

"Unmade?" he asked, but she didn't explain and he assumed that she spoke of her ruined reputation.

She stopped her gentle inventory at his waist, pausing for a moment to draw breath, and then deliberately began to unfasten his trousers. Her hands shook a little as she worked, but she did not falter.

Stephan wondered for a moment how she would deal with his boots and then decided that it didn't matter. Whether he was shod or unshod, the moment was upon them with all its sweet inevitability. It finally occurred to his bemused brain that it behooved him to stand ready to help her if she faltered.

Belle pushed his clothing aside and then paused again to study him. What was in her eyes as she beheld him unclothed for the first time—approval or dismay—he could not see; her long lashes veiled them.

"You have made me naked first, my sweet. Is your modesty so much greater than my own?" Stephan asked, barely able to hear his own voice over the

167

pounding of his heart, yet trying to make it gentle. It was probably a lost gesture, for his body was behaving in anything but a gentle manner, and it gave his true nature away. "This is what you want, is it, Belle? Or have you changed your mind?"

Belle shook her head, apparently not trusting her voice. She sat up slowly and reached for the tapes of her gown. It was also put aside, leaving only the thinnest chemise between them.

Hot blood rushed through his veins. Stephan felt harder than stone and more powerful than a god. The last of his brain's warnings were pushed ruthlessly aside. True, he wanted her promise of trust, and it had not escaped him that she did not like the stakes of this game. But this interlude had gone way beyond a mere bid for distraction. Whatever was moving Belle to this new boldness, it surely was not a desire to escape a losing hand of cards.

Gown disposed of and modesty apparently at last forbidding that she shed any more clothing without some encouragement from him, Belle laid her cheek against Stephan's galloping heart and then rolled her head so that she might kiss the centerline of his chest. Her warm breath sighed over him, the softest of caresses that nevertheless raised gooseflesh along his arms and tightened his nipples. Her hair and silk skirts brushed over his groin, softer than velvet, and he thought he understood what Belle had meant by saying she felt unmade. His ability to think was coming unraveled, his feelings tumbling in one on the other until there was no order to them.

Stephan rolled over, placing her beneath him where he might see her face. But in this study he was again foiled, because Belle slid her hands into his hair and held his lips against hers, mating her mouth against his own. She pressed into his heat, melting against him in a series of tiny shivers until the pleasure of their near-joining was closer to agony than bliss.

Unable to bear any more, he pulled back far enough to pluck at the ribbons of her chemise, loosening them so that it could be thrust aside. It was a pretty bit of nothing, but Belle was more beautiful still, and this lily did not need the gilding of silk.

Belle murmured encouragingly as he ran his hand up her thigh in a long stroke that ended only at the shadow below her gently curved belly. He touched her once, caressing the moist heat that waited there.

He reminded himself that she was a virgin and the moment called for gentle thoughtfulness. Resisting the urge to end his own discomfort immediately, he drew his hands from her legs and journeyed back up her body to pay homage to her lovely breasts, intending to suckle and tease until she knew want at least half as strong as his own. Perhaps then she would not be shocked with the violence of his desires.

"Stephan." Her voice was low and hoarse. Belle's hands left his hair to glide down his back to his buttocks, making him clench with need. "Please, now."

Again undone by her touch, Stephan returned to the shadow between her thighs. Belle shivered as he touched her gently there and then retreated, only to return once more to devour her heat.

"Stephan! Please." Her fingernails bit into him.

He groaned.

She was ready, and she wanted him. Restraint was completely stripped away and replaced with mindless need. He had thought her beautiful in the moment of surrender but could say now that nothing was more glorious than to see Belle so emboldened with desire for him that she made such demands.

Her legs shifted wider apart and he accepted her invitation. He had once thought to seduce her, but instead *he* was being ravished. He might pierce her body now, but he realized that she had pierced his heart, and that those emotional penetrations struck deeper than any physical act. The new ties binding them changed all that he had ever thought about what could pass between lovers. It seemed that somehow they gave him strength, but he sensed that they also made him vulnerable.

If this was Belle's experience, too, then she was doubly right about feeling unmade, for she hadn't even physical defenses to raise against him. He thought hazily that he would have to find a way to protect them both.

He settled between her legs, half expecting some belated show of fear in her beautiful eyes, which he would have to honor even if it killed him. But there was none.

With a soft smile and a long sigh that was his name, syllables uttered as if there were no other words for what she was feeling, she accepted him into her body, wrapping herself about him as though made for this purpose and no other. If there was any pain for her it never showed on her beautiful face or in her voice.

Stephan capitulated to the loveliness of the moment, thinking of nothing that might disturb the unique magic of being wanted by Belle, and becoming instead a creature of the baser senses, which could enjoy sensation without cold calculation.

Belle moved with him, happily meeting his demands as he drove into her, arching up when the sweet fire took her and telling him of her pleasure with body and sighs.

Then fierce ecstasy claimed him, too, stripping away everything but the fact of Belle beneath him, looking up at him with huge, radiant eyes.

When he returned to himself it was to find that he was in the soft cradle of Belle's thighs with his hands tangled in her silken hair. He was half-stunned by bemusement and the growing—and unwelcome—suspicion that he would never be heart-whole again.

"Belle?" He raised up on his elbows, looking down into her face. He demanded almost angrily: "My sweet, why? Why did you do this?"

"Stephan, please," Belle whispered, pulling him

close so that she might nibble his ear, and in doing so managing to hide her expression from him. "Please, just be with me now. Can we not have this one perfect day?"

Her hands traveled gently down his back, her legs tightening slightly as though to prevent his escape. Weakened by a returning craving for the mindless forgetfulness he had just had, Stephan allowed himself to be distracted once again.

They would talk about this later, he promised his untrusting conscience, and Belle would fully explain what she was thinking.

Stephan allowed his own eyes to close, shutting out sight so that he could enjoy his other senses more fully. The silk of her hair, the velvet of her skin, the perfume of desire.

And the music of her voice . . . He loved the way she said his name. It sounded as though she had forgotten all other words because in that moment they could not possibly matter to her. Others might cry out to God; she cried out for him.

Understanding his unspoken pleasure, Belle whispered his name again. Her fingers and lips caressed him, impossibly returning him to a state of desire.

Across the grassy meadow, the trees' shadows shifted from east to west and grew long as the lover's joyful minutes blended into hours, giving Stephan time to open his heart to the possibility of love and for Belle to lose hers completely.

Chapter Ten

The perfume of crushed hyacinths and Stephan still lingered on her skin as a sensual reminder when Belle stepped into her bedchamber and found the boxes from the dressmaker lying on the bed.

"Oh no." Her hands crushed the folds of her skirt and she blinked in the hope that they had deceived her.

But the boxes were not an illusion. Her time had run out! Now that her clothes had arrived early, there was no more reason to linger at Ashlars. Stephan would want to leave for Scotland on the morrow.

Which meant that she would have to institute her plan of escape that very night.

"But I'm not ready," she whispered, still feeling the delightful phantom touches of Stephan's lips and hands upon her body. "Please, not yet. I need time to consider . . ."

"Belle, is something wrong?" Stephan returned to her door and laid a hand upon her shoulder. The warm palm was both distressing and comforting.

"No, nothing is wrong. My dresses have arrived. I just wish that the girl had unpacked them instead of leaving them to wrinkle in their boxes."

"There is hardly any point to her doing that as she would only have to pack them up again," Stephan said, pulling aside her loosened hair and bending down to bestow a kiss on her neck.

"I suppose that is true," Belle forced herself to say through the shiver that ran down her spine which was as much fear as pleasure. She added lamely: "It is just that I wanted to see them."

"Then have a peep. Choose something pretty to wear to dinner tonight," Stephan said, smiling at her reaction to the graze of his teeth upon her nape. "You shall wear the rest in the fullness of time."

"Yes." Belle's voice was flat, but she couldn't help it. Life and warmth seemed to be draining out of her.

Stephan pulled her hand out of the folds of her skirt, and from the corner of her eye, Belle saw him frown.

"Your hands are cold, my sweet. And your fists are clenched so tight that you are driving your nails right into your palms."

"Are they cold? I hadn't noticed." Belle forced herself to relax. It would not do to make Stephan suspicious now. She had to hide her unhappiness and nerves for the next few hours until she was away.

"We had best ring for your maid and have some hot water brought up. I shall yet regret this afternoon if I have caused you to take a chill."

Belle turned to Stephan, hiding her guilty face in his shirt. "Hold me."

Immediately, his arms closed about her.

"Belle, are you feeling ill?"

For a moment Belle hopefully considered claiming illness as a delaying tactic. Then Stephan added: "If you are, I shall send at once for a physician."

Schooling her features to what she hoped was innocent blankness, Belle forced herself to look up at her lover and smile.

"Don't be silly. I am just slightly chilled. A hot bath shall set me right in next to no time."

Stephan looked down at her, his own expression suddenly arrested. "Then we have nothing to worry about," he answered after a moment. "But you look most pale, so as a precaution I will have dinner brought to your room."

"That isn't necessary," Belle said hastily. "Truly, I am fine."

"You must let me be the judge of this. I would never forgive myself if something happened to you now. I will see that you are looked after the entire night. A maid shall stay with you."

"I don't want a maid. Do come and dine with me so I will not be lonely," Belle said, a bit desperately.

"And after we can finish our game of cards."

Stephan considered this suggestion gravely—too gravely—and then nodded, dropping his arms and stepping over to the door that divided their rooms. He took hold of the bell-cord and gave it a tug.

"Have your bath," he said, opening the door to his own chamber. He almost seemed angry, though Belle could not imagine why, unless it was annoyance at a possible delay in travel. "And I shall arrange for our dinner to be sent up in an hour."

"Very well." Belle forced herself to smile, though her lips wanted to tremble. "I shall see you soon."

"Aye, that you will."

Stephan was both angry and disappointed, though he was careful not to let any sign of his perturbation show as he closed the doors between their rooms.

"Bloody hell." In spite of what had passed between them that afternoon, Belle intended to run from him again!

The thought was enough to send him pacing. *How could she?* However careless men might be about sexual relations, women did not behave thusly. It was true that for him the act of sex had never previously meant anything of import, but in this case it was different. Her desire for him could not have been a lie. No one was that good an actress. She had looked up at him with wide eyes, offered herself completely and without reservation. Their lovemaking had been a binding thing. There was no going back and pretending that it hadn't happened.

"Damnation. I shall never understand the workings of the female brain." Suddenly recalling another, even more treacherous female, he touched his cheek and added bitterly: "Whatever it is the seat of, it is not honor and reason."

He hadn't wanted to resort to any more trickery, but for her own sake Belle had to be stopped. She obviously had not considered the possible consequences of their lovemaking. But he had. And if there was one thing that he resolved with all of his being, it was that he would not be responsible for bringing another bastard into the world. He absolutely would not have it.

Stephan went to the small chest on the desk and opened the lid. He removed a small twist of paper that had the sleeping powder he had procured from the chemist. His lips tightened as he stared at it.

Really, this was the lesser of evils. The only other thing would be to lock her in her room or tie her to her bed, and that would cause her shame and probably ignite another scandal. Angry as he was, and however deserving she was of the treatment, he could not find it in himself to hurt her so.

Belle did not always finish her wine, but she was fond of the sauces prepared by Ashlars' chef. He would mix the powder into her dinner. She would fall asleep soon after dining.

Once she was asleep, the maid could pack up her

belongings, except for her traveling dress. It would be painless, except for a bit of dry mouth in the morning, and would not cause either of them any embarrassment. It was the kindest way to deal with her defection.

Possible defection, the voice of justice reminded him.

Stephan paused in his mental recriminations and drew a long breath. Distrust was a habit with him. He had to recall that she was not proved guilty. He did not know Belle all that well yet. It was just barely possible that he had misread her behavior.

Yes, it was possible that he had misunderstood her sudden fear at leaving Ashlars. In which case, the sleeping powder was more than ever a good choice of dealing with a potential problem.

Stephan exhaled slowly, letting go of his disappointment. There was the possibility of some other explanation for her distress. He wouldn't condemn her and ruin the memory of their afternoon by leaping to conclusions.

He looked again at the powder and debated about putting it away.

No. Belle was not proved guilty, but she had not been proved innocent either. He would do it. Belle might have a bit of head in the morning if she also drank any quantity of wine, but she would be too groggy to protest when he bundled her into the chaise and started for the border.

With any luck, she would sleep until they reached

Gretna Green. And whatever her intentions, she would have no opportunity to disappoint him, or get herself into trouble.

He assured himself that they would both be happier to have it this way.

Belle watched from the desk as Stephan personally removed the covers from the trays on the small table the footman had brought up and busied himself with the arrayed dishes. While he was occupied, she took the vital packet from her robe pocket and undid the screw of paper. Hurriedly, she upended the powder into one of the glasses she had taken to her desk. Making haste, she poured out some of the wine from the heavy bottle and sloshed the beverage around, trying to mix the red and white together. She returned the cup to the tray with a shaking hand and made a note of which glass was intended for Stephan.

"Come, Belle," he said, turning toward her suddenly. His voice sounded distant and his smile perfunctory. "Let me serve you. We have here a delicious capon in wine sauce made with apricot and cardamom, and some boiled mushrooms and spring peas, which I know you like."

Belle's guilt was running amok, making her view Stephan's actions with shame-ridden eyes. Tonight he did not seem like her lover but rather as a jailer. With hands that wished to tremble and confess their sin, she picked up the wineglasses and handed one to Stephan.

"Here is your wine," she said, and watched, her heart in her throat, as he took the first sip of his downfall.

She told herself that it was not poison she was giving him but only a sleeping powder, which would leave him with a dry mouth and perhaps a bit of headache. True it was a largish dose, but surely a man as big as Stephan would need more than a lady. And since she had been unable to explain this to the chemist, she was left with having to guess upon a proper measure. Twice the usual portion seemed correct, as she did not want him to awaken early.

"Sit down, my sweet," he said, pulling out a chair for her. "What shall I fetch first for you?"

"Anything will be fine."

Feeling a little ill with apprehension, Belle sank into the seat and allowed Stephan to arrange the delicacies on her plate. He gave her but a small helping of peas and mushrooms, instead filling her plate with capon and a generous portion of thick sauce.

It struck her as odd that for himself he took a much larger serving of vegetables, a small amount of fowl and almost no sauce at all, but perhaps the drugged wine had affected his appetite in some manner.

"Eat up, Belle. You'll need your strength. There's a long journey ahead of you tomorrow."

That was true, *Belle thought with a pang*, though Stephan did not realize how very much she would need both strength and will to leave him once he had fallen asleep.

Belle sipped at her wine, trying to ease her parched mouth, which grew worse with every bite. It helped very little. The lovely capon, even with the rich wine sauce, tasted like bitter ashes in her mouth. If it would not have caused suspicion, she would have refused to eat at all, but under Stephan's steady and unsmiling eyes, she obediently ate her way through the meal.

Her only consolation, as the horrid repast drew to a close, was that Stephan had swallowed the sleeping powder with never a pause, and followed it up with yet another glass of wine. He should sleep soundly while she packed her belongings and left for the stable.

"Shall we play some cards now, Belle?" Stephan asked when the meal was through. Casting aside his napkin, he rose from the table. Thinking of the promise of trust he had failed to extract he queried somewhat harshly: "Do you recall the stakes we wagered?"

Belle blushed suddenly and tucked her head as though afflicted with shame.

Stephan, in that instant recalling that Belle had changed her wager from a hat to making love to him, was ready to kick himself for being insensitive.

"Don't you still want your bonnet?" he asked more gently, resolving to discover from Becky Claremont where this hat shop was and to purchase Belle's bonnet for her before they left town. It was an inadequate apology for drugging her food, but he hoped that she would never realize what he had done to her, and would simply accept the gift as a thoughtful treat.

"It doesn't matter," Belle said, and Stephan was appalled to see a single tear slip down her cheek and fall onto her folded hands. "But I will play cards with you, if that is what you wish."

It wasn't at all what Stephan wished, but he felt too great a cad already to even suggest that she curl up in his arms while a drug he had fed her coursed through her body and sent her into involuntary sleep. Almost, he wished that he could take back his decision.

"I would like it very much, Belle," he said gently, taking her arm and leading her carefully to a chair near the fire. He fetched a coverlet from off the bed and tucked it in around her.

To his horror, Belle's head remained bowed and the slow tears continued to fall, each wet trail on her pale cheeks a stinging reproach for his unkind words and untrusting deed.

"Please don't cry, Belle. We needn't play cards if you don't like the notion."

Belle sniffed and then yawned widely. Her eyelids fluttered down. Stephan wondered what she would dream of when her eyes were closed. Would her thoughts be painted with the day's shames and joys? He hoped that she would dream of beautiful things.

"I am sorry, Stephan. I do not know what is wrong with me. I must be more tired than I thought." Belle blotted her cheeks with her sleeve and smiled up at him. Her breath released itself as a sigh as her head tilted backwards, too heavy to hold up it seemed, showing her pale throat with its delicate tracery of veins where her pulse beat slowly. "But see! I am all better now. Do not look so wan. We may play or do whatever you like."

Stephan looked at her loosened hair, one wayward tress curling into an indolent question mark against her cheek, and knew exactly what was wrong with her. And he cursed the chemist for not telling him that the drug might make her despondent. He had thought that he was only giving her a mild sleeping potion, not something that would upset her mind.

He yawned in sudden sympathy with her expressed weariness. Perhaps the extra wine with dinner had been a mistake. He felt more tired than he had on the night he met Belle at Lord Duncan's masked ball. All he wanted was to curl up beside Belle and have a nap.

"Do you mind dealing out the cards?" Belle asked slowly, her words somewhat muffled as she slouched down in her chair. "My eyes feel terribly heavy just now."

Again, Stephan was so in sympathy with her, that his own eyelids seemed to grow weighted with the need for sleep. It took great effort to shuffle the cards and deal them out on the tiny table. With every moment that passed, the light in the chamber seemed to dim and the shadows to grow, urging him to sleep.

Belle made a slight effort to sort her cards, but presently laid them down and then rested her head on the smooth wood before her.

"Stephan . . ."

She looked at him for a moment, as though trying to say with her eyes what her lips could not articulate, but her lids closed before he understood her message.

Feeling equally bleary, Stephan decided that he would join her for a short catnap, and likewise rested his head in the cradle of his arms, which he laid upon the table.

"Good night, Belle," he mumbled, but got no answer. "We'll talk on the morrow and all will be well."

The maid who arrived an hour later was rather surprised to find her mistress's guests sleeping by the hearth in the wife's chamber. Normally she would have retreated, but she had been given careful instructions about preparing for the next day's journey, and she set about silently packing Missus Kirton's clothes into a generous trunk.

In the other chamber, she could hear Sykes performing the same offices for the sotted Mister Kirton.

It was odd, them wanting to leave so early like—but people from the south were odd. The present mistress of Ashlars was a piece of proof all in herself. It was to be expected that she would have peculiar, foreign friends who practiced heathen ways. Still, this falling asleep over a gambling game was not what a respectable girl liked, and she would bet that her mum would have something pointed to say when she told her about the latest goings-on at the big house.

Mum always did have something to say to everyone. A great one for knowing the gossip, she was.

Chapter Eleven

Belle sat up slowly, painfully stiff from sleeping at the table, and peered blearily at the foggy room. Eventually noticing that the haze before her eyes was not uniform and that there was something rectangular half-blocking the vision of her right eye, she reached up and peeled the knave of hearts off her cheek. After staring at it for a full minute in growing comprehension, she flung it down upon the table.

That appeared to be the signal for awakening in her body a whole chorus of aches and pains, and it started a symphony of woe by setting up a drumming in her skull with a heavy stick. Belle groaned and began rubbing her throbbing head with unsteady fingers.

Once her eyes were able to remain fairly focused, in spite of the pulsing in her brain, she looked across the table and gave the still slumped Stephan a dismayed glance. She then turned to the empty wine bottle, which she gave a withering up and down, even though it was innocent of wrongdoing.

She must have given him the wrong glass and drunk the sleeping powder herself! Nothing else could explain her intense headache.

Belle silently cursed her own carelessness and had to wonder if her heart had betrayed her by stealth, forcing her to drink from the wrong cup so that it would not be parted from Stephan.

It seemed a reasonable explanation. For it was the nature of the heart to put its wants ahead of good sense. And it had been a successful ploy, for there was certainly no way that she could escape Ashlars without Stephan now. She would likely crash the carriage if she attempted to drive, and the mere thought of swaying over rough roads was enough to make her stomach roil.

"I feel like I've died and gone to hell," she moaned, dropping her head back into her hands. "Is it possible for one person to be so unlucky?"

Stephan, forcing his eyes open at these plaintive words, could only agree with Belle about feeling like the tormented damned. He felt ghastly, his eyeballs scorched, the bones of his body disarranged into some grotesque configuration. Turning his head on a neck that creaked like rusted hinges, he glared at the remains of the sauced capon whose discarded bones were lying in a congealed puddle.

"Being dead could not feel half so bad," he muttered. His voice was thick and his tongue clumsy. He, too, began massaging his temples.

The gentle caresses helped, but as immediately as his head cleared of some of the pain, he began to experience the lashings of remorse. If he felt this drugged from the little bit of sauce he had consumed, then Belle must be well nigh sick with poison. He was fortunate that she was not dead. He had used a large dose of powders, not knowing how much of the drugged food she would eat, and obviously the dose had been dangerously large.

Considering his actions by the sane light of morning, he saw that they were the height of irresponsibility.

He paused long enough in his self-castigation to heap a few curses on Mister Frye and the vicious Casker for putting the notion of a sleeping powder into his head in the first place.

Belle moaned again, interrupting his guilty wallowing.

It took an effort, but Stephan staggered to his feet and groped his way toward the dressing table. His parched mouth felt like it was stuffed with rags and could only imagine how parched Belle must be. Catching a glimpse of himself in the glass, Stephan was shocked to see that the haggard man in the mirror looked like he had spent the entire night participating in the wildest forms of dissipation.

Shuddering at his reflection, he heroically poured

out a glass of water from the carafe and carried it over to his abused love.

"Here," he croaked. "This will help with the dry mouth."

Belle looked up with dull eyes. Her hair gleamed like sunlight on a still pond, but her complexion was decidedly pasty. She accepted the water gratefully and didn't comment on the breach of etiquette when he drank directly from the carafe.

"Stephan," she finally managed to say in something approaching her own voice. "I am not certain that I can travel today. I truly feel most vile."

Stephan looked at her woebegone face, a pale imprint of a heart shadowing her cheek, and nearly agreed to forego their journey.

But, if he relented and they stayed another day, he would once again be forced to use some drastic means to prevent Belle from running away, just in case that was what she intended. And his options still seemed limited to desperate acts, which could only enrage any right-minded female. He had not been married before, but common sense told him that he simply could not add any insult to what was already an injury and expect to enjoy any sort of a felicitous union with Belle.

Certainly, if any man served him in such a way he would meet him on the field on honor and put a bullet in him.

"I'm sorry, my sweet," he said, and meant it sincerely. He pulled back the curtain and gestured at the unpleasantly bright morning. "But as you can see from the sun's placement, the hour is well advanced. The curricle and horses will have arrived. It isn't good for the horses to be left standing. We must leave at once."

"But I have not packed—" Belle began, only to notice that there was a large trunk standing in the middle of the room.

Stephan followed her gaze.

"The maid did it for you. I left instructions last night so that you would not be bothered," Stephan explained, letting the curtain fall and then crossing to Belle's side to pour her a little more water.

"Last night? She packed while we slept at the table? But why? And why did you not awaken?" she asked, appalled. She started gathering cards and shoving them haphazardly into the wooden box. "Stephan, what will the servants think? What will Becky think when she hears that we were found in a drugged-*drunken*—stupor over a game of cards?"

From the corner of her eye, Belle watched Stephan stiffen.

"What did you say?" Stephan stared at her, his already taut expression hardening. Distrust came roaring to life. "Did you say *drugged?* Why would you use that word?"

Belle jumped and colored guiltily. "Perhaps I did say *drugged*," she admitted. "I *feel* drugged. My mouth is so very dry."

Stephan stared at her for a long moment, and

Belle, feeling the enormity of her sin, was unable to keep from glancing at the table where the wine bottle and glasses sat.

Stephan followed her line of vision.

"How odd, because so, too, do I feel drugged," he said slowly.

Belle looked down, her cheeks burning.

"And I don't see how that can be when I had very little of the . . . unless you drugged me!" Stephan sounded incredulous and looked it, too. His tone was pure outrage when he said: "Answer me at once, Belle! Did you have the audacity to drug me?"

Belle carefully put the lid on the card box and didn't answer.

"What was it in? The wine?" Stephan snatched up his glass and held it to the window. The white sludge at the bottom was clearly visible. "What was the size of the dose you gave me? It takes little more than a pinch of this stuff to put someone to sleep. With what was already in the food—You could have murdered me, Belle! You could have killed yourself!"

Something inside of him that felt betrayed made him add: "Or was that your plan? To be rid of me forever?"

Feeling at a disadvantage with Stephan towering over her, Belle also leaped to her feet, though standing made her feel exceedingly queasy. "To be rid of you?"

Then with the import of Stephan's words becoming clear, she looked at the remains of the capon, which were adhered to the apricot wine sauce on the plate. It also had a residue of powder dusting the edge of the plate.

It was Belle's turn to be outraged.

"How dare you stand there and charge me with wrongdoing when you put sleeping powder in the sauce! And a great deal of it. You drugged me! And for no good reason that I can see!"

"There was a very good reason, and we both know what it is."

"You used me! You talked all this time about deserving my trust, but it was all a plot!" she accused, and then in a flash of anger, stored up from a week of worry and frustration, she exploded into action. She snatched up her own wineglass and hurled it at Stephan, shouting the most wounding accusation she could imagine: "Was it not enough that you had me willingly? What horrible thing were you going to do to me last night once I was helpless in your power?"

Though shocked into temporary speechlessness at her outrageous allegation, good reflexes made Stephan duck out of the path of flying glass and saved him from harm. But the unfortunate missile sailed into the armoire where it shattered with a head-splitting crash.

The two of them stood, glaring at each other, for the first time in their relationship each genuinely angry at the other.

They were also unprepared to admit their own

guilt even to themselves, or the injustice of their wild accusations to each other.

"So, I was correct," Stephan said coldly, countering her charges with the text of an old distrust. The devastating words emerged before he could stop himself. "That affecting little scene in the woods yesterday *was* just a diversion. It was not about love. That was trade—a bit of the soft for a bit of the hard, so I wouldn't suspect that you planned to run away."

"You bastard!" Belle gasped, paling at the insult, and feeling like someone had just punched a hole straight through her chest and into her heart. "How can you say that?"

"It is quite true that I am a bastard," Stephan agreed, equally pale except for the scar on his cheek, which was a livid red. "But because of yesterday, you may very well be carrying my child even as we speak, and I will not allow you to run away again. There will be no more Kirton bastards brought into this world."

Belle hunched and looked suddenly very ill.

"Stephan, I didn't mean—"

"And this is the thanks I get for offering some heartless, spoiled heiress my hand and heart. Is your sex entirely composed of jades, seducers and liars?" he asked bitterly.

Another wave of anger washed over Belle. "How dare you compare me with some trollop from your past? I was trying to protect you, you idiot! But no more. I will never have you in my bed again—and I wouldn't have your heart now if I got to hack it out of your chest with a dull axe and burn it as an offering! I would not have your baby either!" Belle shouted in return, then burst into tears at the string of untruths.

"You will *not* cry," Stephan ordered, going completely white about the mouth. "You are not that great a coward, and you are not getting out of this by acting like a *female*. I have played this scene before with others of your sex and know false tears when I see them. *Women!* If you have something to say in your defense, then just say it!"

The words were said with apparent antipathy, though the stricken look in his eyes did not match the tone.

At the unfair observation, which was also a reminder that there had been some other woman in Stephan's life who had obviously made a claim upon his minuscule heart, Belle completely lost her head and snatched up another dish. It also went sailing at Stephan's head. He ducked again, but this time received a splash of mushroom on his cheek and coat sleeve.

"Defend myself! I shouldn't have to defend myself . . . and I wouldn't if you were a gentleman. I can't believe that I gave myself to you!"

"That is enough!" he shouted, grabbing his handkerchief and blotting up the mess.

Running footsteps could be heard outside the door just before the hurried knocking sounded on the panel.

"Missus Kirton?" a worried voice called.

"Go away!" Belle ordered, misery making her voice throb.

"Come in at once!" Stephan countermanded, and since his voice was louder, the wide-eyed maid obeyed.

"Get out! I don't want you," Belle said, turning her tear-stained face from the startled domestic.

"My wife and I will be leaving immediately," Stephan contradicted. "Please have our luggage taken down to the chaise."

"I am not your bloody wif—" she began, spinning back to her Nemesis.

Stephan reached Belle in two strides and clapped a hand over her mouth, too angry to care about what the servants thought of his rough treatment.

"You will be shortly, and in the meanwhile you will behave with dignity," he said through clenched teeth. "One more display of temper, one more flying dish or angry word, and I will bind and gag you."

Belle's wet eyes gazed into his for a brief instant before narrowing.

"Don't do it, Belle," he warned, just as she bit his hand.

Cursing luridly, Stephan dragged her to the connecting door. Slamming it against the wall, he hauled Belle into his room. Using one hand, he pulled the sash from his dressing gown, which was laid out upon the bed, and set about tying her hands with it.

Belle fought, kicking Stephan in the shins and even

195

trying to bite him. The blows from the soft slippers didn't hurt, and all she managed to chew on was his coat, but he pulled off his wrinkled cravat and wound it around her ankles as well.

A timid knock fell on his door as he finished tying her off.

"Hel—" Belle shouted.

Stephan pulled out a handkerchief and stuffed the mushroom-flavored bit of linen into Belle's mouth. He wasn't brutal, but he was not his usual gentle self either. The man standing over her was a stranger, one Belle had had glimpses of but had never thought to meet.

"Come in," he said, stepping away from her and straightening his coat sleeves. As a last thought, he twitched her skirts back down over her ankles, hiding the ties that bound her legs.

Two nervous footmen entered the room, goggling at the sight of Stephan's supposed wife tied up on the bed.

Stephan calmly pointed at his two bags and then said: "Don't forget the trunk in my wife's room."

The two footmen, who were not likely to forget anything about that morning, hurried to obey.

"Are you ready to depart, my sweet wife?" he asked Belle, a trace of bitter irony in his voice. "Then let us be off."

Belle, finally returning to herself from the realm of insane anger, did not fight Stephan as he lifted her up into his arms. In fact, Stephan was surprised to feel her slump against him and tuck her face into the curve of his neck. He was suddenly aware of the chill on her skin, which contrasted sharply with the heat of his own.

Mercifully, they did not encounter their hostess or Mrs. Ratham on their way to the carriage. The butler's disapproving face was quite testament enough to the size of the scandal they were leaving behind at Ashlars, and Stephan realized that he was growing tired of leaving country houses under a cloud of ill-repute.

Belle was tossed unceremoniously onto the seat of the chaise and Stephan scrambled up after her. He ordered the groom to stand away and took off at a brisk trot before any further disasters could befall them.

As soon as they were away from the house, Stephan reached over and pulled the soiled handkerchief from Belle's mouth. Though still angry about what had happened, he was not so livid as to wish Belle any harm or even discomfort.

"Thank you," Belle said, gulping air. "But I am afraid that you will have to stop for a moment."

"We are not stopping until we are out of the village," Stephan said. "We must make up for lost time."

"I know that we are behind our time, but I fear that you will have to stop anyway," Belle said, gulping again. "For I am about to be very unwell."

Stephan turned his head and took in her unhealthy

color. This was not a sham. Belle was clearly *in extremis*. He swiftly pulled the team to a halt at the side of the road, and helped Belle lean over the side of the carriage as she emptied her stomach onto the ground.

When the violent fit had passed, Stephan sat her upright and then blotted her face with the stained handkerchief. He produced his flask and, holding it to her lips, said gruffly: "Here. Rinse your mouth."

Brandy would not have been Belle's first choice of palate cleansers, but she did as he ordered, spitting the brandy over the side when she was done.

Once again filled with self-loathing and guilt, Stephan asked: "If I untie you, Belle, will you promise not to try and leave the carriage?"

"I shall have to leave the carriage eventually. Probably even quite soon," Belle said, shifting on the seat, not meeting his eye. "We left this morning in great haste and I did not . . . comb out my hair or wash my face. I must look like a birch broom."

Seeing her uncomfortable shiftings, Stephan was finally aware that she needed a chamber pot. He had to admit that his own need was also pressing.

"Give me your word that you won't try and escape, and I will stop at the inn at the edge of town and procure some coffee for you while you . . . tidy up." Stephan took the handkerchief and attempted to remove the heart stain from Belle's cheek.

"Thank you," Belle said, ducking her head.

Stephan paused at the rejection of his touch, but after a moment took her chin in hand and forced her face back up so that she had to meet his eyes. "But first you will give me your solemn promise not to try and escape, Belle."

"I promise not to leave you at the inn." Her gaze as she looked into his eyes was still defiant, but Stephan believed her words.

Sighing at the quirk of Fate, which had once again interrupted their journey with unpleasantness, Stephan could only regret that they had not finished their game of cards yesterday in the woods. None of this need have happened if Belle had only given her word to trust him.

"Stephan?" her voice was soft and embarrassed as he untied her.

"Yes, Belle?"

"I think that we had best immediately find some secluded spot."

"Do you still feel ill?" he asked, looking anxiously at her face.

"No, but I have just realized something rather discomforting."

"What is it?" he asked, glaring at his rumpled cravat, uncertain what to do with it. He could not wear it now.

"I am still in my dressing gown and have no shoes. We cannot arrive at the inn with me in my bedclothes."

"No, I don't suppose we can," he agreed, coming to a shocked awareness of the deficiencies of his own dress. He was riding about the country in an open carriage in an evening coat and no cravat.

"Also, you forgot Roi."

"Roi!" Stephan flung his cravat on the top of the baggage. He said in amazement: "I forgot Roi."

"Do you wish to return for him?" Belle asked, glancing nervously over her shoulder, obviously filled with misgivings at the thought of facing the staff at Ashlars again.

"No." Stephan's reply was vehement. "He is happy enough at Ashlars stable. I will send for him later."

Belle nodded, relieved. "As I recall, there is a small copse wood just ahead where we might be private. Perhaps . . ."

"Aye! We'll stop there and dress ourselves. There is also a stream, is there not? It will be cold, but you shall be able to wash your face and so forth."

"Stephan?"

"Yes, Belle?" Stephan looked into her blue eyes, and though they were not filled with the same longing and innocent passion of the day before; at least he no longer felt that he was facing a deadly enemy over crossed swords.

He tried to take consolation in that fact, but was aware that something precious that had been growing between them had been wounded, perhaps to the point of death.

"I am truly sorry about throwing those dishes at you," she said softly. "I have never lost my temper that way. I think that I was a little bit mad. Perhaps it was the powders?"

"Perhaps." Stephan looked thoughtful as he picked up the reins. "And I, too, am sorry, Belle, for causing another scandal."

Their apologies were incomplete, and both were aware of it, yet they could not think how to say more without revisiting the painful misinterpretation of what their act of love on the previous day had meant.

"That is alright, Stephan," Belle said at last, managing a sort of smile. "We both caused this mess. And actually, if you think about it, the scandal at Lord Duncan's was mainly Quincy's fault . . . and perhaps Constance's. We were simply flotsam washed up on the tide of his perfidy and her cruelty."

Stephan glanced down at her and shook his head. "That is true. But I can tell you from experience that most unfortunately, it shan't be Quincy or Constance who is remembered for it."

Belle sighed at this unhappy truth and they lapsed into gloomy silence.

Chapter Twelve

Restored to near respectability by their visit to the copse wood, and then renewed by a light meal at the Hatten Inn, Belle and Stephan resumed their journey in a somewhat more cheerful frame of mind.

Though conviviality of a sort had been restored, they had not engaged in any conversation for several minutes. The peace being a fragile thing, a wary Belle was content to simply enjoy the mild sunshine and the passing countryside in harmonious silence while she conversed with her mother.

. . . and so you see, *Mama, I've done something rather dreadful and am not at all certain how to retrace my steps and return to Stephan's graces. For that matter, I am not certain if Stephan can ever be seen the same way again, since I was briefly made a*

*member of the society of the imprisoned and had him
as my enemy.*

*Frankly, it is all very queer and not in the least
what I expected after reading all those books about
Divine and human love. All those tomes' illustrative
anecdotes about what passes between man and maid
did not once touch on a situation such as this. I
sometimes think that the older poets never wrote
about anything of practical use.*

Belle sighed and abandoned her contemplations
on the deficiencies of Herrick and Donne in favor of
the less painful occupation of watching the passing
scenery.

Stephan was less given to bucolic appreciation, even
though the whiteness of the stands of cotton-grass
waving in the breeze was a sight to inspire odes.
Brow furrowed in thought, he suddenly turned to
Belle and asked forthrightly: "What did you mean
before when you said that you were trying to save
me?"

Belle glanced at him and cleared her throat. "I suppose that we must discuss this?"

"It would be best, I believe. Misunderstandings
only grow with the passage of time."

"Hmm . . . It is complicated. But I suppose that I
meant that I was trying to spare you another scandal
by leaving before we married." Belle turned her head
away and studied the stands of heather blooming
along the road. The scenery was very green and uni-

form beyond the heather hedge, which lined a shallow ditch, but she continued to admire it anyway.

"You were trying to spare me a scandal by drugging your *husband* and abandoning him at Ashlars?" he asked, stupefied.

"Becky would never have said anything," Belle defended. "And even if the servants talked, it would still not have been as large a scandal as what is likely to happen if you actually do break your engagement with Constance Wrawby and marry me. After all, by now I am not merely some unfortunate ruined female from the shops. As far as the world is concerned, I am Quincy's cast-off mistress. And shortly I shall also be Nabob Lydgate's stepdaughter. You might as well marry the whore of Babylon—'twould have the same effect."

Stephan stared at her, his face a little bit hard, but he answered gently enough. "Belle, I have told you that Constance broke with me. And you worry overmuch about the gossip—which is odd for I thought no one minded it more than I. In any event, the fact that you may be with child is paramount now."

"Yes, I understand." She did not sound at all happy, and Stephan supposed that he could not blame her.

Belle added: "But as for the rest, the world does not know about Constance's letter. They will think you a jilt and greedy, and that I am a shameless stealer of other women's men."

Stephan digested this, feeling some healing balm

spread over his wounded ego and even over his heart. Belle might have intended leaving him for ridiculous, melodramatic reasons, but it was not because she didn't care.

"I had begun to suspect that this, or something like it, was what you were thinking."

"Had you?" Belle asked, reluctantly recalling some of the things he had said to her that morning. She tried to banish the painful thoughts before they reopened the wounds in her heart. Her regard of the rapidly passing foliage became more fixed and gloved fingers curled in upon themselves. "That wasn't precisely what it sounded like when you accused me of trying to murder you."

"That was just wild anger talking." He made a frustrated gesture. "You could have easily meant something else by those words—perhaps that you were trying to save me from a loveless marriage with someone who would never respect me," he finally suggested, staring straight ahead.

Belle stared at him with a fascinated eye. "The thought never occurred to me. I have always respected you, Stephan. Once again, I am forced to believe that you have confused me with some other woman. One who obviously still claims your thoughts to a marked degree." She looked away. This time her chin jutted into the air.

"Perhaps I misinterpreted your motivations," he allowed. "But whatever my thoughts, I assure you that no one claims my heart."

Belle looked into the distance and did not reply to this statement, which was supposed to please her.

"We have agreed that the drug-induced madness is in us both, have we not?" Stephan asked, briefly taking his eyes from the road to look down at the piquant face whose color could be seen, even through the veil of her hat, to have improved tremendously with food and sunlight.

Belle digested this for a moment and then lowered her chin to nod. "I do not know what else it could have been. I have never behaved that way before," she admitted. "It was like being caught up in some dreadful play."

"Yes, some dreadful production from Drury Lane! Where else would some heroine accuse her lover of trying to drug her so that they might have sexual congress?" He suggested: "Perhaps, if we can, we should try and put this morning's deeds from our thoughts. Such emotionalism was a never-to-be repeated aberration."

"I am trying not to dwell upon it," Belle replied, fussing with her gloves as another carriage approached on the road. Vehicles were less common now that they were away from town, but there were still enough of them that Stephan had to pay attention to his driving, particularly as he was setting a brisk pace for the border.

"I know that my words and even my actions were not those of a gentleman," Stephan began, prepared in the face of Belle's lenient mood to do the honorable thing and apologize completely.

But Belle interrupted his *mea culpa* at once. She flushed delicately while saying: "Cease chastising yourself. You were not speaking to a *lady* this morning. Anyone who had dishes flying at his head would be pardoned for being annoyed."

"A woman scorned is a terrifying thing," Stephan agreed.

Sensing that he might be making a jest, Belle finally turned to face him. "I felt scorned," she admitted somberly. "And it made me quite insane for a few moments."

"I know." Stephan ceased smiling. "Truly, I did not mean what I said, Belle. It *was* like being cast in some play. For a moment, it was as though I was talking to someone else—and I could hear her saying that she would never marry me. That though I was fine to dally with for an afternoon, I was still . . ."

"You were a *bastard*," Belle supplied, almost sotto voce, her eyes returning to the countryside. "I did say that, didn't I?"

"Yes. You didn't mean your words that way, but that is what some part of me heard. However, it was an hallucination, and you must know that I shall always treasure the gift of your innocence, Belle. Nothing has ever pleased me more." He paused, perhaps waiting for comment, and when none was forthcoming added: "It is to be hoped that with time you shall be able to forgive me for doubting you and saying those unkind things. I shall endeavor to make it up to you."

Moved, but uncertain of precisely what she felt—beyond turmoil—Belle looked away and pondered Stephan's explanation. It had been a morning of discoveries. She knew now for certain that Stephan could actually be ruthless when moved by great emotion. And she had proof that there was a strong ghost that haunted him, a phantom brew of rejection and old shame caused from the facts of his birth. It made Stephan's thoughts travel different roads from other men's, and made his actions in any given situation most unpredictable.

It was near dusk and not too distant from the inn where they planned to pass the night that they came upon a small battle, which was being fought in the middle of the road. It was not at first apparent what was going on, as there were a great many cattle milling about and a deal of disorganized shouting of instructions and threatening curses in heavily accented tongues.

"Damnation! These bloody farmers—" Stephan had barely reigned in the horses on the sharp curve when gunfire suddenly rang out, startling the beasts into plunging terror.

"Stephan!"

"Hang on, Belle!" Stephan hauled on the reins, trying to bring down the horses' heads, but the pair still shied violently, reversing the chaise off the road. Stephan kept them from bolting, but the right wheel pushed through the low hedge and then caught in a hidden ditch. Before there was even time to shout a warning, the unsteady chaise overturned.

Belle was flung out onto the shoulder of the road, fortunately somewhat padded with a drift of the ubiquitous heather, which matted there in a convenient bed. Winded by the blow, but not seriously harmed, she rolled to her knees, pushed her skewed bonnet off her head, and started calling for Stephan.

The search was short and fraught with discomfort and danger. Of Stephan she found no sign because of the dozens of bovïne legs that were suddenly milling about her, kicking clods of dirt into her face and pinning her skirts to the ground with their heavy hooves. Dazed, but conscious enough to understand the danger presented by the cattle and horse hooves falling near her skull, Belle finally crawled to the edge of the ditch and lowered herself into the trench behind the carriage, where she cowered.

There came the sound of a horse at gallop and then further shots rang out. Fresh cries of pain filled the air. The body of an elderly man, dressed in dark clothes and heavily muffled, fell to the ground beside the carriage. In spite of the growing shadows and the dark hue of the man's clothing, the blood leaking from the hole in his chest was quite visible.

"Stephan!" Belle whispered, fingers of panic clutching at her heart.

"What oof the toff?" a rough voice asked, raised

to a near shout to be heard above the unhappy cattle.

"Leave 'im wi' the bodies. He'll coom aboot soon enough if his neck ain't broke, which it don't appear tae be. I'm goin' tae cut the horses loose afore they break a leg."

"And the lassie? She maun be aboot somewhere. She looked a bonnie thing. Shall we take her wi' us fer a bit of sport?"

"Have a wee look aboot for 'er. If ye can find 'er, bring 'er along. But haste ye! We maun be off wi' these cattle. We maun cross the border under cover of nicht or they'll have the sassun guards oot after us."

Guessing that the rough voices were talking about her, Belle squatted as low as she could go and began scuttling down the ditch away from the unfriendly voices. Her heart thundered unpleasantly, and she felt terrible for running away. However, she knew that she had to be ruled by practicality and not sentiment. She had no weapon of any kind, and no hope of not being spotted if she left the ditch to search for one among their scattered baggage.

"Be well, Stephan," she breathed. "I shall return at once, and all will be well."

He would be alright wherever he was until then, she told herself firmly, keeping panic at bay. His neck wasn't broken! The horrid man had said so.

The ditch began to shallow and the heather to thin, offering her less and less cover. Belle began looking back constantly to see that she wasn't followed. So intent had she become on discovering what was behind her that she crawled into a pair of hairy breeches before realizing that they were standing in her path.

"Hullo, lassie. Sae here ye be." Belle gasped as a giant hand reached down and pulled her out of the trough by her left arm. "Coom along now. Nae need fer crawlin' aboot like a beastie."

Belle found herself looking into a matted beard of red and gray where she suspected pests might be nesting. The eyes above it were red and frightening. The creature's breath was like a blow from a blunt instrument, and he had muscles bulging out of his filthy clothes in every direction. He was also swaying slightly and studying her with a disturbed air, clearly under the influence of some alcoholic ingestion.

It was obvious to Belle, even with reason and wits still absent from their thrones, that she was being hounded by the forces of darkness. It was not a moment for half-measures or ladylike hesitation. She might not have wanted to do Stephan a serious hurt and therefore had not fought with her all, but this was another matter. Doubling up her fist as she had seen pugilists do, Belle cocked her free arm back and hit out at her captor's stomach with all her might.

But instead of toppling as he ought to have done, the monster simply grunted and stooped long enough to put a shoulder to her midriff and hoist her onto his back like a sack.

"None of yer games now, lassie," he scolded. "We maun be off."

"Put me down at once," Belle commanded, gasping at the smell of the shirt, which was thrust against her face and trying in vain to twist away from the vise that anchored her legs. "How dare you abduct me? You shall hang for this!"

Her captor snorted. "An' they find us, we'll hang any road."

"Put me down . . . or I shall be ill! Immediately!"

"Be ill an' ye maun, but we cannae wait fer ye tae mince along in yer silly shoes," the behemoth said. "Asides, yer a perfect prize fer the young laird. He said tae bring home mair than coos this trip, so I'll not be lettin' ye go free."

Belle swallowed, a difficult task when hanging upside down. "Are you cattle thieves? Is that what this horrid mess is about? Cows?" She demanded, pounding on the creature's back with ineffective blows, which he hardly seemed to notice.

"Aye, reavers we are. Been reavers for many a year noo," he said proudly, striding down the road with the gait of one of Lord Duncan's inferior horses. "Taking back wha' the mulcting English stole frae us, we are."

"What happened to Stephan?" She gasped, beginning to feel dizzy from hanging about upside down and fearing her previous threat of illness might well become fact.

"Yer man? He's well enough. Just knocked aboot the head a bit. If the cattle didnae trample him he'll be aboot in nae time. And the horses are aen fine fettle. Ye shall have one tae ride."

"I want to see him," she said faintly, her head pounding and her vision beginning to cloud. She stopped fighting and used her hands to hold her face away from the suffocating shirt.

"We've nae time fer that," the giant said, hurrying past the bodies, which were scattered about the road. Belle looked about desperately and was relieved to discover Stephan there, and to see that he did not have any blood on him. He at least had not been shot.

"Please let me go to him," Belle pleaded one last time. "He's hurt."

"Nay, ye just forget 'im now. Yer goin' to the home of the laird and he'll be lookin' after ye."

Once again Belle found herself wishing for a pistol so that she might shoot the dumb animal she rode. But the only weapon in sight was the handle of a knife thrust through the creature's belt just beyond her reach. She would keep trying to liberate it, but was not entirely certain that the giant would even notice if she stabbed him.

Stephan regained consciousness slowly and was uncertain, even when he opened his eyes, that he was not dreaming; instead of a canopy over his head, he was looking up into a sky bright with stars and the rising moon decked with lacy clouds, which thickened toward the horizon.

"Bloody hell!" he exclaimed, sitting up abruptly.

The world shifted on its pins, for one moment spinning away, and then righted itself once more.

"Hey! This one's alive yet," a voice said, and two stout shadows bearing torches approached.

"Where is Belle?" Stephan demanded, pushing himself to his feet. The two shades, growing slightly more detailed, halted an arm's length away and exchanged glances.

"Belle?" one repeated.

"My wife! Where is she?"

"We've found no lady, sir. Mayhap she was took off with them thievin' Scots." The man's voice was muffled because he wore a scarf up over his face.

"Thieving Scots?" Stephan repeated in a voice of incomprehension. He looked about vaguely and seeing the overturned chaise, he staggered over to the upended equipage and began hunting for Belle beneath it. There was nothing there but a lump of straw and some veiling, which had been her hat. "Belle?"

"Aye, the cattle reavers. They come down to steal back their cows from Farmer Huggate. They took your horses it seems, but left your luggage," one of the two men volunteered. Stephan noticed that he, too, had his lower face concealed.

"Your missus ain't under there," the other one said. "We looked already."

"Bloody hell," he said again, finally noticing that their bags had been stacked neatly at the side of the road.

Stephan picked up Belle's muddied bonnet and

then leaned on the side of the carriage while he glared up at the sky. Was his relationship with Belle opposed by the gods? Fate had certainly been against them at every turn. The machinations of some ancient and ill-natured goddess would explain the sheer numbers of disasters that befell them.

"It doesn't matter," he said aloud, feeling in dangerous humor as he cast the ruined bonnet aside. "I'll have her anyway. You plot and toil in vain."

And he meant it. He was going to find Belle and marry her if he had to defy a whole pantheon of gods and cattle thieves to do it. He was through trying to be a gentleman. The next man who stepped in his path was a dead one—as were the creatures who had taken Belle.

However, his desire to do instantaneous harm to the author of their iniquities was impractical, so he put aside cursing and dark rumination in favor of more immediately useful action.

"I need a horse. May I buy or borrow yours?" he asked. Noticing finally that his clothes were wet, he turned about, and with a note of outrage creeping into his voice, he demanded: "Has it been raining again?"

Somewhat taken aback, one of the men answered: "Aye, just a small shower a space back."

Stephan ground his teeth together and muttered: "Of course it rained. It shall likely rain again before we find shelter." Then more loudly: "I would be much obliged if our luggage—particularly my wife's clothes—could be taken to the Cowder Inn, and the theft of our horses reported to the innkeeper. Doubtless he will alert the authorities as to what has happened."

"Mayhap we could," one of them agreed with obvious reluctance, "if we was so inclined."

"There is room in the dray for your traps," the more talkative and better spoken of the two men added after a moment. "But it shall have to go with the dead. A friend of ours was cut down, do you see? We are taking him for burial so he don't end in the quicklime."

"The bags will hardly care who they ride with," Stephan said, straightening. "Just let me get my pistols, and then you may have them."

"You've a pistol?" The man sounded impressed and perhaps a bit amused. "In your bags?"

"Aye, two of them. And it is high time I used them, too. Apparently one's needs must be armed at all times in these parts."

"Well, yer a man after me own heart! I feel just the same. Ye may take my horse—as a gift. He's strong enough and knows the country to the north," the less talkative man volunteered. "I think he may have come from up there and would like as not enjoying going home."

The other man snorted and muttered something incomprehensible.

"Thank you," Stephan said, opening his valise. He did not ask how it was that the man did not know the origins of his own horse. Given the pains they were taking to conceal their faces from him, Stephan doubted that it was wise to ask. That they had the sort of friend who would be buried in quicklime did not recommend their character either. He would count himself lucky if they did not unburden him of his purse before they went on their way. "I am very much obliged to you. Please bring your torch closer. I cannot see—ah!"

The dueling pistol had a long nose and gleamed coldly in the wavering torchlight. The two men stared at it in hushed respect.

"That's a beautiful barker, that is! Always wanted one like it." The voice held lust and envy.

"Hush, Lydd! There'll be none of that talk. So, ye'll be planning to get yer wife back then, will ye?" the horse lender asked at last.

"Aye. That I will. And before morning, too." Stephan removed a second pistol.

"Then ye best be off. They are about three hours ahead of ye. And don't worry about your bags. They'll be waiting safe and sound at the inn for ye as yer doin' us a service."

"They will?" Lydd asked.

"Aye, they will," the other said firmly. "It's the least we can do fer the man what's going to kill Lydd's murderers."

"Well . . . aye, I suppose it is."

Stephan, who did not actually plan on shooting any

more men than was necessary to rescue Belle, did not correct their slight misapprehension.

"Thank you," he said again, walking swiftly to the horse and pulling himself into the saddle. His head swam with the minor exertion, but he refused to acknowledge any hurt. "I am grateful for the assistance you have rendered me. Perhaps someday I might be able to do something for you."

"I doubt it, but we thank ye for the sentiment. We don't often meet with polite gentry. Perishing rude most them are. God speed ye, sir."

Stephan nodded, but said under his breath: "I'd feel a sight better if all divine beings let us be just now. Somehow I suspect that their aid is likely to prove more deadly than the ailment."

Chapter Thirteen

Belle was confident that Stephan had started on her trail just as quickly as he regained consciousness—which with any luck would not have been too long after they left him as it had begun to rain and the cold water should have been an effective restorative. It certainly kept her feeling alert!

Though Stephan's doggedness had, in the past, been something she deplored, at the moment Belle found herself grateful for this reliable trait. It meant that rescue was probably at hand. And, much though it galled her to admit it, she would require rescuing.

Circumstances presently favored her and Stephan, but there was no way to know how long Fate would side with them. The cattle had had a difficult day, and they refused to be hurried on their journey home through the sometimes inclement weather. They were also in digestive distress, having wandered into a turnip field where they'd eaten unreservedly, and they were leaving ample evidence of their unhappy passage for any rescuers blessed with either nose or eyes to find.

Further in their momentary favor, now that the squall had passed, was that it was a bright night without too many clouds so Stephan could find the way even after the moon set—though with any luck he would have caught up with them long before then. She had to pray that it was so, since the reavers might well stop for the night once they had crossed the border, and Belle placed no reliance upon them *saving* her for the laird.

Belle's nervous thoughts were interrupted by another plaintive bellow and a fresh explosion of manure from the beast in front of her. Though she might curse the cattle for being so noisy that she could not listen for sounds of pursuit, she took comfort from the fact that her captors could not hear anything either, and they had to keep their eyes on the path immediately before them or else risk slipping in the awful green sludge.

Though angry enough at the preposterous kidnapping to commit mortal sin, Belle behaved herself, meeting all of her captors' suspicious looks, which could not be avoided with an expression of utmost limpidity, and she was chewing holes in her tongue so she did not say anything to provoke them. There had been some argument about whether to take her, kill her—*a half-hearted suggestion from a stunted misogynist with a squint in his right eye, probably supplied by his long-suffering wife*—or let her go. Two of them had favored freeing her, but the giant, Idiot Angus, had been determined to fetch her north, so the others had reluctantly given in.

Their trust in her docility was still not absolute, but clearly they thought her a negligible threat for her hands were bound before her in a sloppy manner, allowing her to grip the horse's mane as it was led across the open fields by the smug Angus.

Had it been any of the three other men who made up the raiding party at the horse's head, she would have attempted to break away and trust the darkness to hide her from their bullets, but the behemoth was nearly the same size as the beast she rode and had his meaty fists wrapped stoutly on the horse's mane. A single twist from his hands and the horse would end with a broken neck. Situated as she was, Belle could do nothing but remain prepared to react swiftly to whatever favorable circumstances came her way.

In preparation for the impending rescue, Belle was careful to keep her eyes turned away from the lantern that the lead man carried to investigate the terrain. She did not wish to see only spots before her eyes when the moment of liberation was at hand. She also had a firm grip on her mount's mane so she would not be thrown if the beast—or *she*, herself—shied at the sound of gunfire.

It spoke of her confidence in Stephan's possessive nature that she expected gunfire.

And, Mama, should I be—when I am—rescued, I swear that I will do my utmost to make Stephan happy. This shan't be a union purely of necessity, at least not on my part. I've tried suffocating my feelings, but they keep crawling out from under the blanket of indifference. I must accept that they are not to be so easily extinguished.

And I know that though it is duty that now compels Stephan, with time we can achieve a strong marriage. I esteem Stephan, and I know that he has never cared for an absence of wits in his companions, so he will not insist that I stifle my thoughts. I shall be allowed to be a person.

And perhaps, in time, he will even come to love me.

Stephan took in the scene with a calm eye and then carefully shifted his aim from the shambling creature who walked beside Belle to the man holding the lantern. Much as he wanted to shoot the other individual for daring to stand so close to his woman, it made more sense to get rid of the man with the light. The others would likely rush forward to see what was amiss with their friend, and he would have the best chance to get at Belle, since they would likely hesitate to shoot back into the herd of cattle for fear of panicking them into flight.

Moonlight gleamed on the pistol's sights as Stephan held his breath against the prevailing odoriferous wind. He squeezed the trigger, prepared for the flash and the loud report. As planned, the lead man crumpled with a satisfying cry and the others immediately started for him with loud exclamations of alarm.

Stephan didn't hesitate but spurred his horse into the milling cattle, heading directly for Belle. His mount, as promised, was sure-footed and swift, but before he had ridden even half the distance that separated them, Belle had pulled her mount's head about and, throwing one leg over its back so she might straddle the horse, she rode away at a full gallop that made no allowances for terrain or the large beasts milling around her.

"Good girl!" he applauded, seeing how she laid down flat, making herself the smallest possible target for the reavers. Though he might want further revenge on the men who waylaid them, Stephan immediately switched directions and followed her.

Concerned as he was for Belle's well-being, he was doubly grateful to be away from the slippery, malodorous ground. Not only was it an assault to the nose, it was dangerous to ride upon.

Dodging the panicked cattle, which were conveniently bolting in every direction, Stephan made a note to never again tease Belle about her skills as an equestrian. Her mount was not accustomed to bearing a rider, but she clung to that carriage horse like a burr to a blanket, weaving through panicked beasts with her hair streaming out behind her like a golden banner of war. She looked magnificent. He vowed to gift her with the finest of hunters and take her on a fox-hunt next season.

There came another shout, this one angry, and then the belated explosion of gunfire behind them. Stephan did not look back. All his attention was focused on catching up with Belle, whose terrified mount was clearly intent on running into the cover at the heart of the woods. She had a great seat, possibly the best he had ever seen, but without any sort of saddle or bridle, she would have difficulty in controlling the runaway horse and could end up badly hurt if thrown into a tree.

"Hang on, Belle," he urged, riding up beside the crazed gelding and matching its frantic pace.

"Stephan!" she exclaimed, turning her head to smile at him. Her face was streaked with mud, but her expression was exultant. "I was sure you would come!"

"I've got you now. Let go," he ordered, plucking her off the horse's back and pulling her onto the saddle before him. At once he veered for the nearest edge of the woods where the trees were not so closely placed and the ground hidden with snaring deadfall.

Belle grunted once as she hit the saddle bow and caught at his leg to steady herself. Though he wished to abate the punishing pace, he did not dare slow at all until they were under some sort of cover between them and the reavers. It would be foolhardy of the raiders to follow them, but they had two other horses, from which they could give chase and send bullets after them. Of course, it was dastardly to shoot at a woman, but they had already demonstrated their contempt for English life.

"Hang on for just a moment more, love. We must get into the woods where we will have some protection. We'll tend to any injuries then."

"I am unhurt," she assured him. "I shan't be unhorsed either. Just ride."

Belle righted herself as best she could with her bound hands, again dragging one leg across the mount's back so that she could ride astride. It was much easier to do with Stephan's supporting arms about her, though the saddle was badly crowded.

Stephan, for the first time seeing the ties about her wrists, was both horrified and awed at the risk she had taken.

"You are quick of wit, my sweet," he praised her, ducking his head as they entered the small copse wood. "And we again owe your first stepfather a debt of gratitude for teaching you to keep a level head at all times."

"I knew you would follow," Belle answered, also lowering herself a trifle to escape the junior limbs that snatched at their faces with damp twigs. She was glad to have Stephan's larger body behind her, protecting her from the trees and cold. "I was just waiting for the signal to escape."

There came another volley of gunshots. Belle

flinched and then began hurriedly working on the knot with her teeth.

"I do believe that those idiots are following us," Stephan said in amazement, listening to the bushes crashing behind them. They were easily outstripping those who followed on foot, but he was still annoyed enough to turn in the saddle and send a bullet flying back.

Belle barely flinched.

"Are they completely mad?" Stephan demanded. "They must know that the families of those they killed will be out for their blood. It isn't likely that my rescuers went to the authorities, but at the very least, the landlord will have summoned the soldiers from the border garrison. They have their cows— sick as they are, poor beasts—and a chance to escape, why would they chase after you?"

"It's probably just the giant," Belle said, craning to look behind them as she pulled the ties off her hands. "He had a notion to take me back to their leader as a present, and he is most tiresomely stubborn."

"Obviously he is another male who hasn't heard about the end of slavery in the British empire," Stephan muttered, heading for a clearing.

"Well, he is a Scotsman," Belle answered, trying to be fair-minded. "I don't think they pay much heed to English law. Besides, he is quite horridly stupid. He may even be the village idiot."

"A giant idiot—why not?" Stephan asked. "We've seen every other sort of fantastical creature today."

226

"Stephan? Should we not be heading the opposite way? We shall never make it back to the chaise this night if we keep on much longer in this direction."

"The horses are gone and, in any event, the chaise may not be fit for travel. I didn't stop to examine it. I was in too great a hurry to get after you, and I feared that if I lingered, temptation might get the better of the footpads who found me."

"Footpads?"

"Or highwaymen. They might have been either."

"Oh dear! What dreadful luck we are having."

"Eventually we'll return south to the Cowder Inn, Belle, for I believe that the two hedge birds were sincere about leaving our baggage there. But we are very near the border now, and I truly think it wise to wake up the nearest smith and be married as soon as possible," Stephan said with rare feeling. "You may call me superstitious, Belle, but I have lately had the feeling that we are being dogged by organized disaster."

"Yes!" she exclaimed, almost gaily, still bubbling with the delight of having escaped from her kidnappers. "I have thought this very same thing almost from the start. I have never heard of an elopement so plagued by adversity. All that is left is for us to be abducted by pirates and shanghaied away to sea—or perhaps to be attacked by a headless horseman or dragon."

"Don't even think it!" Stephan warned. "We are not safe yet."

"Are you truly concerned about pirates or—or anything else?" Belle demanded, suddenly uneasy. She peered anxiously at a twisted bush that looked rather like a crouching bear.

"Nay, but there is plenty to fear from the reavers and the soldiers chasing them. These thieves will never expect us to travel north, and that might be the safer course for the time being. Otherwise, we could ride smack into the soldiers who are likely pursuing them with blood in their eyes. I should hate to end up getting shot by our countrymen."

Stephan slowed his horse's gait to one less dangerous given the deep shadows in the forest. Feeling suddenly exhausted, Belle abandoned her search of the underbrush for fantastical beings and slumped back against Stephan.

"I don't suppose that you brought a comb with you?" She asked with a sigh, reaching a hand for her disturbed hair and pulling it over one shoulder. Feeling the caked mud on her cheek she added: "Or a clean handkerchief?"

"Nay," Stephan said, feeling some of the tension leave his body as he finally realized that Belle was truly safe and in his arms again. He looked down at his own dirt-encrusted coat and shook his head, which had suddenly begun aching. "I shall buy you one of each as a wedding gift if you like, when we reach the next town."

"Thank you," Belle said, quickly plaiting her hair and tying it off with her former bond. The results were far from perfect, but she had never tried to dress her hair while riding on horseback in the dark. "Do you know, Stephan, I am really quite tired of arriving at strange towns and inns looking like a ragged gypsy. What has the world come to that two people cannot travel safely to Scotland?"

"We do seem to be making a habit of this unfortunate behavior," Stephan agreed, tightening the arm about her waist. "But at least this time we will be making a conspicuous entrance in another country. And perhaps the dark will hide the worst of the damage."

"Somehow, this does not entirely console me. It was never my ambition to be notorious in three lands."

"Three?"

Belle looked over her shoulder and smiled wryly. "Aye." She ticked them off on her hand. "England, Scotland, and by next week, the East Indies."

"You have an excellent point. And one that settles the debate. We must marry immediately. I can deal with the gods of misfortune, murdering innkeepers, footpads and cattle thieves, but I feel totally unprepared to face your stepfather without being properly bound and hidden behind the shield of holy wedlock."

Belle nodded.

"Pirates would be less dangerous," she agreed, and then, looking up at the portion of sky visible through the leafy canopy: "Do you think that it will rain again?"

"There are no clouds overhead just now, but it is almost inevitable, don't you think?" Stephan asked, pulling Belle closer to the warmth of his body and bestowing a quick kiss to her mussed hair.

Belle nodded wearily and then shifted uncomfortably. She was beginning to feel the bruises from her earlier, unceremonious ejection from the chaise. She wiggled her feet, trying to bring some feeling back into her frozen toes, and then made an unpleasant discovery. "Stephan, would it distress you to have a wife who uses profanity?"

"I should not like it to be habitual, but under these circumstances, I think it might be allowed," he answered broad-mindedly.

"That is fortunate, for I seem to have lost my bloody damned shoe!"

Suddenly Stephan began laughing. The spasm of hilarity made his head hurt, but he persisted for a long moment regardless of the pain.

"I am sorry, Stephan, but I do not see the humor of being shoeless. My feet are cold, and this makes things even more awkward."

"Ah, Belle! My apologies. I shall buy you new shoes as well. They are likely to be ugly peasant things, but they will go well with your ruined dress and my muddy coat." Stephan added: "My head aches abominably. I just realized it."

"This isn't a nightmare, is it? We shan't wake up in the morning and be back at Ashlars?" Belle asked, staring fretfully as they left the woods cover for another open field. There were clumps of boulders and stands of shrubbery where any number of desperate persons might lie in wait for them.

"Nay, but we're both alive to see another the morning—something that might not have happened—so I'll not complain about the rest of it."

"I suppose that you are right." Belle sighed. "Give me your pistols, and I shall reload them. We may not complain about adversity, but I think it behooves us to be prepared for it."

Stephan handed her his pistols, making no comment on her knowledge of firearms. Belle's resourcefulness had ceased to amaze him.

Chapter Fourteen

The smith in the village was not at first entirely happy to be woken before dawn by the innkeeper of the coach house. But he was prepared to forgive the English trespassers when the situation was explained and Stephan proved generous about dispensing bridal largesse. In fact, so pleased was the village celebrant with the offering that he volunteered to wake his cousin, the shopkeeper, and procure a handkerchief, comb, and brogues for Belle, as well as taking a bit of broken bridle he had in the shop and forging it into a wedding ring while the bridal couple broke their fast.

Accustomed as the villagers were to the irregular marriage trade, fed mostly by those English who wished to immediately plight their troth and avoid a reading of the pesky banns or the fees for a marriage license, they were assured that there was no difficulty in finding two witnesses who would be willing, for a coin, to stand with the smith at the coaching house anvil and observe the short dawn ceremony.

A kindly young woman at the coach house gave Stephan and Belle some strong tea and a plate of cold bannocks, and a place at the freshly made-up hearth where they could rest while the ceremony was arranged.

Stephan's coat was taken off for brushing, and the children sent into the dew-damp meadow behind the inn to quickly gather a nosegay of wood sorrel and cowslips so that Belle would have flowers as well as shoes when she married.

In the space of less than an hour, everything was prepared. The sun was barely up and shining through the branches of the horse chestnut where a family of inquisitive red squirrels lived when Belle and Stephan, titivated as much as they were able to be in their fate-assaulted attire, walked out to the warm smithy attached to the coach house to say their wedding vows.

The ceremony began without preamble.

"I am a forger," the smith intoned, looking his clients over with watery blue eyes, which were slightly clouded with cataracts. "As I marry metal tae metal, so do I forge the bands of marriage between this lad and this lass wha hae plighted their troth before witnesses . . . Do the ring now, lad, and plight your troth."

The smith nodded encouragingly at Stephan who hesitantly slipped over Belle's finger the clumsy bit of reworked metal that was her ring. He made a mental vow to replace the ugly band as soon as possible.

"I plight thee my troth," he said obediently, looking into Belle's eyes, hoping—*foolishly*—to see something joyous there.

"And ye also, lassie," the smith said. "Tell yer man that ye are plighted."

"I plight thee my troth," Belle murmured, her tone and expression rather dazed by fatigue. Stephan could not imagine anyone who looked less like a bride.

"Then you are now man and wife," the smith announced. "This is the law of marriage in Scotland, and so mote it be."

The hammer clenched in his leathery fist clanged down over the anvil with a resounding clang, and thus quickly the marriage ceremony was over and they were ushered out of the shop.

Though exhausted, Stephan and Belle politely declined to take rooms at the inn to consummate their marriage, hire a guide for trout fishing, or sample the local whiskey in a bridal toast.

They did engage in a last bit of commerce, hiring a mare for Belle to ride, an arrangement made possible because the landlord at the Cowder Inn was some sort of cousin by marriage to the innkeeper at Powsail and was assured of having his hack returned.

They took the journey in easy stages since Stephan's mount had been worked so hard the night before. Though the village of Powsail was not on the main road to England, there was still a fair amount of trade between the two countries, and Belle and Stephan had periodic company, both on foot and mounted, for their short journey back to their own country.

The hillocky way where the heather grew deep was very quiet on that sunny day, so there was ample opportunity for the bridal couple to esteem the graceful roe deer and delicate dragonflies that favored the small fields and fens of the north countryside.

They also had a chance to admire the many stands of handsome Kingcups and wild thyme that they had been unable to appreciate the night before. As the morning grew warmer they even saw a daring kestrel, who briefly mounted the brightening sky and attracted the eye upward to the lacy clouds gathering in the blue.

Unfortunately, Stephan was not in a particularly appreciative mood. The peace that he had hoped to achieve by making this marriage still eluded him. Perhaps it was because his whole thought had been fixed upon getting Belle to Scotland and wed, and not upon the life they would lead thereafter.

The thought of further complexities made him frown slightly and rub his tender head.

Mayhap part of the difficulty was that they had not followed the rules of social order, and therefore did not have the structure of ritual to rely upon as a guide. In their courtship—*if such a word could even be applied to their strange situation*—all things had come in reverse. Adversity before the wedding, carnal knowledge before the vows, near-carnal knowledge before acquaintance—and now here they were turned loose alone upon the world; man and wife, but without a home or even family to celebrate the event.

They had not even had a wedding breakfast to mark their nuptials, having consumed their bannock cakes before the strange ceremony.

Of course, he had to admit that the lump on his head and the bruises on his body might be contributing to his less than optimistic mood, and it behooved him to suspend judgment until he was rested and healed. Perhaps things were not as bleak as they seemed.

"Are you well, Belle?" he asked, belatedly solicitous of the woman who truly was, now and forever, his life's companion. The thought, even with all the vexations that attached to it, still pleased him mightily.

"Quite well, aside from some bruises," Belle answered politely. Looking up at the sky, she added: "And perhaps dreading another wet and blowy evening, which I believe we shall have."

"But you are also rather dazed and uncertain of what to do next?" he guessed.

"Yes," she admitted, glancing over at Stephan. She managed a small smile. "I was just wondering if we should not have taken rooms at the Powsail, had a few drinks and then hired a guide to take us fishing. It would have been a celebration of sorts."

Relieved that Belle felt as much as he did, Stephan also managed a smile.

"I had thought of that, but soon you'll be lusting after your new dresses—which you haven't even seen—and a coach house is no place for a honeymoon."

Belle looked into the distance at the abandoned cemetery and derelict church they were passing. The ancient headstones were leaning drunkenly against one another, unsettled from upright dignity by years of neglect and the miles of burrowing hares' tunnels, which riddled the fields about them.

She felt a bit like one of those mossy, tilted stones. Circumstance had undermined her and she was still uncertain of what she felt. It seemed unbelievable that she was actually married.

"I don't suppose that we dare return to Ashlars for a spell, do we? It was so lovely there."

Stephan, recalling the servants' shocked faces on the day they departed, shook his head.

"I am sorry, but I fear that I've turned craven in my old age, Belle," he confessed. "I can face bullets but not your friend's staff."

Hearing the note of humor in his voice, Belle straightened a bit and made an effort to be a better companion. What was done was done, she told herself. All they could do was make the best of things.

"It is fortunate that we traveled to Scotland by backroads," she said, "For we may now return by the main thoroughfares and have a much more comfortable journey back to . . . to London?"

"Aye, to London—at least briefly. But after I have seen the Kelpie Lass off I should like to take you to my country home, Warkworth, in Kent. It is a lovely place in the spring, and I should like you to see it when it is at its best."

"I would like that very much," Belle said sincerely, responding more to the image of *home* than the promise of springtime vistas. She had actually had quite enough of nature for the time being.

"Later in the year, when the seas have moderated, we could plan a trip to see your stepfather," Stephan suggested.

"Perhaps." Belle frowned slightly at the mention of her stepparent. "I suppose that I shall have to write to him from London and apprise him of our marriage. Certainly I shall have to speak to our people there and allay their alarm at my disappearance."

Stephan grimaced in sympathy. "I shall write to your stepfather as well, though what might be appropriate to say to him is at present eluding me."

"Epistolary brevity may be the order of the day. Simply relating the fact that we are married may be sufficient for an introductory letter. Even that much is likely to initiate a flurry of correspondence."

"And what will you tell him?" Stephan asked, suddenly curious about the relationship Belle must share with this legendary recluse.

"I intend to relate all of Quincy's perfidy," Belle said bluntly. "Normally I should not be so unkind as to bring my stepfather's wrath down on anyone, but I think for our own sakes that Marvelle should be offered up as a sacrifice, don't you?"

"Without question. If your stepfather kills him it shall save me the effort."

Belle frowned at him. "Do not jest about this."

Stephan opened his mouth to assure Belle that he was not jesting, but then thought better of commenting.

"Done carefully," Belle told him, "Papa may even come to be grateful to you for saving my reputation."

"Perhaps, provided he never hears about how I helped to destroy it in the first place."

Belle nodded agreement. "That is true. And I do not think that I will mention anything about our meeting with a Bow Street runner—or anything that happened along the road—though it was very heroic of you to rescue me from those reavers, and I shall always be grateful."

Stephan flushed. "No, it is best that you put these incidents out of your mind completely, especially what passed at Casker's Chance," he said gently. "And I did nothing heroic. You all but saved yourself. That was a masterful piece of riding. I shall enjoy hunting with you."

"Of course you were heroic," Belle contradicted,

much to his pleasure. "Oddly enough, I had forgotten about meeting Mister Frye until just this moment. Being abducted by those horrid men quite distracted me from all manner of smaller problems."

"It did rather focus my thinking as well," Stephan said a trifle grimly.

"Yes?" Belle smiled mischievously and peeped up at him. "Ah, but you had the added pleasure of meeting up with highwaymen. What an adventure! You may dine out on that tale for a month."

"Highwaymen or footpads. They parted so quickly with this horse that I cannot help but suspect that it was only recently stolen—damnation!" Stephan said in vexation.

"What?" Belle demanded. "What is wrong?"

"Nothing of import. I have only just recalled that there is no way to return this beast to his owners—whomever they might be. And as sure as I ride out upon him, he will be recognized and I shall be accused of horse thievery—possibly even blamed for the cattle thefts." Stephan's tone was gloomy. "I suppose it is inevitable that I end on the gallows."

Belle chuckled.

"Ah! That is true. Doubtless we shall both hang. I don't suppose that your new friends will come around to claim him either and spare us. A pity, for I should like to meet them."

Stephan sent her a reproving glance. "It isn't likely that they would come around, and I shouldn't introduce you if they did. Perhaps it would be best if I

240

offered him up to the man who rented the chaise in replacement for the two we lost. He is a very good beast."

"Or perhaps they will know the beast at the Cowder Inn, and we shall be able to return him after all." Belle exhaled heavily, her light mood abruptly abandoning her. "We must retrieve Roi from Becky as well. And then there is the task of informing your uncle and Constance about our marriage." She shook her head. "This isn't going to be a pleasant few days, is it?"

"Well, don't fret, my sweet. I shall have it cleared up in no time. I'll place an advertisement for our nuptials in the papers as directly as we return to town. That will end some of the wildest gossip and answer many people's questions."

Belle shook her head again, this time more emphatically. "No. An advertisement shall take care of the Marvelles and Duncans, but we shall have to clear up some of these more feral rumors in more personal ways. You must correspond with your uncle and tell him some version of the truth, and I must write to Becky before she hears some garbled version of the story and feels betrayed."

Stephan reluctantly conceded the point. "I had hoped that the first weeks of our marriage would be more pleasant for you, Belle," he said wryly, thinking of his plans for their honeymoon.

"Don't chastise yourself, Stephan," Belle said, leaning forward to pat her mare's neck. Her ugly ring

241

caught the sun and glinted dully. "This is only what I expected would happen. We shall simply have to make the best of it."

On that somewhat deflating observation, the two of them lapsed back into exhausted silence.

Mama, our marriage has actually begun. We can but hope that this means our adventuring is finally over. I pray it is, for I am so very tired!

Riding along here and thinking about the day's event, I have had a sudden outburst of what I think is family feeling. This wasn't the wedding ceremony that you would have wanted for me, I know—but how I wish that you and Papa had been there to see it! It was shameful and scandalous, but I can't help thinking of that bit from Shakespeare about chamomile being the sweeter for having been trodden upon—only it should have been hyacinths or narcissus, don't you think? In any event, for all that we arrived at the anvil bruised and looking like a pair of gypsies, perhaps in years to come the moment will seem sweeter for all that we went through to get there.

Mama, one last thing. You would laugh to see my ugly wedding band, but I must tell you that even if I do not wear it in public, I shall keep it always. For some reason I find that I value the thing above rubies or pearls, though not—of course—above Stephan.

Chapter Fifteen

Stephan discovered, much to his chagrin, that he was a folk hero. Fortunately, no one in the taproom had yet recognized him so he was allowed to drink in relative peace and listen to the gossip.

In his quest for news, a disconcerted Stephan soon found that the local costumers who visited the Cowder Inn's taproom were only too happy to discourse upon the recent murders in their district. They were, in fact, inclined to discuss nothing else but the murders and the man who had struck the reavers down.

One loquacious oldster was so given to indignation at the incursion by the Scots that he made the rounds to all the tables saying: "Brethren, remain sober! Remain vigilant! Our adversaries, those Scottish devils, goeth about like thieves in the night, seeking out honest Christian men to rob! Our only hope is this avenging hero who has released these demons from their earthly flesh."

The innkeeper, perhaps because of having cousins in the north, viewed the speech with a jaundiced eye and soon ordered the oldster to finish his drink and depart until he had slept off his potation.

But the oldster's banishment did not empty the room of colorful patrons. The tapster, Henry Jones, who had taken an unaccountable liking to Stephan, was quite happy to identify the local personages for his new friend and give him some personal histories.

"See 'im, the one in the rough tweed? That be William Tudge, the pig gelder. He says that if he is late for supper the rib'll nag 'im all night. And if he's out a' night she won't speak to 'im for a week. Looks as though he is makin' the extra effort to be very late tonight. Must be that 'is sister by marriage is visitin' again. They don't speak. Haven't fer nigh on a decade now."

"I see. And the peculiar man in the brown moleskin wescott?" Stephan asked idly, glancing at the mantel clock and wondering if he had allowed Belle sufficient time to bathe and prepare for bed.

He was very aware of the gift he had in his pocket. It was a wedding ring, a plain gold band that he would probably replace once they reached London, but he wanted that ugly bit of iron mongery off Belle's finger immediately.

"Ah, that be Jock, the dubious meat vendor. My sister says as how she wouldn't buy a roast from 'im as ye might notice the taste, but 'is wares makes up alright in stews and pies."

Stephan made a mental note to decline any dinner invitation from the tapster's sister should such an honor arise during their stay. Casker's Chance had cured him of eating in places that served *dubious meats*.

"Ah, William must be feelin' frisky tonight. He is goin' to favor us wi' a song," the tapster said. His tone made it clear that Stephan was in for a real treat.

Unfortunately, the lyric was delivered in local dialect whose accent was so strong that Stephan could not fathom its meaning. Adding to the confusion was the fact that the dubious meat vendor insisted on singing along with the chorus in a ghastly atonal voice, and having no sense of rhythm was given to random banging on the table with his empty tankard.

Stephan, his headache returning at the sound of the cacophonous din, decided that Belle had had ample opportunity to bathe and change, and it was time for him to retire upstairs also to soak and prepare for bed. They would be leaving first thing in the morning, once again, only one step ahead of gossip and identification.

Making his excuses to Henry, he departed.

As he neared the bedchamber, Stephan discovered that he was feeling somewhat trepidatious. Though he now had every right to come and go as he pleased, he paused outside his assigned chamber door and knocked softly.

"Stephan?" Belle asked.

"Aye."

"Come in." She pulled the door open. "The water is still warm if you wish to have a bath."

Stephan entered the room, his eyes fixed on her. She was attired in nightrail and dressing gown in a shade of deep russet. Bare feet peeped out from beneath the edge of the robe and her hair was unbound. The domesticity of the moment again brought home to him the fact that he was truly married.

"There is a screen," Belle said, dropping her gaze under Stephan's concentrated scrutiny. "Or I can dress and then go down to the parlor while you bathe, if you prefer to be alone."

"No!" Stephan cleared his throat. "No, I do not mind if you remain. Anyway, you do not want to go downstairs again this evening. There are a great many drunken men singing what I think are bawdy songs."

He also did not want her to hear any of the nonsense they were saying about him.

"I wondered about the noise." Belle turned away. "Very well. I shall just fetch the screen for you then."

Stephan found himself smiling at her unexpected show of modesty. "What is this, Belle? A sudden attack of nerve? From you?"

Belle blushed at the accusation. "I do not know why it should be so, but I am suddenly aware that this is our wedding night. And I am . . ." she paused, peeping up at him uncertainly.

"Go on," Stephan said, taking a chair by the fire and pulling off his boots.

"And I am not a virgin anymore," she explained in a rush.

Stephan knew that he was looking at some of the damage he had inflicted that ever-to-be-rued morning at Ashlars. Though he wished that the moment truly could be allowed to sink uncommented upon into the mists of oblivion, he knew that, until Belle was reassured, this memory would always come between them. However uncomfortable or difficult the conversation, it was time to repair some of the harm he had done.

"Ah. That is true," he said matter-of-factly. "But it need not bother you, Belle. Recall that I was the man you lost your virginity to. And truly, I wouldn't give you back your innocence even if I could."

"You wouldn't?" Belle's gaze was hopeful.

"No, I would not. That is the most precious gift I have ever received, and I am glad that we had that moment alone in a meadow instead of in a marginal bed at the Cowder Inn. What a horrid place to begin a bridal trip. It is I who should be apologizing to you." Stephan stood and shrugged off his coat. "Come and sit here by the fire and talk to me while I bathe. I can think of nothing that I would enjoy more."

Rediscovering her courage, Belle came nearer to the hearth and took the proffered chair. Heat from the blaze infused her tired muscles and made her relax enough that she could watch with interest as Stephan disrobed. Shirt, stocking and then breeches were peeled away.

Her eyes widened slightly as he turned around to face her. Somehow she had not taken in all the particulars that day in the meadow and was fascinated by his appearance. It wasn't simply that Stephan was larger than she was and so obviously male. It was the definition of the muscles in his legs and abdomen, and the dark hair of his chest that arrowed down the length of his body, which proclaimed him a man.

"Will you come and wash my back and hair, Belle?" Stephan asked, stepping into the tepid water of the tub. "I find that these bruises make raising my arms difficult, and I've a cursed headache as well."

"Certainly," she said, turning her chair so that she fully faced him. "I saved a canister of water here on the hearth so that you would have something clean to rinse with."

"Thank you," Stephan said. "I shall need to rinse or go about smelling of lavender water."

"It is the soap," Belle explained in apologetic tones. "I bought it in York. It's French. I had no thought at the time that you might be using it."

"It is very nice. On you." Stephan handed her a cloth and leaned forward so that she might scrub his back.

After a moment's hesitation, Belle removed her robe and then rolled back her sleeves. She picked up the cake of soap and dampened it with water.

Though she saw no obvious bruises, she was careful not to be rough in her touch since Stephan had complained of sore muscles. Down she traveled the expanse of back admiring its powerful lines and the sleek skin slipping beneath her fingers.

When his back was done, Belle happily abandoned the cloth and started on Stephan's hair. Like Sampson's mane, his dark locks had great power in them, at least over her. She found them irresistible.

Using a bit of water from the canister, she dampened his tresses and then, soaping her hands, she used the pads of her fingers to work the pale lather into his black hair.

Stephan sighed languorously, his face at smiling ease. "I knew that I would like married life," he said as his headache disappeared.

Caught up in the pleasure of running her fingers through his hair, Belle didn't answer. Up and down his nape her fingers traveled, seeking out tight muscles and coaxing them to relax. She caressed the shorter locks at his temples and behind his ears, drawing her fingernails over his scalp and watching with interest as each caress made gooseflesh form on his arms.

"I did not know that my touch could affect you so. Look at your skin. It is rather marvel—Stephan!" Belle's fingers stopped at his crown she discovered a small knot. "You did not tell me that you had a lump on your head."

"It is nearly gone now and doesn't hurt much," he

assured her, opening one eye. "Please go on. My headache is nearly gone."

"But perhaps I should not touch you . . ."

"Large boast, but small roast, my sweet," he taunted when she still hesitated. "I haven't any gooseflesh on my legs yet. I'll wager you can't manage that feat either if you don't finish my hair."

"Oh, you think not?" Belle asked. She at once slid off her chair and onto her knees, bringing her face even with Stephan's. Their eyes met, Stephan's gaze quizzical, her own unwavering and firm in the face of his challenge. "And what shall I win if I disturb your body and put gooseflesh on your legs?"

"A new bonnet?" he offered, amused at her competitiveness but feeling very lazy under the effects of her massage.

Belle nodded.

"Done then. I accept the wager." She reached over and picked up the canister. "Close your eyes."

Slowing and carefully, she directed the warm stream over his head, following the water's path with gentle fingernails.

Stephan groaned, not bothering to hide his pleasure at her touch. "Are you quite certain that they have ended slavery all over the empire?" he asked. "I should quite like to make you my permanent bath attendant—even if you don't cover me in gooseflesh."

"We shall see. Keeping me in new bonnets could be expensive."

Belle put down the empty canister and carefully wrung the water from Stephan's hair.

"That was wonderful," he told her. "Too short, but exquisite. However, observe that there is no gooseflesh on my legs. I think that this round is mine."

"Sit back now," Belle ordered, picking up her soap. She smiled at the play of firelight over Stephan's wet skin. He was beautiful, a pagan sultan waiting to be pleasured by a concubine.

Stephan complied immediately, happily allowing her access to his shoulders and chest. Inch by inch the circling hands worked their way down his body, leaving both relaxation and a certain tingling excitement in their wake. He stretched dreamily, laying his arms along the tub's rim, giving more of himself up to her touch.

Belle didn't hesitate to stroke him. She was enjoying all the textures of damp skin and water and crisp fur made slippery with soap. Again, feeling the solidity of muscle beneath her fingers, she was made aware of the differences between their bodies.

Seeing telltale movement beneath the soapy water, Belle smiled wickedly. There was perhaps another way to win the wager. It was possibly somewhat unfair, but Stephan had not said anything about how she was—or was not—to give him gooseflesh. Hesitating for but an instant, Belle reached for the soap.

Stephan made a shuddering out-breath as Belle's hands skimmed over his stirring manhood, her touch slick and warm, over the tip, down the shaft and a light brush below that had him drawing up like a startled cat.

The momentary contact was ended far too quickly to be an act of deliberate arousal, he decided. Belle had not made him an invitation to lovemaking, probably it was only an accidental touch, he explained to his body.

But the memory of the delicate sensation was as frustrating as it was delicious and brought a continuing change to his manhood.

Afraid that she might cut short her delightful ablutions if she noticed his arousal, Stephan opened his eyes and ordered his penis to behave. The water was cool. He should easily remain in control.

However he soon discovered that his body was acting autonomously. For the moment, his manhood was deaf and stubborn, and simply wasn't biddable to his command. It wanted Belle's hands back, and it was seeking her out in mute appeal.

"Oops." The soap splashed into the water and sank in its murky depths. Belle leaned down to retrieve it, allowing the neckline of her nightrail to gape enticingly.

Stephan closed his eyes against the tempting sight of Belle leaning over the side of the tub, trying to sink deeper into the cooling water. But the bathtub was only shallowly filled and did not completely hide him no matter what posture he assumed.

As though unaware of the havoc she had wrought, Belle finally retrieved the soap and went on with washing his legs, pressing her soapy fingers into the muscles and then unhurriedly rinsing him off with the cloth.

He cleared his throat as she began the return trip up his body.

"Belle." He opened his eyes again. "I think that perhaps I am clean enough."

"Patience, Stephan." Belle reached for the soap, rolling it between her palms for a long moment before putting it aside. "We are nearly done. And you must let me try and win our wager."

"*Wager,*" he repeated blankly. Stephan had never realized that watching a woman use soap could be such an excitant. Too much of an excitant. He closed his eyes tightly, hoping that out of sight would mean out of mind as well.

As he half-feared—and also half-hoped—Belle again touched him while soaping his inner thighs. She skimmed over him lightly, unhurriedly . . . *mercilessly*. Once, twice, a third time. Finally realizing that her touch could not possibly be accidental, Stephan opened his eyes and stared at her in mock reproach.

"Belle!"

She was watching him, wearing a mischievous smile. "You suddenly look quite cross, Stephan. Aren't you enjoying this?"

"Aye. What man wouldn't? But if I *enjoy* it anymore, our wedding night shall be over before it is even begun."

"Are you certain?" she asked, looking down at his body, mildly dismayed and also clearly disappointed at this bit of news.

Stephan found himself chuckling. "Well, it would be over for a while," he amended. "A short while."

"But only for a short while?"

"Aye, I suspect a very short while."

"Then I wish to go on. It is only fair."

Stephan considered it.

"Very well," he agreed finally. "If you are convinced that this is what you want." *She had him convinced. It was definitely what his body wanted.*

"I am quite certain," she said softly, returning to her soapy caresses.

At the first firm touch, sensation gripped him everywhere, like invisible fingers spreading out from a giant hand, pulling him tight and raising the hair on the lower half of his body.

Sensing that a harder touch was now needed, Belle curled her fingers about him, making her strokes more deliberate. Almost immediately climax seized him. He cried out as his seed burst forth, painting his belly and Belle's hand in convulsive jets.

As the ecstatic contractions finally eased, Stephan opened his eyes and looked into his wife's face. He saw a general glow of delight.

"You enjoyed that," she said softly, dragging the cloth over him in a way that was more teasing than cleansing.

"I did," he agreed. "And I believe you did, too, little wanton."

Belle nodded and looked up. "And since you enjoyed it, you likely won't mind that I won this game," she said, beginning to smile.

When he looked blank, she pointed to his limbs, which were covered in gooseflesh. "There is gooseflesh all over your legs *and* arms. You owe me a bonnet."

Stephan stood up, reaching for a folded linen. He dried himself perfunctorily. "No, I don't mind that you won as there will be a rematch, and we will not quit until you are likewise given to gooseflesh."

Rinsing off her hands, Belle stood also. She was still smiling. "I have a feeling that whatever happens, I shall win this contest also."

"We both will," he promised. Stephan reached for his cast-off clothing. "There is just one more thing we must see to."

"And that is?"

Stephan didn't answer with words. Instead he took her hand and removed the crude silver band. In its place he slipped on the plain, but beautiful gold ring.

"Stephan, thank you!" Belle said with genuine pleasure. "It's lovely."

"Perhaps now you will feel more like a real bride," he said, raising her hand to his lips.

It was dark and peaceful in their room, the inn having retired for the night, and the only sound in the darkness being the gentle tapping of rain against the glass.

A sense of well-being filled Stephan as he enjoyed the fact that Belle was again sleeping safe in his arms. Her body was cuddled against his in a lazy S, her hair fanned out on the pillow, and on her left hand the new wedding band glinted.

There was only one small area of discontent that clouded his thoughts and kept him from blissful sleep.

It had nothing to do with their lovemaking. As much as he generally avoided situations that overwhelmed his reason and made him lose all sense of control, Stephan freely admitted that he couldn't wait to lose himself again and again in the blinding, deafening passions Belle called forth.

But somehow, in spite of their marriage, and in spite of Belle's endless generosity in offering up her body to him, it wasn't enough. As wonderful as the night had been, filled with tenderness and ardor, it wasn't sufficient. And he feared that it would never be enough now that he understood what he wanted from his wife.

Taking a deep breath, Stephan finally named this new desire.

He wanted love. He wanted to tell Belle of his feelings for her, and eventually he wanted Belle to tell him plainly of her regard for him.

Surely she *had* some regard for him!

Stephan sighed, baffled. Never in his life had he so desired something. But he had never sought out, or even thought of wanting, such an admission of feelings from another person. It was extremely disconcerting to discover such needs now.

The only question was how he was to obtain what he wanted. A bald plea for tender feelings from Belle would never do! It would make him look weak and stupid. He would not be seen as such a needy creature!

But how else was he to tell her of what he sought and ask her to answer this need?

Stephan fell asleep still pondering the question.

Chapter Sixteen

Stephan and Belle were well aware by this time that a public parlor at an inn could be filled at any hour of the day with people of any and all social conditions—and most often would be, if the place was a busy one like Cowder.

And though they had no acquaintance in the area who should be looking them up at breakfast time, it somehow seemed inevitable that Belle and Stephan should enter the dining room the next morning and find Mister Oliver Frye of Bow Street seated behind a large dish of ham as though just waiting for the opportunity to speak with them.

It also seemed like predetermined fate that the landlord should come into the room only a moment behind Belle and Stephan, and that he would address the two of them as Mister and Missus Kirton when he wished them a pleasant morning and assured them that their rented nag would be returned to Scotland upon the morrow. He also wanted Stephan to know that the owner of his *borrowed* horse had been located and was very grateful to have the assurance that it would be returned.

"Good mornin' to ye both," Mister Frye said, after the landlord had quitted the room with a promise to send the serving wench in immediately.

"Good morning," Stephan answered because Belle seemed, for once, incapable of speech.

Mister Frye rose a few inches from his chair and went so far as to drink to their health, taking a large swallow of ale and then wiping his mouth on a dirty sleeve. His florid face beamed at Belle once his chin was clean.

Stephan supposed that it was inevitable that the runner should look at her with admiration, for no normal man could fail to admire her that morning. She looked like a bit of spring, dressed in a gown of palest blue sky and her golden hair falling like sunshine in soft curls over her ears and onto her lovely white shoulders. The only thing wintry in her appearance was her too-pale face except for the hectic color that burned high on each cheekbone.

"Mister Frye," Stephan said politely, seating a stiff and blushing Belle at a table.

She did not look again at Mister Frye, having first dropped her tiny reticule on the floor where it had to be retrieved, and then becoming involved in the task of arranging her dress, taking perhaps slightly unnecessary pains to see that her skirt was not crushed by the table's sharply carved legs.

"It seems we meet again at a wayside inn. Much better food they have here. Good ale, too. No fear of drinkin' this brew." Mister Frye, receiving no response from Belle, finally transferred his smile to Stephan.

"Indeed," he answered noncommittally, taking a chair beside Belle so that he might keep the runner in his line of sight.

Mister Frye stuffed another forkful of ham into his mouth and masticated thoughtfully. "Odd that ye should be in the district when another tragedy occurred," Mister Frye pursued through a mouthful of food. He was apparently oblivious to the unsubtle hint that Belle and Stephan did not wish to be engaged in conversation. Or, more likely, his profession had accustomed him to being unpopular, and he had learned to rise above the hostile snubs. "But it couldn't be aught but coincidence, could it?"

"Very odd and completely coincidental," Stephan agreed, accepting the serving girl's offer of coffee with a tight smile.

"Aye, you were visiting friends in Northumbria—and in York—on yer way to Scotland as I recall."

"Just so," Stephan's voice was growing more wooden, but it didn't deter Mister Frye.

"And I'm told by very reliable sources that congratulations to ye and the Missus are now in order as ye tied on the shackles while ye were in Scotland."

"That is correct."

"Ah! Well, I am mighty glad to hear it. Glad to have a chance to wish ye well before I leave. You'll doubtless be sorry to hear it, but I'll be headin' back to London soon to make my report to the gentleman what hired me to come here."

The serving girl also left the room, freeing Belle from her paralysis. "Someone in London was worried about the cattle thieves?" Belle asked, at last taking part in the conversation.

"Not that I know of," Mister Frye replied. "I was sent after a desperate criminal, a real fiend—handy with his pops—what had kidnapped a young heiress from a country estate and was forcing her to a scandalous marriage over the border in Scotland."

Belle nearly dropped her coffee cup. "Really? How unusual!" she said, swallowing hard and then asking: "If you don't mind my inquiring, Mister Frye, who was this person who came to Bow Street with this tale? It wasn't a Mister Lydgate of the East Indies Trading Company, was it?"

Belle and Stephan both stared into Mister Frye's twinkling eyes and waited anxiously for an answer.

"Nay, it was not Mister Lydgate. My client is some chub with flash manners and a weak chin. I don't trust a man that don't talk like a man but squawks like some shrewish woman. I couldn't tell ye his name—even if I remembered it properly—it not being discreet and all to discuss what I do in the line of duty."

"I see."

"However, it seems that I am too late to stop the desperate criminal from having his evil way with the lady, so the flash chub will simply have to be sorry that he caused his own woes by being ungentlemanly to start with . . . and a good riddance to him, I say. Any road, it seems that the lady is of age. There isn't anything else to do, regardless."

"I am certain that the lady would thank you for not interfering," Belle said earnestly. She added without looking at Stephan: "Your client was likely mistaken in his facts. Surely no one could forcibly abduct a woman in this day and age. And by now the matter is moot as the couple are wed."

"Aye, I believe he was mistaken. Men with weak chins often are. And had he not abandoned her at that den of iniquity of Lord Duncan's he'd have nothing to complain of anyway." Mister Frye scratched his head. "Of course, to my way of thinkin' it would have been a shame had the lady not taken it into her head to run away from Lord Duncan's. A strong-minded lady should never marry a man with a weak chin. Now, yer husband here has a nice strong chin. He's sound as a roast—Mister Oliver Frye can always tell. And I tell you, Missus Kirton, I don't forget my debts to folks neither."

"Stephan *is* sound as a roast," Belle agreed, hiding a relieved smile in her coffee cup.

Stephan cleared his throat.

"And ye've a pretty sound bottom yerself, Missus Kirton, if ye'll allow me the familiarity of sayin' so," the runner went on.

"Certainly," Belle said, not knowing the turn of phrase he used, but correctly divining that this was praise of no mean order.

"I don't suppose that there is any chance of the er—*flash chub*—coming up north himself?" Stephan asked casually, toying with his cutlery.

Mister Frye looked at Stephan, testing the edge on the table knife and then said shrewdly: "There is no knowing what a flash chub might do, particularly one who has a weak chin. But men of sense don't go about litterin' the countryside with corpses. It is one thing to shoot a cattle thief in a heathen land—especially one what might have stolen a man's wife and horses, but eyebrows would be raised if flash chubs started turnin' up dead in a civilized country whether they be little better than vermin or no."

"I wasn't suggesting that the young cur would end up completely deceased," Stephan answered, smiling reassurance at a newly alarmed Belle. "But I can't help but think that he would probably benefit from a beating."

The runner ruminated as he sipped some more ale. "Aye, reckon he might be improved for having someone darken his daylights for him," Mister Frye finally allowed as he popped a last piece of ham into his mouth. He added thickly: "I should enjoy seein' it,

263

too, but don't suppose that my superiors would be too happy if I let him be milled down though."

"Stephan, I thought we had agreed to let my stepfather deal with the Marvelles," Belle reminded her husband. Her tone was stern.

"We have. And a very comprehensive punishment they shall suffer in the fullness of time, I am sure. It is only that if Quincy should choose to make a pest of himself . . . well, do be reasonable, Belle. A man must protect his wife, after all," Stephan continued, his expression virtuous. "Mister Frye understands that even if you don't."

"Perhaps. But I am a married lady now and should be best pleased to not have any new scandals attach themselves to my name, which would certainly be the case if you trounced Quincy. You know how this is, Stephan. It isn't fair, but they would blame you."

Stephan sighed. "I wouldn't mind just one more scandal."

"Well, I would."

"Married for only two days and already you are nagging—ooph! My sweet, you just kicked me."

"Did I? My apologies, I am apt to move about abruptly when I am upset."

Mister Frye grinned at the exchange and rose from the table. "Well, I'd best be shovin' off back home to my own ball and chain. She gets nervy and out of sorts when I'm gone too long." The runner reached for his slightly battered hat. "London is a big city and full of people, but I have a strange feelin' that ye and

I shall be meetin' up again, Mister Kirton."

"One cannot foretell the future with any accuracy," Stephan answered. "But forgive me if I say that I do most sincerely hope that you are mistaken. If I never again encounter you in the course of one of your investigations it will still be too soon. Our little adventure at Casker's provided us with quite enough excitement for one or even two lifetimes."

"Don't blame you a bit, Mister Kirton," Mister Frye said, plopping his hat on his head and donning his furze coat. He walked over to their table. "Most folks don't like having dealin's with Bow Street, nor murderin' innkeepers either. Still and all, you have a certain air of trouble and danger about ye, Mister Kirton. And ye also, Missus Kirton—Mister Oliver Frye always knows. We'll be meetin' up again one of these fine days. Wait and see. Good day to ye now."

Mister Frye reached into his capacious pocket and carefully removed a badly burned scrap of paper. He laid it on the table.

"A present for ye." The runner bowed quickly and then sauntered from the room.

"Bloody hell," Stephan said as the door closed behind the smaller man. "The very thought of seeing Mister Oliver Frye again is enough to keep me out of London indefinitely."

Belle could only nod in agreement. "What is that he gave you?"

Stephan picked up the remains of Constance

Wrawby's letter, which could only have been had from the fireplace at Ormstead.

"I believe that this is my acquittal. My uncle will have a difficult time arguing my decision not to marry Constance after he reads this. Hopefully—"

Stephan was interrupted by Mister Frye's abrupt reappearance in the room. The runner closed the door with a brisk snap and flattened himself against it, hands braced on either side of the frame. His eyes were wide and looked a bit wild.

"There is no beatin' this nose of mine. It always smells trouble," the runner announced with grim satisfaction as he did his best to mimic a human barricade.

"What is it now?" Belle asked, a certain fatalistic dread settling over her heart.

"It's the weak-chinned chub, arguifying with the landlord about gettin' a room fer the night and trying to winkle some news about you two out of the man at the same time." Mister Frye seemed to know that this was a particularly inflammatory remark and lowered his voice respectfully while he delivered the news.

"I see!" Belle stood, throwing her napkin on the table. A militant light kindled in her eyes, making them blaze in an alarming manner.

"Have a seat, Belle, I will deal with this," Stephan ordered, but he was talking to his wife's poker-straight back before the sentence was done.

"Stand away from that door, Mister Frye," Belle

requested, her heels rapping on the wooden floor as she stomped toward the taproom.

Seeing the aggressive gleam in her eye as she eyed his braced hands, Mister Frye was brisk about obeying.

"Dammit, Belle, where are you going?" Stephan demanded, stowing away his letter and hurrying after her. He fixed Mister Frye with an unfriendly eye and added: "And why did you let her by?"

Mister Frye opened his mouth to reply and then shrugged helplessly. He hurried after them.

"Belle, what are you doing?" Stephan called, alarmed at her posture as she approached Quincy Marvelle. The man, who had turned about at that shout, was standing with his mouth hanging open in surprise.

"I have had quite enough of you, you nosy, lecherous beast," Belle announced in a clear voice, either unmindful or uncaring that there were patrons in the lobby. She stopped less than an arm's length from Quincy and fixed him with an unblinking eye. "It is thanks to you and your treachery that I have suffered the worst week of my life—and if you say one more bloody word I shall let Stephan shoot you after all."

Quincy's goggle-eyed gaze shifted from his former fiancée to the rapidly approaching Stephan. Foolishly, he began to sneer at the other man.

Fortunately for Mister Frye, Quincy did not seem to notice him standing behind the larger, angrier man, and it seemed that the runner was about to have his wish to witness Quincy's trouncing gratified.

"Kirton! You cad, you have stolen my affianced," the young Marvelle announced in tones of high drama.

"He did nothing of the sort," Belle said stoutly. "And I told you if you said a word that I would let my husband shoot you. Stephan, I have heard enough from this pest. Get your pistol."

Quincy gasped, startled out of his posturing by the outrageous remark.

"Belle," Stephan said, striving for a tone of moderation. "We are at an inn. It would be highly irregular to shoot someone right here. Think of the mess it would make of the floor."

"Well then, you may shoot him outside. I've no wish to inconvenience anyone."

There were one or two quiet sniggers from male guests and one strangled guffaw from Stephan's friend, the tapster.

Quincy sent Belle a look of loathing down his rather long nose. "I might have known that you would make a vulgar spectacle, you unnatural female. But even bastard Kirton knows—"

Belle had lately had opportunity to practice her pugilistic skills, and Quincy was not a giant Scotsman hardened by a life of physical labor. Her roundhouse punch was doubly devastating because it was completely unexpected. Quincy went down under her blow with a satisfying whoosh of air followed by the hard thump of his backside hitting the floor.

"Don't you *ever* speak of my husband that way again, you chinless coward!" she yelled at him, all restraint leaving her as she drew back her foot, preparatory to inflicting more damage.

"Belle, stop right there! You cannot strike a man who is down." Stephan added hurriedly: "It is against the code of honor."

Belle paused, foot drawn back as she weighed doing what Stephan wanted against her own impulses.

The tapster snorted out a short laugh, and Stephan, who had been prepared to break Quincy's jaw for calling Belle unnatural, found himself with nothing to do but join in the general hilarity that overtook the room in an impolite rush. He stopped short of actual laughter since it might enrage Belle, but a small smile tugged at his lips and a silent chuckle shook his frame.

Mister Frye, sensing that the moment of violence had come and gone, stepped out from behind Stephan and peered down at his bleary-eyed client. He shook his gray head sadly. "Well now! This is certainly a new one for the occurrence book."

"I'll have the magistrate summoned, by God!" Quincy wheezed angrily, clutching his stomach as he rolled onto his knees.

Belle looked longingly at his backside, but managed to restrain herself.

"I'd reconsider the matter," Stephan advised the fallen "flash-chub," taking Belle's arm and giving her an admonitory squeeze as she continued to stare fixedly at the inviting target of Quincy's behind. "You've already made yourself into a laughingstock with your stupidity. Such an act would only confirm your idiocy to the entire world."

"Aye, that ye have done, I must say. I've never seen the like for moonling behavior. Up with ye, my lad," Mister Frye said, hauling Quincy to his feet with a none-too-gentle hand. "I'd not be calling in the magistrate either. There is no knowing what might happen if he were to ask me about how it was I was sent after a respectable married lady like Missus Kirton. Why, he might arrest ye fer plottin' something indecent—and fer getting drunk and causing a ruckus in this house."

"What?" Quincy asked, astounded, staring in shock at the sudden appearance of his runner. "But that's a lie! I never sent you after a married lady. And it wasn't I who caused a ruckus. It was this creat—"

"Be very careful what you say next," Stephan warned, his tone steely. "You are speaking of my wife."

"Your wife!"

"Well, this here is the woman what used to be Anabelle Winston-Wrexhall-Lydgate," the runner said in an officious tone. "And she is now Missus Kirton, espoused of Stephan Kirton. And I knowed them as a married couple as far back as a week ago—and so I'd have to say to any magistrate. I don't doubt that the law would take a lenient view of this lady defending her virtue from a man what was persecuting her so particular-like."

"The law would probably even understand if I shot you," Stephan said, his tone deceptively mild and at variance with the expression in his eyes. "After all, I still owe my wife a bridal gift, and she has expressly asked me to save her from you."

"That won't be necessary, Mister Kirton," Oliver Frye said in reassuring tones as he hauled a staggering Quincy toward the door. "Mister Marvelle here is sorry fer the misunderstandin' and is just departing. Ye and yer lovely wife will be troubled no more."

"It's no trouble at all if he changes his mind," Stephan said. "I have a pair of pistols right upstairs, and you would be welcome to act as a second."

Mister Frye shook his head and tried to look severe, but his pale eyes were smiling. "Dueling is illegal in this country, Mister Kirton, so I know that is not what ye meant—but I thank ye kindly for the thought all the same."

Stephan and Belle watched as the suddenly silenced Quincy was hauled away. Belle was rubbing absently at her hand, flexing her assaulted fingers.

"Belle, my sweet," Stephan finally said, taking Belle's arm and urging his wife in the opposite direction. "This has been a most memorable day, but I do believe that it is also time for us to depart."

Belle, at last recalled to their public surroundings, looked about guiltily at the collection of grinning faces staring at them and muttered a hasty, but heart-felt apology.

"Think nothing of it," Stephan answered cheerfully as they mounted the stairs. "This is one scandal I shan't mind in the least."

"Truly?" she asked, still feeling a bit mortified for involving Stephan in another public spectacle.

"Truly. I have never had anyone defend my honor before. I'll treasure the memory of it forever." Stephan paused long enough to raise Belle's bruised hand to his lips and salute her with a grand air.

Below them, the witnesses applauded the final act of the short drama.

Chapter Seventeen

After the relative bleakness of the largely treeless north, Belle found it a relief to be back in the luscious meadowland of the midlands where there were still generous tracts of unharvested forest. It was in early afternoon that they saw their first clusters of the ancient trees dotting the grassland, offering pools of shade to the clumps of brave bluebells and tufted lawn daisies that were fighting against the onslaught of late rains. They also sheltered the tired mothers of the fat white lambs, and occasional high-spirited calves that frolicked in the fields.

They soon passed a tumulus—impossibly large and prehistoric—flanked by a row of venerating pines planted eons ago. Up in their dark and gently swaying boughs birds called continuously, hard at work on some avian project. There were harsh-voiced rooks guarding the highest branches of their domain, cooing cushats seated on nests, and closer to earth, the indignant sounds of the odd pheasant and partridge which their wheels' nearby passage flushed from the low shrubs.

Belle wondered happily if night would bring a chorus of philomels. She had not heard the haunting sound of nightingales song since early childhood. The very thought of the nightly serenade made her yawn with remembered contentment.

As they went deeper into the country, there grew a diffused though wholly unalarming sense of being observed by some invisible being, which was most present when they passed through the ancient trees' shade. Belle, feeling very sleepy in the unexpected noon heat, could only suppose that any ghosts or magicked folk that might live in the antique barrows and pines were friendly ones.

They journeyed at an unhurried pace to the Leidham Hotel, an attractive but largely unknown country house that Stephan knew had recently been bought up by a man of business and converted into a hotel. It was situated deep in a wooded downland a few miles off the main road. The grand brick building, standing at the top of an upward sloping greensward, would have been considered the handsomest of the area's attractions, but for the fact that in the spring it rose out of a field of wild narcissi and therefore looked a bit of a red excrescence in an otherwise pristine meadow.

The road eventually curved back on itself, and they passed through a pair of handsome gates, hung on carved stone gateposts, which depicted horses rearing in battle. The drive had not yet been civilized and was lined with giant wild cowslips, easily tall enough to reach Belle's knees, and the air was scented with the richness of flowers and fresh mown grass.

They entered a drive of old cobbles, due to be replaced as they had grown rutted, and stopped before the main doors of the hotel, which were great carved relics of another era studded with iron nails and hinges thick as a man's fist.

The grand entry to the house also had a large stone placard, placed on the south-facing side of a pyramidal monument, surmounted by the heads of three fine horses, proclaiming proudly that Leidham House had been built in 1621.

Belle, looking about with a pleased eye while Stephan surrendered their chaise to a groomsman, thought everything about Leidam to be very nice. She happily welcomed the better accommodations, but did wonder why the unusually silent Stephan had been so insistent that they drive out of their way to stay at this place when there were other, more conveniently located inns along the road.

It was all rather puzzling. Ever since the incident with Quincy at Cowder Inn, Stephan had been acting oddly. He was thoughtful and protective, but also silent and given to ruminations, which made him frown in a distracted manner. While before he had seemed in a tearing hurry to return to his business in London, now he seemed to be inventing reasons for delay.

Their host, Mister Clarkham, came out to greet them, interrupting Belle's futile contemplation of indecipherable matters. He was a small, balding man with stick-thin legs, but he still looked very dapper in his blue serge coat and was blessed with twinkling eyes. Having been a man of business he also spoke in a cultured way.

Ushered in with all possible pomp, Belle and Stephan passed under an impressive carved lintel, which marked the grand entry. They discovered the interior of the E-shaped inn to be handsomely paneled in old heartwood, polished to a gentle glow, and quite generously endowed with light that came in through the glass of the western wall, which faced into the setting sun. So endowed with casements was that side of the house that on first glance Belle thought it was actually all window and no wall.

Knowing how panes were taxed in England, she could only marvel at the new owner for not counting the cost and bricking some of them up.

The entry also had a beautiful oaken staircase built in the Italian style, which was added, the landlord told her, upon seeing her fascination with the renaissance piece, by the famous Indigo Jones.

Missus Clarkham joined them then. The charming master of the house was blessed with a spouse who was a loquacious soul. Receiving encouragement from Belle, she was happy to regale their guests with a history of the hotel while she showed them to their rooms.

The Leidham Hotel had a colorful record, including a hidden cupboard, and a secret cellar and stair used long ago for the purpose of hiding Catholic priests and Jacobites, but now—the landlord interjected, assuring them most earnestly—not used at all.

Belle, no longer so innocent about what could go on at even the nicest hostelries, reserved judgment about the landlord's honesty until she had an opportunity to taste the quality of the wine and brandy offered. They were a bit far inland to be on the main path of smugglers, but as she had been made aware, there was such a thing as land smugglers. And she had seen through the windows the pond and the strange iron cage that sat on its pier. It occurred to her that the water would make a convenient place to submerge stores if the hotel were ever investigated by the likes of Mister Oliver Frye or some official from the boards of tariffs and taxation.

The rooms in the top wing of the E where they were finally shown were plenteous and spacious, and for the moment, largely unoccupied, although a small party from London was expected the following morning, and in their honor, vases of fragrant narcissi were being arranged and distributed through the house.

Belle took Missus Clarkham's words as an invitation to bend down and sniff at the flowers whose aroma made her nearly giddy. Looking over the top of the bouquet, her eyes smiled at Stephan.

Stephan, drinking in the smile that Belle sent him, was more than pleased with her reaction to the hotel and glad that he had recalled its existence. It was the perfect place to begin a honeymoon. Not that his memories of Cowder Inn would not always be fond ones! Thanks to Belle, he would never view bathing in quite the same light. And he had been sincere when he told her that he would treasure the memory of her defending his honor to Quincy Marvelle and the town at large.

However, this was the moment when they would begin their marriage in earnest, and he wanted everything to be perfect tonight. Such perfection could not be had at any common roadside inn.

The thought of what he planned to do made Stephan feel a bit awkward and foolish. However, he could not think of how else to ask Belle to love him. It was not romantic to win a girl's heart in a game of cards—indeed it couldn't really be done. But it was a way to inaugurate what might well prove a difficult conversation.

There was, of course, always the danger of such a request being rejected or met with damning silence, but he truly did not want to go on any longer without knowing where he stood with her. Whatever her answer, whatever her thoughts, he wished to know them. Belle understood about honoring debts. A victory at cards would compel her to speak.

"What a beautiful bed!" Belle exclaimed, walking over to the giant, posted assemblage. The dark wood was waxed to a glassy shine making the carven fruit of its posts glow.

"Charles—the First—is said to have slept in it. But to the best of my knowledge it is not haunted," Mister Clarkham hastened to assure her, as a maid entered and began unpacking Belle's trunk. "Not like that other bed in Wright."

Missus Clarkham sniffed.

"I expect that the king slept in a lot of beds through the years," Belle answered briskly. She added mischievously: "It's a bit disappointing that his presence doesn't linger here, but the poor man was not as broadly traveled as Charles II, and we can't expect him to haunt every bed he slept in."

Stephan felt himself begin to smile. He loved this practical side of his bride. Most women, at any suggestion of possible ghostly manifestation, would have demanded some other couch to sleep in, but Belle simply took things such as ghosts in stride. Even went as far as to laugh at them. He thought, not for the first time, that a man could do a whole lot worse than to have such a courageous woman at his side.

"Do you by any chance have nightingales here?" Belle asked suddenly.

"Aye, that we do. Doves sing to wake us in the morning, and the philomels sing us to sleep. It is very different from London."

"I imagine it is a change, and surely one for the better."

"Aye, that it is, I must say. Now if you need anything, simply ring the bell. We've had them all rewired in the last fortnight." Missus Clarkham frowned. "Odd that. We used to get bells ringing at all hours. The locals say it is the resident ghosties, but in all likelihood it is only birds or mice getting at the wires. Neither Mister Clarkham or I have ever seen anything the least bit haunting here." This was added with a disappointed sigh.

"How unsatisfactory," Belle commiserated politely. "To buy a house this old and not get a single ghost."

"Aye, that it is. Still and all, it is a lovely place," Missus Clarkham said as she finally left the room with her slightly embarrassed husband.

"Mister Clarkham obviously doesn't approve of his wife's interest in ghosts," Belle commented. "I am glad that you are not so hidebound."

"I don't blame him for discouraging such talk. It could be bad for custom. But you may entertain any number of ghosts in our home if it pleases you."

Then thinking of his plan, Stephan hastily excused himself and hurried after Missus Clarkham. He wanted to make arrangements for a special dinner to be served in their room that night—tender peas and mushrooms for Belle, and if possible a green goose roasted with apples. And a shrub for after. He hoped that Leidham House ran to such luxuries as brandy and oranges for he wanted Belle to be pliant and yet not divorced from her senses, and this was the very posset for the task.

Belle, finally left all alone with the giant bed and its feather tick mounded up like a fat rain cloud, was completely unable to resist taking a skipping jump and flinging herself down on the velvet coverlet. Not expecting there to be anything other than linen sheets beneath, she was not prepared when the smooth silk slipped beneath her weight, and taking off like a new shoe on ice, it tumbled her onto the floor in an undignified heap.

Belle gave an involuntary giggle and pushed the coverlet off her face.

It's hopeless, Mama, she thought, staring at the gilded ceiling. *Your daughter has sunk beneath reproach—brawling in inns, jumping on beds like a hoydenish child. You must admit to being relieved that I am now Stephan's problem instead of yours.*

Stephan . . . Belle sighed.

Apologies and explanations are so tiresome, but must be made when we have wronged someone. Stephan says that he does not mind the scandal I caused at Cowder Inn, but I most certainly mind. I shall have to endeavor to do better in the future.

To begin with, I shall have to learn how to make a happy, peaceful home for us. It most likely won't be like any home I've had before. But however challenging, I must succeed.

Why?

Because I am certain that I am in love with him. And I want him to learn to love me.

Love . . . It isn't at all what I expected. Falling in love with Stephan has been a bit like tumbling down a steep slope. I meant to be careful, but somehow I put a foot wrong and then I was off. And nothing has called me back.

So, there it is. I tumble into love. I tumble into adventure. I even tumble out of beds. Let's admit to the fact, name the Devil and shame him. I am simply a fallen woman.

But I can do better—I am certain of it. And I promise you—and Stephan—that I shall.

"Belle?" Stephan found her on the far side of the bed, looking sheepish as she crawled out from under the costly fabric pile with her hair again in disarray.

He grinned at her. "I had thought to offer you a turn through the gardens, but I see you have discovered your own form of exercise."

"Not at all," Belle said, hurriedly smoothing her skirts and then grabbing the linens to remake the bed. She said with a show of dignity: "I should love to see the gardens. They must be quite superior."

"Of course—but if you are not yet done inspecting the sheets . . ."

"Don't be a beast. Come help me right this mess before Missus Clarkham or the maid sees the jumble. Velvet crushes so easily! I can't imagine why they have anything so impractical in the rooms."

Stifling a smile, Stephan took a corner of the coverlet and helped smooth it into place.

As Belle predicted, the gardens were superior, but not in any expected manner. Beyond a tame herbaceous hedge and knot garden, the more exotic transplants of the previous owner had been allowed to run amok, rampaging over ruins built in the Eastern style until they resembled some long-abandoned Persian seraglio of lore.

They had for company in their wanderings, at least for a time, a cat—a great orange thing—that seemed to find the scent of wildflowers ambrosial. And it was he who guided them through a small shadowy maze and into the red-and-gold blaze of the rose garden. Coming from the relative dimness of green shade, Belle could only blink her eyes at the dazzlement of colors.

Bordering the forgotten garden was a Chinese wisteria, which had all but smothered some unidentifiable tree whose shaggy bark was seamed with scars. The barely opened blue blossoms were aswarm with industrious bees who hummed happily as they worked at tearing open the blooms and harvesting the nectar.

Narcissi were there in abundance, too, their petals more translucent than the lightest parchment and glowing the sheen of porcelain held up to the sun. But it was the early blooming roses that most perfumed the air and ravaged the senses and bewitched the eyes. There were citrines, carmines, pinks and red in every shade from deep blush to pigeon blood and ruby. There were medieval blossoms, shaded from cream to peach whose petals were so densely whorled that they had to fight one another to unfurl. They snuggled up with the more modest wild roses who held up the simple white cups to the sun.

Stephan and Belle never noticed when the cat abandoned them.

Taking Stephan's hand Belle pulled him into the garden, laughing delightedly when a sudden breeze disturbed the wisteria and sent a blue rain—softer and warmer than butterfly wings—to flutter down upon them.

Belle pulled off her bonnet and turned her face up into the breeze. One stray lock of living gold fluttered across her cheek.

"Stephan, we must have a rose garden like this! I've never known roses to bloom so early," she said, eyes closed as she enjoyed the caress of wind and sun. "And the perfume! Nothing could ever be half so wonderful."

"Aye, we must have a garden for you," he agreed, knowing that the bespelling likeness of Belle's face kissed by sun would haunt his dreams forever. With a feeling of gratitude, Stephan slipped the image away into the place where he kept his few cherished memories.

"Would it be theft, do you think, if we took some

roses back to the house?" she asked without opening her eyes. "I should dearly love to take some cuttings with us when we leave."

"It would be a forgivable theft," he answered. Then with a practicality he was far from feeling, he added: "I am glad I brought my knife."

Belle finally opened her eyes and smiled at him.

"And I am thankful that I brought a handkerchief. The flowers are beautiful but the thorns will not be so forgiving in surrender. However, together I am certain that we shall prevail."

Together. Feeling at once more hopeful and light-hearted, Stephan suddenly snatched Belle up in his arms.

"Stephan!" she cried in surprise and then began laughing as he spun her about like a child.

Stephan laughed, too, storing up her delighted mirth against that evening when his hopes for their future might be taken from him.

Chapter Eighteen

Dinner, Belle assured Stephan, was gustatory perfection, the side dishes delicious, the green goose divine. But so distracted was he by what was to come after their meal that Stephan hardly tasted any of it. The afternoon's delightful optimism had faded upon their return to the house and he was feeling the breath of grim reality on the back of his neck and it quite ruined his appetite.

Getting up from the table, Stephan wandered over to the fire and began poking at it absently with the fireplace tongs.

Why should Belle love him? What reason had she? What right had he to even ask this of her? She might be his wife, but she had been forced into wedlock against her will—to a bastard who was still, in spite of their physical intimacy, largely a stranger. She'd been subjected to every sort of humiliation and discomfort.

He had thwarted her plans.

Drugged her.

Enraged her to the point of throwing crockery.

Indeed her very life had been imperiled on more than one occasion since they began their association.

Was he insane to wish that she would reach for him right now, to pull him to her with her eyes, her body, her heart open?

Had anyone served him such a trick he should have done his utmost to see them vivisected, not invite them to make love to him.

Yet—*said a last small ember of optimism*—in mitigation to this slate of charges was the fact that she *had* cared sufficiently about him to offer her body, gifting him with her innocence even before they had married. He had thought at the time that making love with a near-stranger was something that an experienced woman might do, but not an unmarried one with a moral upbringing. The act had to have some meaning for Belle.

True, she had planned to run from him later—but she said that this was to protect him. And there was her seduction of him at the Cowder Inn.

And her attack on Quincy.

And yet, all too often in the past few days he had looked at her and sensed that there were unshared thoughts moving through her mind. What they could be he did not know, but he wanted them. All of them.

her memories, speculations, hopes and plans.

Even if they did not include him?

Yes, he thought, even then.

Back and forth his thoughts traveled, making him grow more quiet with every moment that passed.

"What is troubling you, Stephan?" Belle asked softly as the last of the covers were removed and the servants went away. "You've not been yourself the entire day."

"Bothering me? Nothing," he denied, turning from the fire and allowing himself a moment to appreciate how lovely Belle looked in her sherry-colored gown with a matching ribbon threaded through her hair. Her mouth—those wonderful lips that had so eagerly kissed him—were offering him a shy smile.

The thought of again kissing Belle glittered in a distracting manner and it took Stephan a moment to recollect himself. Yes, he wanted her body. He would always want her body! But tonight he was after something more important. He could not give in immediately to the bright shimmer of attraction.

"I thought that tonight we would enjoy a *shrub*—they do have excellent brandy here—"

"I rather thought they might," Belle murmured, looking significantly at the handsome ewer left standing on the table.

Relaxing, Stephan grinned. Belle was gifted with the talent of moving him from dark brooding to amusement with utterance of one dry sentence.

"You noticed the iron cage out at the pond."

"It was rather difficult to miss. Perhaps someone should tell the Clarkhams that it is unwise to leave it in the open."

"I already have."

"It isn't that I approve of smuggling," Belle began.

"Of course not," Stephan said, humoring her.

"But I like the Clarkhams, and starting a new business venture is expensive. And many of the tariffs on liquor are quite unjust—and the navy coastguard is quite arrogant about searching vessels and deserves the occasional humiliation. My stepfather has often said so."

"Just so. Most seamen would agree with him, I am sure." Not wanting to be diverted into a political discussion, he added quickly: "By the way, that is a lovely gown."

Belle blinked. "Thank you. I chose the fabric because it was the color of your eyes." She added before he could think of a reply: "I've never had a shrub made with anything but rum. My stepfather is not partial to brandy."

She sniffed appreciatively at the ewer's contents and then leaned back so that Stephan could pour out two generous cups.

"My eyes are honored." Stephan tried not to sound delighted at Belle's light words. It was likely only polite flirtation. "If I had the talent I would write an ode to both."

"Nay, it is the gown alone that is flattered," she answered gaily. "But have you been hiding a poetic gift under a bushel? I must admit that I would love to hear an ode to my gown or your eyes."

"You likely would, but it is doubtful that you would want to hear any ode of my composing. I've never had the knack for speaking in measured periods." Stephan, not caring for this topic either, cleared his throat and began again. "You will find that this is a gentler drink by far than any made with rum. The brandy is subtle enough to let the sweet of the oranges and sugar come through."

"It certainly smells delicious," Belle answered courteously, but there was a perplexed frown gathering between her brows as she studied him.

Stephan handed Belle a glass and made a small, silent toast. Prepared at last to actually begin, he said: "I had thought that tonight we might have a game of cards."

"Yes?" Belle smiled cautiously. "That could be nice. Of course, you will recall that you still owe me a bonnet for our last game. And a miniature, too."

"I recall it," Stephan assured her. "And you shall have them."

"Good. Well then! What shall we play tonight? All Fours again?"

"Nay. I thought tonight that we would play something else. A game called *lansquenet*."

"I don't think I know this game. It sounds Italian and I do not know many foreign card games since my stepfather detests them," Belle admitted, as Stephan went to fetch the cards and a branch of candles. She added idly: "What beautiful tapestry to use on these chairs. It is almost a crime to sit upon them."

"The chairs are doubtless more honored than either my eyes or your dress," Stephan said gallantly.

A dimple appeared briefly in Belle's cheek and then was gone. "Flattery will not distract me, Stephan. Nor promises of an ode to a chair. So cease this formal speech and tell me, how does one play lansquenet?"

"Have I been formal?" he asked, knowing that he had retreated into social manners as a defense against his own desires.

"Quite. You are beginning to alarm me. The last time you were this way was when you were trying to lure me into Lord Duncan's garden to seduce me."

"I promise that I am not trying to lead you into the garden."

"Don't be so literal," Belle scolded, toying with her wedding ring. "Just sit down and tell me how to play this game."

Unable to abandon his defenses, Stephan answered: "You were correct in your guess. It is an Italian game that has grown popular in France. The rules are not difficult. I can explain them in a trice."

Stephan returned to the table and began to shuffle the cards. Left with nothing to do, a suddenly restless Belle reached out to adjust the candelabra more to her liking and then took a sip of the infused brandy.

"This is very good," she complimented.

"I believe that I saw paper and ink inside the desk, if you would be so good as to fetch it."

Belle raised a brow, and Stephan realized that he still sounded ridiculously formal.

"Please."

"We are to have a written wager tonight?" Belle asked, surprised.

"Yes. Tonight, in honor of our dignified surroundings, we shall play more formally." Stephan tried to sound calm, but couldn't tell if he entirely succeeded because of the over-loud beating of his heart. Apparently it was growing concerned at his latest enterprise and sounding an internal alarm.

"Very well." Belle went to fetch the paper and ink. "Shall we have quarters again?"

Stephan shook his head.

"Nay, just halves. Tonight we play only for what we want to win."

Hearing the thread of deadly seriousness that ran beneath the light words, Belle glanced sharply at Stephan before tearing the sheet of paper in two.

"Why do I feel that I am about to fight a duel instead of play a game of cards?"

"Perhaps because cards are a way of dueling that doesn't end in bloodshed."

"What a comforting thought," Belle murmured. "Perhaps we should have seconds in to examine the cards before we begin."

"Don't be absurd. I was only speaking of cards in a general way. Let us get on with play."

Stephan was brisk as he wrote down what he wanted from Belle. The simple words, so short and plain seemed to swim before his eyes as he reread them. Hastily he folded the note and set it to the side. This was not the time to be undermined by apprehension.

Belle also looked rather nervous as she hesitated, began writing and then hesitated again. She did this three times before finally writing down what she desired. She folded her paper with slow deliberation and hands that trembled, making Stephan maddeningly curious about what she had scribbled there.

Suddenly, he wished that he had suggested some other game, one that allowed for skill and not just the happening of luck. To trust the outcome to random chance was an act of folly!

"I am ready." Belle reached for her cup and took a healthy swallow. The quick gulp suggested to Stephan that she was recruiting her strength rather than savoring the brandy's bouquet.

"Very well. The game is played thusly. I lay out two cards upon the table. One for you and one for me." Stephan turned over the queen of hearts and placed in front of Belle. His own card was the knave of spades.

"Are these good cards?" she asked, a shade of nervousness entering her voice.

"There is no numeric value assigned to cards in this game. And no strategy. All cards are equally good as it is comes down to random luck."

"Then I don't suppose that one can cheat."

"It would be difficult, but not impossible," Stephan answered. "However, from here forward, you and I shall always deal honestly together, shall we not?"

Belle nodded, her face very serious and her eyes wide. It occurred to Stephan that neither of them looked or acted like friends passing the evening in simple entertainment. The game had indeed become a duel.

"Now I begin turning over cards. Whichever comes up first, a queen or knave, will determine who wins."

"And that is all there is to it?" she asked.

"Aye, that is all. Are you ready?"

"Yes." Belle said calmly, but her skin appeared a shade paler and her eyes were wary.

One by one the cards fell, both players growing steadily more tense and serious with every card turned, until Stephan had to admit that the play had become an odd sort of torture. Pistols at thirty paces had never seemed so worrisome.

The spacious room felt suddenly close. Time stretched to unnatural lengths, and every breath had to be drawn in by force against the constrictions of the chest.

Finally, Fate chose a winner and a second knave revealed itself.

Belle exhaled and fell back in her chair. She touched a hand to her bosom as though to secure her heart in place. She was so pale that her skin appeared translucent.

"Belle? Are you well?"

"Certainly. I just do not appear to have the nerves for this particular game."

"We needn't ever play it again," he said reassuringly, hoping this would chase away the air of distress that surrounded her.

"Thank you. I shall hold you to that promise."

Stephan did not indulge his relief at having the game end so far as to fall back into his seat, as the difficult part still lay ahead, but he did permit himself a deep breath and a quick sip of the infused brandy before reaching for a paper.

"Which wager shall you open?" Belle asked, her voice trembling slightly.

Stephan, who had had every intention of selecting his own paper, was once again arrested in his intent. Recalling how Belle had reacted when he chose her paper instead of his own, he paused long enough to make a reassessment of the course he had chosen.

Slowly, watching Belle's expression, he reached for his own choice. Shockingly, her face showed relief.

Stephan paused again, now thoroughly intrigued—and perhaps even a trifle worried—and then he stretched his hand across the table.

Involuntarily, Belle made as if to snatch the scrap back, but Stephan was too quick for her. Belle's empty hand fluttered back into her lap.

"You should have what you want this time," Belle

said desperately. "It is only right since you won. Choose your own wish."

"But I believe that this *is* what I want."

"No." Belle shook her head, her eyes pleading as she leaned forward. She sounded like someone certain that they were about to be cut to the emotional quick. "It isn't what you want right now. I was feeling a little mad. The shrub made me giddy. You do not want to read what is on that paper. You don't want the burden."

"But I do want to read it, Belle. I want to know your giddy choice," he said gently. "And I cannot imagine anything you could ask for that would be too great a burden for me."

"Stephan . . ."

"Please trust me, Belle."

"I do trust you, Stephan. I wish that you would not choose that one, but if it is your will . . ." Surrendering on these words, Belle again fell back in her chair, watching him with almost frightened eyes.

Feeling a bit like he was plucking whiskers off a kitten, Stephan unfolded the note. Four short words were written there: *I want your love.*

"I wanted to know if you could love me just a little instead of thinking of me as an honorable obligation," she said softly.

"An honorable obligation?" Exhaling in relief, Stephan reached for his own paper and pushed the scrap across the table. "Once again we are backwards in events. Go ahead. Read it."

With hands that shook, Belle picked up the scrap. She unfolded it slowly and read. Her face was flushed but hopeful as she looked up.

"You have my love, Belle," Stephan said gently, watching her eyes as he spoke. "My heart has been yours almost from the first."

Belle shook her head from side to side, looking as much dazed as denying.

"That surely can't be. You wanted to make a respectable marriage to a lady of good birth," she whispered. "We wed only to avert a scandal."

Stephan shook his head.

"It is the truth. It might have been that poisonous wine of Duncan's that slowed my ambition enough that it had time to appreciate you—or perhaps it was the letter from Constance, pushing me away from an old but shallow goal of a society-approved wedding— but whatever it was, I knew from the moment I saw you that something profound had changed in my life. I saw you at the dining table and all my past plans got shoved aside, making room for a new dream to grow. And, Belle, I never want to hear you speak of your birth as being unrespectable. It isn't true."

"Stephan?" she asked tremulously, reaching for him across the table with the hand that wore his ring.

Stephan took her hand and squeezed gently.

"I shall be eternally grateful that destiny took a hand and brought you to my notice, Belle. You fetched me out of the wasteland of empty ambition."

After a moment, Stephan broke off his gaze and

freed himself from Belle's clasp. He cleared his throat and then asked bluntly: "And what of you, Belle? Will you ever be able to bestow your heart? On me?"

Belle rose from her chair and came around the table in a soft whisper of skirts. She laid her hands on his cheeks, and smiling unsteadily said: "Stephan, you've had at least a part of mine perhaps since I was a child."

He absorbed her words, taking hope from them.

"And now, Belle?"

"And you have all of it now. I resisted as best I could, thinking that it was wrong, but the part of my heart that I kept was miserable, mooning about like a ghost in an empty ruin. It was glad finally to go to you. Stephan, you have all of my heart. I love you, too."

Belle sealed the sweet words with a kiss that was sweeter still. Shockwaves of relief went through him, the percussions shattering doubt and fear and replacing it with euphoria. Her words of love were a radiance of warming light that illumined the dark and frozen places in his soul.

"Thank you, God." Stephan sighed, also standing so that he could take her into his arms. "I don't deserve it, but I am grateful."

Chapter Nineteen

Belle plucked the ribbon from her hair and threw it aside as Stephan caught her up and moved quickly to the bed. He laid her down carefully in the feather billows and settled on top of her.

He didn't say anything for a moment, apparently fascinated with the spill of her hair on the velvet coverlet and over his arm, which cradled her head. But even had his face and its blazing eyes been hidden from her, his body's sudden rigidity would have attested to how much he wanted her.

Her body accepted the testimony and answered with its own. But rather than growing harder as Stephan had, Belle's limbs became soft and pliant.

"You are beautiful," he said. "I don't think that I have told you this before."

Belle smiled, but shook her head. " 'Tis dark here. You cannot see me."

"I can see you. But that doesn't matter, cloaked in darkness or bathed in brightest light, you will always be beautiful to me."

"And you to me."

Stephan dropped his head and nipped her ear, sending a shiver down her body and making her nipples tighten. Pleased with the reaction, he did it again.

Belle moaned and shifted under him. She could feel him pressed against her, every beat of his heart marked with a throb where loin met loin.

"Stephan—"

"How restless you are, my sweet. There is no need for haste."

Belle did not agree. Her body said that there was every need. Kicking off her slippers, she brought her legs around him. She drew her stockinged feet up the back on his calves but was forced to stop by the constrictions of her skirt, which was tethered beneath Stephan's legs.

"Stephan?" Belle tried to tug herself loose.

"Aye, my sweet?" He nibbled again at her ear, sending a third shiver down her spine. He truly seemed in no hurry to consummate his declaration of love.

Belle was not so patient. All the day she had thought about little else, and now with the words of love spoken between them, making their marriage real, she wanted Stephan to make love to her.

"You are lying on my dress again," she said breathlessly. "I cannot move."

"I rather thought that I was lying on you. It certainly feels like you; soft and warm and welcoming," he answered prosaically, though there was a teasing laugh behind the reply that Belle sensed even if she could not actually hear it.

"The result is the same, since my dress is upon me. And you are cruel to tease me so. It would serve you justly if I simply went to sleep right now," she scolded. But the threat did not carry any weight as she curled her fingers into his hair and strained upward to kiss him even as she made it.

Stephan did not resist. Belle found that the meeting of their lips was very much like the joining of fire to dry tinder. His lips eventually abandoned her mouth, traveling down her throat. The scrape of teeth made her neck bend back over his forearm, arching her body into his. Stephan's lips ventured farther, pausing at the pulse that hammered there before journeying down to her breasts.

He murmured something as he bit the soft flesh that was trying to escape its décolletage. The nips he bestowed had enough force to tell Belle of Stephan's diminishing sensual restraint.

"You play the very hell with my good intentions, Belle," he complained. "I have yet to act the gentleman with you. One kiss, a touch, and I am turned to some sort of mindless beast."

The admission was a signal to Belle to let go of all thoughts of moderation. Tugging Stephan's mouth back to hers, she returned the nibbling caress.

"I like the beast. Let him go."

It was Stephan's turn to shudder and grow taut. All aspect of teasing fled as he kissed her in earnest. First lips and then tongues mated, Stephan's breath mingling with hers, their sighs tangling.

At the relaxation of modest constraint, the scorch of new desire spread over Belle's flesh with the speed of a flashfire, and tiny shudders passed through her body and into his where the passion seemed to redouble. Her nails bit through the fabric of his breeches as her hands flexed involuntarily into the solid muscle of his flank.

"Very well, I shall liberate you, since you have asked so nicely." Stephan's voice was smoky, his eyes narrowed. He rolled to his side, not just freeing her clothing but quickly helping her to disrobe.

Every brush of fingers against skin brought another flare of heat along her naked flesh, marking the path his hands had traveled. She felt feverish, but still shivered as with cold.

Stephan began shedding his own attire. She reached to untie his cravat and then unfastened his shirt, but the emotion seething in Belle made her tremble and her fingers were clumsy as she tried to aid Stephan in ridding himself of his clothes. Frustrated with her ineptness, she finally pulled away and simply ordered him to hurry. Anticipation all but shimmered in the air.

With a quick grin of pleasure, Stephan complied, being careless of seams and buttons as he hastened to obey. In less than a minute he returned to her arms. They sank back into the feather tick, and this time there was nothing between them, nothing to slow the sensual fire as it consumed them, nothing to hamper exploration.

Belle moaned softly, welcoming Stephan's weight, his kiss and his entry in equal measure. Unencumbered by fabric or modesty, she wrapped herself about him.

Stephan at first moved slowly, as though fearing to rush in case he hurt her, but Belle had no such hesitation. The fit was close, and nearly unbearable in the heat and frustration it caused, but it was also perfect and exactly what she wanted. It was in such a crucible that love was wrought.

Turning her head, she whispered into his throat. The words were not coherent, just a plea for more of the fiery feeling that was spreading through her.

Accepting her invitation, Stephan shifted forward, going deeper, moving more quickly. A small starburst of heat raced through her body in a wild rush from breast to loins, tightening her like a bow. Reflexively, Belle's legs shifted higher, wrapping themselves about his waist. And her hands traveled restlessly from back to flank. His skin was fevered to the touch.

He drove into her again and again. Belle could feel the tremors that shook him each time he slid into her.

A small convulsion seized her, and then another. Stephan gave a broken groan and in the next instant, the world went away, leaving only fire. Belle threw herself into the blaze. The conflagration spread, burning away everything but ecstasy. A second hoarse cry from Stephan told her that he, too, had found the fire.

"So, you are grateful for me?" Belle teased, smiling into Stephan's chest as they cuddled. "We'll see what occurs after you meet my stepfather."

"At the moment I feel like I could sack Carthage. Facing one angry stepfather—even when he is Nabob Lydgate—would be a bagatelle."

Belle looked up, her eyes shining in the light of dwindling fire. Her lips were slightly swollen and her cheeks retained a trace of blush.

"I see. So this was something in the nature of a pillage?"

Stephan kissed her briefly. "It was not in the nature of anything. It was an act of love. It is hardly my fault if you make me feel like conquering the world so I might offer it to you as a present."

Belle began to answer, but stopped when the sweet yet haunting sounds of nightingale song floated into the room through the slightly opened window.

"That must be the most beautiful sound in the

world," Belle whispered when the symphony at last fell silent.

"Nay, there is a sound more beautiful still," Stephan said, rising on to an elbow and looking down at his wife. "And that is the sigh you make just before you kiss me. Come, kiss me again, Belle."

And she most happily did.

THE MASTER

MELANIE JACKSON

Long ago the hobgoblin Qasim was turned to darkness, was made a master of evil. His newest plot is a sacrifice of unspeakable horror that will mean full-fledged war between all species.

There exists hope to fight back. Nicholas Anthony, an ER doctor, doesn't know of his own fey blood, or that others of his kind are massing in the Nevada desert. Alienated from himself, he is a man about to discover his destiny. Magic will draw Nick to his true self—and to Zee, an enchanting beauty with dark secrets yet to be revealed. To these two is entrusted the fate of the world, their kind, and salvation from...*The Master*.

IONA

MELANIE JACKSON

Isolated by the icy storms of the North Atlantic, the isle of Iona is only a temporary haven for its mistress. Lona MacLean, daughter of a rebel and traitor to the crown, knows that it is only a matter of time before the bloody Sasannachs come for her. But she has a stout Scottish heart, and the fiery beauty gave up dreams of happiness years before. One task remains—to protect her people. But the man who lands upon Iona's rain-swept shores is not an Englishman. The handsome intruder is a Scot, and a crafty one at that. His clever words leave her tossing and turning in her bed long into the night. His kiss promises an end to the ghosts that plague both her people and her heart. And in his powerful embrace, Lona finds an ecstasy she'd long ago forsworn.

___4614-8 $6.99 US/$8.99 CAN

Dorchester Publishing Co., Inc.
P.O. Box 6640
Wayne, PA 19087-8640

Please add $2.50 for shipping and handling for the first book and $.75 for each book thereafter. NY, NYC, and PA residents, please add appropriate sales tax. No cash, stamps, or C.O.D.s. All orders shipped within 6 weeks via postal service book rate. Canadian orders require $2.00 extra postage and must be paid in U.S. dollars through a U.S. banking facility.

Name_____

Address_____

City_____ State_____ Zip_____

I have enclosed $_____ in payment for the checked book(s).

Payment <u>must</u> accompany all orders. ❑ Please send a free catalog.

CHECK OUT OUR WEBSITE! www.dorchesterpub.com

NIGHT VISITOR

MELANIE JACKSON

All self-respecting Scots know of the massacre and of the brave piper who gave his life so that some of its defenders might live. But few see his face in their sleep, his sad gray eyes touching their souls, his warm hands caressing them like a lover's. And Tafaline is willing to wager that none have heard his sweet voice. But he was slain so long ago. How is it possible that he now haunts her dreams? Are they true, those fairy tales that claim a woman of MacLeod blood can save a man from even death? Is it true that when she touched his bones, she bound herself to his soul? Yes, it is Malcolm "the piper" who calls to her insistently, across the winds of night and time . . . and looking into her heart, Taffy knows there is naught to do but go to him.

___52423-6 $6.99 US/$8.99 CAN

DIVINE FIRE
MELANIE JACKSON

In 1816, Lord Byron stayed at the castle of Dr. Johann Dippel, the inspiration for Mary Shelley's Baron von Frankenstein. The doctor promised a cure for his epilepsy. That "cure" changed him forever.

In the 21st century, Brice Ashton wrote a book. Like all biographies of famous persons, hers on Lord Byron was sent to critics in advance. One Damien Ruthven responded. He suggested her work contained two errors—and that only he could give her the truth. His words held hints of long-lost knowledge; were fraught with danger, deception...and desire. And his eyes showed the experience of centuries. Damien promised to share his secrets. But first, Brice knew, she would have to share herself with him.

STILL LIFE
MELANIE JACKSON

Snippets of a forgotten past are returning to Nyssa Laszlo, along with the power to project her mind. Each projection thrusts her into a glowing still life of color and time, and her every step leads deeper into undiscovered country. Things are changing, and dangerously so. She is learning who she is—whether she wants to or not. She is also learning dark things are on the rise. From the Unseelie faerie court to Abrial, the dauntless dreamwalker who pursues her, the curtain is going up on a stage Nyssa has never seen and a cast she can't imagine—and it's the final act of a play for her heart and soul.

THE COURIER
MELANIE JACKSON

In the alternate world of the Wildside, earth is populated not only by humans but creatures of dark, seductive magic—pookas, sylphs, goblins and more. This wonderland is in delicate balance. And the goblins are always plotting.

Lyris knows all about goblins. But is Quede, the strange owner of the plantation Toujours Perdrix, the biggest threat in New Orleans? Or is it Romeo Hart, the fey who laughs at death and quickens Lyris's blood? This courier mission she's just been assigned is trouble. No question. Lyris is in danger of losing her life, her soul, or her heart—but by the time she discovers which, it will be too late.

OUTSIDERS
MELANIE JACKSON

Cyra Delphin never felt quite right in her skin. As a child, her parents made her hide her gifts. What others are afraid to acknowledge—the modern world's seedy underbelly, its Wildside ruled by dark magic and goblins—doesn't simply go away. And when that darkness comes to call, Cyra seeks sanctuary in the Nevada desert.

She finds Thomas Marrowbone. Beneath his tormented shell lurks something powerful and inhuman, but also something primal and erotic. Cyra recognizes it, and for love she follows the enigmatic loner into the depths of Hell. The journey tests both their bodies and hearts . . . but their quest's success promises salvation and a happiness Cyra has never known.

TRAVELER
MELANIE JACKSON

Evil forces are on the rise, and Io is part of a secret association dedicated to stopping them. Lutins are replacing society's bigwigs—no one is safe. The only solution is to travel beneath the Motor City into the hordes thronging Goblin Town, rendezvous with Jack Frost and uncover the plot.

The quest will force Io through labyrinths of vice and challenge every aspect of her incomplete training. And if enemies aren't enough, her ally will imperil her heart. Jack Frost is much more than a simple sorceror: He rules the realms of love and death. Yet in Jack's hands, a little death could be a very, very good thing.